A

He wrapped hi   to cry. Slowly, the sobs   hitches in her breathing, but Kate didn't move. When was the last time she'd been held with such tenderness, such caring?

It felt so right, so good to be in Robin's arms that she didn't want to leave. But she had to. He was only being kind.

She pushed against his chest in an attempt to step away, but his hold remained firm. Surprised, she looked up, then caught her breath.

Fire blazed in his eyes, his gaze searching her face until it rested on her mouth. Her lips softened in response and she moistened them with the tip of her tongue.

His arms tensed around her. "Kate." Her name emerged as more of a groan. He cradled the back of her head in one hand as he drew nearer, his warm breath caressing her skin . . .

Prince
of
Charming

KAREN FOX

JOVE BOOKS, NEW YORK

MAGICAL LOVE is a trademark of Penguin Putnam Inc.,

PRINCE OF CHARMING

A Jove Book / published by arrangement with
the author

PRINTING HISTORY
Jove edition / December 2000

All rights reserved.
Copyright © 2000 by Karen Fox.
Cover illustration by Franco Accornero.
This book, or parts thereof, may not be
reproduced in any form without permission.
For information address: The Berkley Publishing Group,
a division of Penguin Putnam Inc.,
375 Hudson Street, New York, New York 10014.

The Penguin Putnam Inc. World Wide Web site address is
http://www.penguinputnam.com

ISBN: 0-515-12974-7

A JOVE BOOK®
Jove Books are published by The Berkley Publishing Group,
a division of Penguin Putnam Inc.,
375 Hudson Street, New York, New York 10014.
JOVE and the "J" design
are trademarks belonging to Penguin Putnam Inc.

PRINTED IN THE UNITED STATES OF AMERICA

10   9   8   7   6   5   4   3   2   1

To Torie—

may you always believe in yourself.

And to Kathy Carmichael—

thanks for letting me mutate your name.

And as always, to the Wyrd Sisters.

Prologue

"Your charm won't help you this time, Robin Goodfellow. You'll remain trapped for the rest of eternity." Titania finished her spell, her arms slicing the air for emphasis.

Robin couldn't run. There was no escape. Already the coils of magic surrounded him, transformed him, forced him into his prison. He could not speak, could not move. He could only watch . . . and listen.

Was this to be his fate forever?

When Oberon appeared, long after Titania's departure, Robin took hope. His father would save him.

Oberon's serious expression destroyed Robin's hope. "You should have come to me before facing Titania. I cannot undo what she has wrought. But I may be able to change things . . ."

One

~

"There must be some mistake." Kate Carmichael shot out of her chair and planted her palms on the lawyer's desk. "I know Nana left a will. She gave her house to me."

"As I just explained, Miss Carmichael, if Zelma St. John had a will, it has yet to surface." Stan Bennett's expression didn't deviate from his bland mask. "She didn't file it with me."

Kate dug her fingernails into her palms, her stomach twisting into knots. This couldn't be happening. "But she promised I'd be taken care of. She knew how much I love that house."

"I'm sorry. Without a will, all of Mrs. St. John's possessions go to her only living relative, Adam St. John." The lawyer motioned toward the man sitting in the chair beside Kate's vacated one.

Adam St. John. He hadn't changed much from the young man she remembered, other than the gray at his temples.

He met her gaze. "You knew this would happen, Kate."

"But it's not fair. I love the house. You don't."

He gave her a smile that didn't begin to reach his eyes. "But I'm the only *blood* family Nana had. Just because she was soft-hearted enough to keep you after your father deserted you doesn't—"

"My father didn't desert me," Kate cut him off, tightening her fists. She didn't . . . wouldn't believe that. "He's dead."

"Whatever." The quick twist of Adam's lips showed he didn't care one way or the other. "For years you've mooched off the old lady. I think you've had far more than you deserve."

Kate bit her lip. His words held an element of truth. Dad had asked Nana to watch her for a month, maybe two. Only the two months had turned into twelve years. "But at least I *cared* about her. *I* was the one who took care of her when she got sick. *I* was the one who held her hand when she died." Tears pooled in her eyes and Kate blinked them back. She couldn't afford to display any weakness in front of him. "Where were you?"

"I had business."

"And that was more important than Nana?" Trust Adam to put economics ahead of his grandmother. In the past he'd enjoyed visiting her, but since his father had died three years ago, he'd only come to see Nana once. Making money was more important, especially since he'd married Cordelia.

"You'd been saying she was dying for the last two years. How was I to know she really would kick the bucket this time?" Adam brushed a piece of lint from his tailored suit coat, avoiding Kate's angry glare.

"You couldn't come say good-bye, but you can find time to take over her house?" Her voice rose as her pent-up emotions spilled over. "Ever since I've known you, all you cared about was money. I can see you haven't changed."

"Look who's talking." Adam scowled at her. "As far as the law is concerned you're nothing but a freeloader." He speared the lawyer with a glance. "Isn't that right?"

"I'm afraid in this case, Mr. St. John has all the rights, Miss Carmichael." Bennett's expression softened enough to appear apologetic. "Without a valid will, you're entitled to nothing."

"I see." Though anger vibrated through her body, Kate

carefully straightened and slid her purse strap onto her shoulder. "Then I guess I need to find it."

"If it even exists." Adam's final taunt followed her out the door, but it only added to Kate's determination.

She stalked down the sidewalk, momentarily glad she'd decided to walk the mile to the lawyer's office. She needed the physical exertion to ease her rising frustration.

Nana wouldn't have told her she'd be taken care of if it wasn't so. Since the disappearance of Kate's father, the elderly woman had been the only person Kate had dared to trust . . . and love. And, as always, everyone Kate cared about left her.

Her mother had passed away when Kate was eleven, following a two-year battle with cancer. Though Kate understood her mom had escaped the suffering and gone to a better place, she never could grasp the unfairness of it all. Mom had been a good person, always giving, ready to help others, smiling bravely to the end.

After her mother's death, Kate had drawn even closer to her father. He'd always had time for her and she'd never doubted his love. Until he left her.

The medical bills had bankrupted him. Always convinced that Carmichaels were blessed with faerie sight, Philip insisted he knew how to find some of the fae creatures' gold. With it, he could pay all the bills and provide for Kate. He'd left her with Nana, a close friend of his deceased parents, and ventured off on his quest. Kate never saw him again.

At that time, Kate had firmly believed his tales of magic. She'd had no doubts he would do as he said. But she'd matured since then.

Arriving at Nana's large Victorian house, she paused outside, her chest tight. Framed against a backdrop of tall elm and maple trees and the majestic beauty of the Rocky Mountains, the house resonated with dependability, security, and comfort. The house had been the one thing Kate thought would always be there.

And now Adam intended to take even this. With his connections, power, and money, what chance did she have of winning? Nana's promise that Kate would be taken care of meant nothing to anyone but Kate.

Approaching the wide front porch, trimmed with gingerbread and broad slats, Kate breathed in the serenity of the place, the air filled with the scents of spring—blooming daffodils, new grass, and budding trees. It gave her a sense of renewal, of life, of hope.

She loved this place. It was home, the only place she'd ever lived longer than a few years.

And dammit, she wasn't going to lose it. The will had to be here someplace.

Striding through the front door, Kate tossed her purse onto the heavy oak bureau in the hallway and paused. Where would Nana have put it?

She started with the sunroom, a small alcove off Nana's bedroom, where the elderly woman had spent most of her time the last couple of years. A thorough search of the desk and shelves revealed nothing, as did a larger sweep of the bedroom itself.

Blast. Where was it? Nana hadn't walked much in the past year, only from her bedroom to the main room downstairs. If the will wasn't here, it had to be downstairs.

Kate hesitated at the wood sliding doors that led into the living room. Of all the rooms in the house, this was her favorite. Large, multi-paned windows admitted brilliant sunshine, creating rainbows on the textured-papered walls as the light danced off the stained glass in the doors. Heavy wood furniture, most of it dating back to Nana's mother, dominated the room. Though well-worn and not always the most comfortable, the furnishings suited the decor. Kate had spent much of her time here, surrounded by history and books.

Where to start? She searched the crevices of the furniture to no avail. Kate eyed the bookshelves built into the walls on either side of the wide stone fireplace. Nana had always loved to read.

Kate resorted to removing books to check behind them, even flicking through the pages of some of Nana's favorites.

While she did find a long-lost recipe card tucked inside one novel, she didn't locate the will.

Desperate, she dragged a padded bench over to check the top shelves. Nana never could have gotten up here herself, but Kate had to check everywhere. Wherever she didn't look was where the will would be.

Jean, the housekeeper, hadn't cleaned up here for a while. Kate ran her hand over the shelf and sneezed as a thick layer of dust filled the air.

Still nothing. Damn.

With a sigh, Kate propped her elbow on the shelf. Now where?

Her change in position brought her face-to-face with the portrait. Ah, him. The handsome one. Involuntarily, Kate smiled. How could she not when looking at that face?

The portrait had hung in this spot over the fireplace since long before Kate's arrival. Nana's mother had brought it with her from England when she and her husband came to the United States as newlyweds following the first World War. Both Nana and Kate had spent many hours musing over the man's identity and staring at him for the pure pleasure of it.

They didn't make men like that anymore.

And that was assuming he'd once been real. His black hair, cut just above his collar, curled about his head, framing a face that was too perfect to be true—high cheekbones, a sleek aristocratic nose, dark eyebrows above chocolate brown eyes that held a glint of deviltry, and perfect lips, the bottom one sensuously full, the top finely arched.

His was a mouth made for kissing. And this man without a name, who existed only in this old portrait, had spoiled all other men for her. As a teen, Kate had been totally infatuated with him. No ordinary boy could compare.

She'd spent hours talking to the portrait, spilling her secrets, heartaches and desires where she knew they'd be safe. The man in the portrait had become her confidante, her friend, her unrequited love.

Kate sighed and reached out to trace the outline of his face. Even now, when she was long past childish dreams, she still held a fondness for him. For a mere picture, he appeared amazingly alive, his cheeks glowing with good health, his eyes twinkling with mischief, his lips curved with the hint of a smile. The artist had skillfully captured this handsome young man's vitality.

"I don't suppose you know where Nana hid the will." As the words left her mouth, she gasped.

Of course. Nana knew of Kate's love for the portrait. She must've put the will somewhere nearby.

With renewed eagerness, Kate ran her fingers along the edges of the engraved frame.

Nothing.

She pulled the heavy painting away from the wall and peeked behind it. Was it stuck to the back? No. She scowled. The will had to be here. There was nowhere else it could be.

Before she could replace the portrait, a strange glimmer on the back caught her eye. Squinting, she leaned closer, almost losing her balance to examine it. Words were scrawled against the back of the canvas. How unusual.

Teetering on one foot, she made out the erratic scrawl. "Ro . . . Rob . . . Robin. Good . . . Goodfellow. Robin Goodfellow. What does that mean?"

"Actually it's my name."

As the deep voice, shaded with a definite English accent, spoke behind her, Kate whirled around. The bench teetered, knocking her off-balance, and she plummeted toward the floor with a cry. Strong arms caught her in mid-air, wrapping beneath her knees and shoulders to cradle her close to a very solid chest.

Her heart hammered so hard, speech was momentarily impossible. Kate glanced up at the man and lost any remaining breath. It was him—the man in the portrait. He was gorgeous, definitely too handsome to be true, with a sensuous smile on his lips that matched his dancing dark brown eyes—eyes that looked at her with more than a little interest.

He couldn't be real. She had to be dreaming. Men didn't look at her that way. And they didn't hold her as if she was a lightweight either.

Realizing he still held her nestled against his powerful body, she forced words through her closed throat. "I . . . I . . . you can put me down now."

"If I must." He set her slowly on her feet, a twinkle in his eyes.

As her feet touched the carpet, Kate stumbled backward, unable to stop staring at this extraordinary man. His clothes looked odd, as if he'd stepped from an old movie. His pants clung to his muscular thighs, stopping at the knee where they met high stockings. His coat was long and trimmed with ornate buttons, his shirt silky with lace ruffles falling from the neck. He should've looked silly, but instead he looked . . . wonderful.

Kate shook her head. What was wrong with her? "Who are you?" she demanded finally. "Where did you come from?" How had he managed to get inside the house?

With a courtly bow, he took her hand, then pressed his lips against the back of it in a kiss so warm Kate felt certain it had left an imprint. "My name, sweet Kate, is Robin Good-fellow, and I thank you from the bottom of my heart for setting me free. I'd begun to fear I would be trapped in that portrait forever."

Portrait? Kate blinked, studying him. The resemblance *was* unbelievable, but he couldn't be . . . She glanced over her shoulder at the painting, then did a double-take, the blood draining from her head, leaving her dizzy. The painting did appear to have lost some of its vitality. This was insane.

She faced the stranger again. His smile greeted her confused gaze. He looked *exactly* like the man in the portrait, down to the clothing he wore. "I must be dreaming."

That had to be it. After years of fantasizing over this man, she'd fallen asleep and brought him to life in her dreams—not the first time she'd done so. But she didn't feel like she was asleep and the warmth of his lips still lingered on her hand.

Kate extended her trembling fingers until she touched his jacket. It felt real, the material smooth, the buttons hard and cold, the man beneath it solid and warm.

"You can't be real." She spoke aloud, half-hoping to convince herself.

"Ah, but I am." He caught her elbow in his hand, his grip firm, reassuring. "You've gone quite pale. Come, sit down."

The whirling in her brain made her agree. Better to sit now than pass out at his feet. She sank onto the couch and he dropped to one knee before her, his expression solemn for the first time.

"I should go while I can, but I do owe you an explanation, Kate. Since you set me free, it's the least I can do."

"How do you know my name?"

He grinned, bathing her in warmth. "How could I not know you, sweet Kate? I saw you grow from a young girl to the beautiful woman you are today." His voice took on a seductive huskiness as he said, "You confided in me often enough that I know you very well."

Her pulse leapt into a rumba. She'd have to be a rock to be immune to that voice. "But I . . . I talked to the portrait." Confused, she glanced from his too real profile to the painting, then back . . . twice.

"Aye, and I was trapped within it for the past two hundred years."

"That's impossible." She closed her eyes, convinced he would be gone once she opened them again. Maybe the stress of Nana's death and losing the house was causing her to see things.

"Everything is possible when there's magic about." His smooth English accent made his crazy words believable and she opened her eyes to stare at him.

"There's no such thing as magic." She couldn't keep bitterness from tinging her voice. "My father taught me that lesson well."

"No such thing?" He stood straight, his stance proud, his physique cover-model quality. "You don't believe that."

"Yes, I do." But she couldn't meet his accusatory gaze.

"That's heartache speaking, not you."

She looked up in surprise. "What do you know about my heartache?"

"A great deal, sweet Kate." His voice softened. "I've been hanging over that fireplace for a long time."

The portrait. She glanced at it, half expecting the painting to be empty, but the seductive image remained suspended over the mantel. Only it wasn't nearly as seductive as the flesh and blood specimen before her.

Kate inhaled slowly, trying to steady her rapid pulse. "I don't know where you came from, but it wasn't from the portrait."

His lips quirked in an amused smile. "You shouldn't find this so difficult to believe. The tales I've seen in your picture box show many magical things."

"Picture box?"

He pointed to the large console television on the opposite wall. "There. It's been very helpful in teaching me your speech patterns. It's shown me things even I had trouble believing—flying machines, men in the blackness of space, women wearing less clothing than some I've made love to . . ." His expression reflected his appreciation of that last statement, ". . . and most unusual, people who change from child to adult then back to child simply by eating some kind of food."

Kate laughed. "That's just a commercial."

"Commercial?"

"Advertisements. Don't believe everything you see on TV. It's—" She stopped abruptly. What was she doing? No matter how naive he acted, she couldn't believe his incredible tale.

She crossed her arms, refusing to let his charm and good looks seduce her. "Tell me where you came from, Mr. Goodfellow, why you're here, then leave."

"As you wish." He sat on the couch beside her, far too close for her peace of mind. However, instead of screaming danger as any intelligent mind would, hers concerned itself with the quirk of his eyebrow and the shape of his lips as he spoke.

"I was born in eleven eighty-nine."

"Eleven eighty-nine?" Kate made a scoffing noise. "Right.

Like you're eight hundred years old." She would've guessed more like twenty-eight or so.

He held up his hand, impish lights in his eyes. "Let me finish." When she pressed her lips together, he continued. "My mother was a simple country maiden who happened to catch the eye of Oberon, King of the Fae. They fell in love and I was born as a result of their union."

This sounded like one of the bedtime tales her father used to spin. A wave of nostalgia swept over her. She'd loved that time with Dad. Against her will, she found herself listening to Robin's crazy explanation.

"My father returned to the magical realm shortly after I was born, leaving me in my mother's care. She told me about him, but I didn't entirely believe her until my magic began to manifest itself."

"How?"

His smile sent waves of heat through her veins. "With my charm, of course."

"Conceited." Even if it was true, he didn't have to sound so confident.

He shrugged, a grin lurking at the corners of his lips. "Only the truth. My magic is in my charm."

At this point, she could believe *that*. He oozed sensuality and mischief, a deadly combination. She raised her eyebrows, the closest she could get to vocalizing her skepticism.

He leaned closer and her breath caught as his face came within inches of hers. "I could persuade the wild creatures of the forest to come to me. And I could convince mortals to do my bidding, as well. Few could refuse me anything."

The husky quality of his voice made Kate think of sweaty sheets and long, leisurely lovemaking. Yes, few probably refused him. Especially women.

She swallowed the lump in her throat. "Around here, we just call that sex appeal."

His grin broadened. "I do have some talent with glamour as well, but my powers of persuasion are my main gift. And my immortality."

"Oh, that's right." Kate gave him a wry smile. "You're eight hundred years old."

"Eight hundred and eleven, to be exact."

He sat back and Kate gulped for air, feeling as if she'd just been released from a spell. What was it about him? His magical charm? He hadn't even touched her, but her skin tingled, her blood warmed and her breasts grew heavy. She shook her head. Nonsense.

"So you've been spreading your charm for all that time?" He probably spread more than a few wild oats as well. A man like him would have women falling all over him.

"About six hundred years actually." Robin paused and his expression lost its animation. "I grew tired of living with mortals. They're born, they live hard lives with too little joy, then they die. After a few hundred years, I no longer wished to continue losing my friends to their mortality. I wanted to talk to my father, so I made my way to the magical realm."

If anything, he grew gloomier. Kate stopped herself from touching his shoulder to comfort him. How could she have gotten used to his smile in so short a time? Without it, she felt bereft. "And you couldn't find it?" she asked.

"I found it . . . and Titania."

Just the way he said the name sent a chill over Kate's heated flesh. "What happened?" In spite of herself, she was as engrossed in this fantastic tale as any told by her father.

"Titania is Queen of the Fae." He twisted his lips in a mere shadow of his previous grins. "And Oberon's wife. I quickly discovered she wasn't happy about his dalliance with my mother. The fact that my mother was long dead didn't sway her. *I* was alive."

He sighed. "Even worse, Oberon had given one of Titania's circlets to my mother. He'd thought Titania would never miss it since it was one of her plainer ones. But she did and had never forgiven him for it."

"What did she do? Throw you out?"

"Ah, that would've been too simple." A hint of pain appeared in his expressive eyes as he glanced at the painting. "I made the mistake of taking my portrait with me. My friend

Tommy had just painted it and I intended to present it to my father as a gift. Since the Fae cannot harm one another, Titania spun a spell that trapped me within the painting for all eternity—a fate worse than any death. I could see. I could hear. But I was inanimate, unable to live."

His despair tugged at Kate's heart. Her active imagination had no trouble putting herself in his place, doomed forever to watch while unable to participate. Her eyes widened as a new thought occurred. Doomed to watch her as she'd passed through the difficult teenage years to adulthood. How many times had she come into this room to bid Nana good-night wearing nothing more than a skimpy nightshirt?

No, she wouldn't even consider that.

"If you were trapped forever, then how did you get free?" she demanded. She had him now, caught in his lies.

"You freed me, sweet Kate." His gentle smile returned. "With help from my father. He couldn't remove Titania's spell, but he did modify it slightly so that if a mortal said my name while in the presence of the portrait, I would be released. To increase my chances, he wrote my name on the back, where you saw it."

"Why the back? Why not the front where it would be more obvious?"

"Ah, more obvious to Titania as well." Robin ran his finger down the bridge of her nose in a quick but affectionate gesture that sent flashes of fire through her blood. "He sent my portrait back into the mortal world, where I waited for someone with faerie sight to read my name. And at last, you did."

"Faerie sight?" Now he was trying to make her believe she had magic as well. Not likely. "Anyone could've read that."

"The portrait went through several owners before Zelma's mother brought it here. None of them saw it."

"I don't—"

He touched her lips, silencing her. "I know. You don't believe. It's no matter whether you do or not. I've done my duty and told my tale. Now I'll be on my way." His eyes twinkled. "I have much to learn about this new era."

As he stood, she leapt to her feet. He was leaving. Wasn't that what she wanted? Then why did she have this irrational impulse to grab his arm and make him stay? She straightened her shoulders. "I think that's best."

"Yes, I . . ." He hesitated, studying her face, his gaze suddenly intense. "It is for the best, but I'll not go without a kiss."

Before his intention fully registered, he closed the distance between them and touched his lips to hers. Kate had been kissed before, but his gentle pressure reduced them all to dim tepid memories. He turned kissing into an art form, his lips seducing hers, the tenderness of his claim shattering Kate's defenses.

Okay, maybe he hadn't been lying about magical charm. Kate's heart thudded so loudly she knew he had to hear it. Her lips softened beneath his and the rest of her body followed suit, wanting to nestle even closer. Without conscious thought, she tightened her hand around his arm. An attempt to hold him in place?

It had the opposite effect. Robin drew back and smiled warmly. "Good-bye, sweet Kate, and thank you again." He gave her a courtly bow, then walked from the room.

Kate couldn't move. Her body simply didn't have the power to respond to mental commands. She stared after him, entranced, until the sound of the front door closing roused her from her stupor.

Good Lord. That man was more dangerous than a loaded weapon. Especially to a woman who hadn't much experience with men . . . a woman a little too Rubenesque to capture any man's interest, she thought.

Forcing herself to breathe evenly, she turned to the portrait. The familiar face looked back at her—the same, yet somehow different. It didn't have the same vibrancy, the sense of almost being alive. Could his story be true?

She didn't dare believe it. Her father had lived for that nonsense once and look where it led him. To his death.

But Robin's resemblance to the man in the portrait couldn't be instantly dismissed. A relative, perhaps? Had he come for the portrait, then left because he'd found Kate there?

She pulled the heavy frame away from the wall in an attempt to look behind it again. The name was there, perfectly obvious, if difficult to read.

"What are you doing?"

Adam's accusing tone made Kate jump and she turned to glare at him. When had he come in? "I'm trying to read the name back here."

Though his scowl didn't fade, Adam joined her in peering behind the painting. "I don't see anything."

"It's right there." Kate pointed to the scrawl.

"There's nothing there." Adam let the portrait fall back against the wall. "What are you plotting now?"

"What?" Hot anger rose quickly. She didn't have red hair for nothing. "I was looking for the will."

"The *fictitious* will." He pinned her beneath his blue gaze. "Even if you produced one, I wouldn't believe it was real."

"How dare—" Kate stopped as she suddenly spotted Robin standing behind Adam. He hadn't been there a moment ago. She'd swear it.

Robin looked equally surprised. His expression held bewilderment as he glanced around the room, stopping at Kate. With a shrug, he grinned and bowed once again. "I was just leaving."

He made it to the front door before Adam turned to look at him. "Who was that?" he demanded. "Your boyfriend?"

"I don't have a boyfriend." Kate raised her chin, daring him to taunt her. "You've told me often enough no man would look twice at me."

A sheepish expression crossed his features, reminding her of the shaky camaraderie they'd once shared . . . before he met Cordelia. "You have a pretty face, Kate. You just need to lose a few pounds."

Easier said than done. Kate didn't respond. Instead, she focused her attention on the portrait. Robin hadn't looked at her as if he found her roundness offensive. In fact, he made her feel sexy, almost pretty. His magical charm, no doubt.

Adam cleared his throat in an obvious attempt to get her attention. She didn't give him the satisfaction.

"Kate, I've talked to Mr. Bennett. I have to return home for now, so he's going to arrange for the sale of the house and its contents."

That brought her about to face him. "You can't sell this place. It's my home."

"Not any longer." His face hardened. "You managed to dupe my grandmother all these years, but the free ride is over."

"I'm not a freeloader, Adam." No matter what he thought. "I've been working and helping to support Nana, which is more than you've done."

"It doesn't matter. The house is mine now."

"That doesn't mean you have to *sell* it." Nana was probably turning in her grave at the thought. "Or is Cordelia the one pushing for the money?"

The sudden tightness of his expression confirmed her suspicions. "I have a house in Chicago. I don't need this one." Adam surveyed the surroundings. "It would take too much time and money to keep it up."

"But—"

"You can always buy it yourself."

His suggestion made her pause. She had some money saved from her meager salary as an elementary school secretary. She'd intended to use it to go to college, to get her teaching degree, but if it would save the house . . . "How much are you asking?"

He named a figure that made her gasp. "I can't begin to afford that."

"That's not my problem." He started for the hallway. "You have a week to move out."

"A *week*?" She hadn't known until today that she'd have to leave. When would she have time to find another place, to pack, to move?

"A week." His familiar scowl raked over her. "If you're still here next Friday, I'll have you forcibly removed."

Kate trembled with rage, her fingernails digging into her palms. "Damn you, Adam."

"You've taken advantage of the St. Johns long enough. My father told Nana to get rid of you years ago. She wouldn't listen. It's up to me now."

Before Kate could come up with an adequate retort, he left, the firm click of the door signaling his departure. Damn him again. Nana had loved her and Kate had returned that love.

Did Adam have a clue how much Kate had contributed to the upkeep of this place? How much time she'd spent taking care of Nana as the woman's health failed? This house had been her home, Nana her only remaining family.

Now she had nothing.

Choking back a sob, she whirled around to run to her room and collided with Robin's sturdy body. His hands caught her shoulders to steady her and she stared at him in amazement. Hadn't he just left?

Twice?

He didn't look very happy himself. "Bloody hell," he muttered. "I'm not free after all."

"What?" Kate blinked back her tears and tried to concentrate.

"Every time I try to leave, I make it no further than the front walk before I find myself pulled back here to you."

"Which means what?"

His expressive mouth twisted in a grimace. "It means that while I'm no longer bound to the portrait, I am still caught by Titania's spell. Only now I'm bound to *you*."

Two

Kate blinked. Surely she hadn't heard correctly. "What did you say?"

"The spell isn't broken." Robin's accent grew more lilting as he continued, making his words difficult to understand. "Oberon modified the spell enough to provide a way out of the portrait, but now I'm tied to whoever released me. You."

"No way." She shook her head and backed out of his hold. This guy was more devious than she'd thought. "I'm not buying that for a moment. You came here to steal the portrait, didn't you? And now you think you've found a way to stick around until you can do that."

"Believe me, I'd prefer to leave." He glanced around. "The house is nice, but I've seen nothing except this room for the past eighty years."

"Then go."

"I can't. I tried. I get no further than the front pathway when I find myself pulled back here . . . to you," he repeated himself.

He *had* looked startled, but . . . no, that was impossible. His whole story sounded like some fairy tale concocted by her father.

"Look, I don't have time for this. A woman I cared a great deal about died recently and I'm about to lose my home." To her horror, her voice quavered and she paused to regain control. "Just go away. Please."

"I'm sorry." And dammit, he did sound sympathetic. "I liked Zelma, too."

He couldn't have known Nana. "How did—?"

Before she could complete her sentence, Robin jerked his head toward the portrait. So he still clung to his preposterous story of hanging there watching for decades. A shiver vibrated down her spine. No, she wasn't about to consider the implications of that.

"I'm not buying any of this." She stalked into the hallway and yanked open the front door. "Now leave."

He followed her. "I can't." He stopped beside her, entirely too close for her peace of mind. "What is the distance from the main room to the front path?" Even when he was serious, his eyes held a dangerous glimmer of mischief.

Kate glanced in the night, thankful for an excuse to look away. The sidewalk was dimly illuminated by the street light. "I'm not sure. About fifty feet."

"If you stand here, can you watch me until I reach a point that far away?"

She nodded, her eyes narrowed. What was he up to?

"Good. Then watch me, sweet Kate." He crossed the porch, leapt nimbly down the steps, then walked with long strides down the front path to the sidewalk. Turning, he paused to wave, then strode along the pavement. If he kept moving at that pace, he'd be out of sight in a few minutes.

Kate leaned forward to watch him, then blinked and looked again. He was there . . . and then he wasn't. Had he run?

"Kate?"

With a gasp, she whirled around to find Robin behind her, his arms crossed. "Believe me now?"

Her mind whirled with possibilities as she struggled to calm her erratic heartbeat into a more even rhythm. How had he done it? For a man to be in one spot in one instant, then another in the next was . . . impossible. Kate swallowed. She sure seemed to encounter that word a lot lately, especially since she'd met Robin.

"If I believe this . . ." Then everything else had to be true, as well. "I'd have to believe your whole crazy story."

His beguiling smile reappeared. "I suppose you would. Is that so terrible?" Before she could reply, he touched her shoulder, his hold firm yet warm, almost comforting. "Come inside. You've gone pale again."

She accompanied him into the house, struggling to make sense of what she'd seen. If she believed Robin was under a spell, tied to her, then she had to believe his story of magic, of actually being trapped in the portrait for two hundred years.

As they entered the living room, she glanced at the painting over the mantel. The resemblance between it and Robin was too uncanny to be coincidental. To keep denying it was foolish. As incredible as his tale sounded, he had to be telling the truth.

"So what happens now?" She sank onto the couch, her senses numb.

Robin sat beside her. "This changes things. I'd decided to stay away from the Fae for the present time, but now . . ." Robin gave her a half smile. "Now I will have to face Titania in order to get the spell removed."

Kate looked at him in surprise. "Why would she consider removing it? You said she hates you."

"True. And I don't expect that's changed in only two hundred years."

"Then—"

He held up his finger. "I had plenty of time to think while I was trapped. If I can locate her circlet—the one Oberon gave my mother—and return it, she may be willing to undo her spell and allow me to stay."

"Her circlet? Does it still exist?" How could Robin expect to find something like that after all these years? It could be buried in the dirt, forgotten in a museum or hidden in some stranger's home in England.

"It still exists. In fact, it's here." He turned to survey the shelves. "In this house . . . somewhere."

Kate frowned. How could he know that? Nana didn't own anything like a circlet, at least, not that Kate knew of. "How . . . ?"

"When I first thought of this idea, I created a simple spell that enabled the portrait to find the hands that held the circlet. Zelma's mother brought both the painting and the circlet with her when she came to this house. The pull has remained all these years, which means the circlet is still here."

"What does it look like?"

He shrugged, a careless gesture that added to his appeal. "It's one of Titania's plainer crowns. Circular, of course, gold, with a simple design engraved around the outside."

Kate did a quick mental survey of all Nana's jewelry. "I don't remember seeing anything like that."

"Then we'll have to hunt for it." He gave her an engaging smile that tugged at her emotions.

"And Nana's will."

"Certainly."

"We—" Kate started to speak, but then caught herself as a yawn emerged instead. Where had that come from? How could anyone yawn with a man as appealing as Robin sitting beside her?

Glancing at her watch, she straightened. Where had the time gone? She'd gone from a full day at work to the lawyer's office to this unbelievable meeting with the man from the portrait. No wonder she was tired . . . and susceptible to Robin's charm.

She stood abruptly. "We can continue this tomorrow. It's been a killer of a day and I'm beat."

Robin nodded slowly, his expression indicating he didn't completely comprehend everything she said. "As you wish."

Where to put him? If their distance limit truly was fifty feet, she couldn't leave him on the couch as she preferred. But having him ensconced on the second floor—even in a different room—was too unnerving. Yet what choice did she have? He wasn't really a threat. Aside from his toe-curling farewell kiss, he hadn't tried anything.

And if he did, would she try to stop him?

Of course she would. Kate gave herself a quick nod for emphasis, trying to add strength to her conviction. *Of course.*

"Come upstairs. There are a couple of empty rooms. You can sleep in one of those." She turned to leave and he joined her.

"A room beside yours would work best."

Her heart gave a sudden lurch. "Excuse me?" Maybe she wasn't safe, after all.

"Do you want to push the limits of how far we can be apart from each other? Rolling over could bring me into your bed." His eyes gleamed with mischief. "You wouldn't want that, would you?"

Her throat went dry. "I . . . ah. . . ." Why did that mental image send her pulse into a record-breaking rhythm? "I . . . no, I wouldn't."

He grinned and raised his eyebrows, but said nothing. He didn't have to. Kate's protest sounded false, even to herself. Blast, how was she going to get rid of this man?

She grimaced. Normally, she couldn't get a man to stick around any longer than it took him to eye her hips. But then, this situation was hardly normal. Robin *couldn't* leave. He'd proven that.

She took him to the bedroom beside hers and quickly put clean sheets on the bed, her cheeks warming when Robin bent to help her. His nearness made her entirely too aware of him . . . and their surroundings. He radiated a sensuality that stimulated her long-dormant desires.

She had to get away before she did something stupid, like throw her arms around his neck and beg for another fantastic kiss. Inhaling deeply, Kate pivoted and hurried for the door, not daring to glance back. "Good night."   ·

"Good night, sweet Kate." His husky voice slid like smooth brandy over her nerves, remaining within her mind as she entered her bedroom.

This was *not* good. Already she could tell Robin was a

charming rogue who didn't believe in committing to any woman—definitely *not* what she wanted. Kate sighed. Why was she even considering any kind of attraction to Robin? The man wasn't fully human, or so he claimed.

Climbing beneath her covers, she switched off the light and nestled deep into her pillow. Magic. She still found it difficult to believe. Was his story some sort of scam?

She recalled Robin's sudden appearance beside her earlier. It had to be magic. Nothing else could explain everything she'd seen.

Weariness pulled at her eyelids. Maybe after she had some sleep . . . maybe in the morning . . . maybe then she'd know what to do about Robin Goodfellow.

Robin opened his eyes to find the rosy rays of morning sun creeping through his window. Ah, he'd slept well. Much better than he'd expected. Reclining on this marvelous cushioned bed after two hundred years of feeling nothing had been a treat.

Remaining on his back, he pounded his fists against the soft padding beneath him. Perhaps this was one of those unusual beds he'd seen in the picture box. A man had dropped a heavy ball and the wooden pins on it didn't fall over. Magic. He smiled. From what he'd seen, magic was very prominent in this time.

He could learn to like it here.

Sitting upright, he pushed back the comforter and swung his feet to the floor. Amazing. The room held no hint of the chill he knew must linger outside, yet he saw no sign of a fire.

Yes, he could *definitely* like it here.

He pulled on his breeches, then paused in reaching for his shirt. People dressed differently now. He'd noticed that as well. In fact, everyone appeared to wear less than he was accustomed to.

Except for Kate.

As a girl, she'd worn clothes that clung to her developing figure. Then one day, she'd stopped. Most of her apparel now

was similar to that she'd worn yesterday . . . male trousers—
something Robin realized women wore in this time—and
loose shirts that concealed her curves. Why?

From what he'd observed in the television, most women
dressed in clothing designed to reveal their assets. Yet Kate
chose to hide hers from the world. Robin quirked one eyebrow in the direction of her room. Interesting.

Hearing laughter outside, he padded barefoot to the window. A man and woman sauntered along the walkway, obviously enjoying each other's company.

Robin studied the man's clothing. He wore the distinctive
blue trousers called jeans that Robin had observed on many
men over the past couple decades. That style must be the
reigning design for this era.

After a moment's thought, Robin touched his trousers,
then grinned as they changed to match those of the man
outside. At least he still retained his magic.

He shifted his weight from one foot to the other, testing
the feel of this odd material. Heavy, strong, yet it fit his legs
every bit as close as his own garment had.

Now for a shirt. He looked out the window again, but the
couple was almost to the end of the block.

Yanking open the window, Robin stuck his head outside.
He still couldn't see them well. The porch roof extended
beneath his window. If he stood there, perhaps he could get
the one good glimpse he needed.

Robin thrust one leg through the open window, then froze
in the act of pulling his body out as an already too-familiar
tingling seized him. He'd exceeded the allowable distance
from Kate. "Bloody . . ."

". . . hell." The remainder of his oath emerged in a small,
bright room, different from any he'd ever seen, but that
didn't claim his attention. The naked woman who whirled to
face him did.

She was beautiful.

Why did Kate hide such treasures? Her skin was flawless,
a smooth creamy color from top to bottom. Her generous
breasts would more than fill a man's hand, her peaked nipples

the color of fresh peaches, begging to be kissed, caressed. Her gently rounded belly and hips hinted at sensuality and passion, more than any of those stick women he'd seen in the picture box.

He continued his thorough examination, unable to look away. Auburn curls capped her Venus mound, matching the unruly curls that tumbled around her shoulders, unfettered for once from a tight braid. Ah, this was a woman made for loving.

Desire slammed into Robin, igniting a painful fire within him. He stepped toward her.

Kate finally moved, crying out in alarm as she jumped into a wide tub and wrapped a curtain around her. "What are you doing here?" she demanded, her cheeks shining beacons of red.

Words failed him. He could only stare, still envisioning the charms she tried to hide, charms he ached to touch.

"Get out of here. Now!" Fear trembled in her rising voice, jerking Robin from his reverie.

He gave her a slight bow. "My apologies."

Fleeing the room, he tugged the door shut behind him, to stand stunned in the hallway outside. He sank against the wall, then slid down it, his senses reeling, until he sat on the floor.

By the Stones, he'd always thought of his Kate as a delightful child who'd grown into a lovely woman, but this . . . this was beyond imagination. After all the women he'd seen through the years, he'd deduced their preferred form had swung from the full curves he preferred to nothing more than skin and bones. Did men now approve of that?

He'd spent many years with Peter Paul Rubens, encouraging the artist in his portrayals of beautiful women. Peter had mentioned more than once that only a woman with such generosity of form as Kate possessed could truly appreciate a man's loving. From experience, Robin agreed.

But as the years progressed, he'd found women forcing themselves into thinner and thinner molds. He hadn't lacked for partners, but he'd found fewer that reveled in lovemaking as he did. That had played a part in his decision to return to the magical realm. He'd experienced too many women, too many mortals who died before ever truly realizing the joys of life.

And now he'd found Kate—beautiful, enticing Kate—who represented all that he sought in a woman and stirred his desire, dormant for two hundred years, to a fever pitch. Yet she was the one woman he could not have.

After years spent listening to her confidences, her losses, her joys, she'd become his friend. He'd never known a woman in that capacity before. Many had succumbed to his charm, cared for him, shared his bed, yet none had touched his emotions.

Except Kate.

He cared what happened to her, wanted her to win this house, wanted her to find the happiness she deserved. And she wouldn't find it with him. He knew himself well enough. He didn't stay with any woman for long. It was his nature, his method of self-protection.

After all, they all died eventually and he was left alone . . . again.

No, better to value this rare friendship than to cater to his lusts and leave Kate with another loss to bear. He could do it. He *would* do it.

Robin crossed his arms over his knees, then dropped his head atop them. He needed to find a way to break this bond that kept him from leaving her. Soon.

Kate refused to look at Robin as she darted about the kitchen, throwing breakfast together. Only his stunned expression when she'd seen him in the bathroom made her believe his story.

That he should've seen her like that, totally exposed, all her flaws revealed, still filled her with humiliation. She'd only ever allowed one man to see her naked—the first and only man to make love to her.

If their act could've been called that. He'd been as inexperienced as she, more eager to get inside her than see to her satisfaction. When she'd cried out at the pain, he'd ignored her, too caught up in his own desires.

Fortunately he'd needed little time to finish. But when she'd complained, he'd been angry, telling her she should count herself lucky that any man would touch her. His parting remark still had the power to hurt her. "The only guy who'd look at you twice is the Pillsbury Dough Boy."

Shaking her head to chase away the memory, she lifted the coffee pot from the burner, then turned to discover that Robin had already placed two mugs on the counter. With muttered thanks, she poured the hot liquid into them.

It wasn't as if she ate a lot. And she exercised regularly. But she was tall, nearly six feet, and big-boned like her father. She would never be a size seven. It was a physical impossibility.

And now Robin—the handsomest man she'd ever seen, the one man she'd lusted over since her adolescent years—had seen her at her worst. She wouldn't meet his gaze to discover his revulsion—or worse, his pity. Now she would lose the one best friend she'd had through the years.

She handed him a mug, keeping her gaze firmly focused on his chest. He'd managed to find a gray-blue polo shirt that fit him perfectly and she concentrated on the three buttons near his collar.

"Thank you, Kate." To her surprise, he took both mugs from her hands and set them on the table, then cupped her chin between his palms and lifted her face.

She flinched out of instinct and refused to look up. As if not doing so would erase his horror.

"Look at me, Kate."

The gentleness of his voice beckoned her. Slowly, she lifted her gaze, then blinked. No revulsion. No horror. No pity. Instead, his gaze held an affection that reached inside her to soothe her, an affection that still spoke of friendship.

"I've said I'm sorry. I didn't mean to intrude upon your privacy. I assumed you were in the next room or I wouldn't have tried to step out the window."

"I know. I didn't think about it when I went to the bathroom." She didn't blame him for what happened. With the bathroom at the opposite end of the hallway, she should've known she was pushing their distance limit, but she'd been too busy reviewing the previous day's events, trying to convince herself this magical visitor wasn't just a dream.

His sudden appearance had quickly convinced her of his reality.

"I just . . . I'm sorry you had to see me like that." Heat flooded her face and she glanced away.

"I'm not." Robin brushed his thumb across her cheek, pausing at the corner of her mouth.

She glanced up, startled. The warmth in his eyes had deepened, changed into a seductive heat that made her breath catch in her throat. Surely he was joking. He looked as if . . . as if he wanted her.

"I didn't think such beauty existed in this era." He smiled, a twinkle replacing the fire. "I'm glad to know I was wrong."

"Beauty?" Kate pulled free. She knew what she looked like. On a good hair day and twenty pounds lighter, she might pass for pretty, but never beautiful. "You don't have to mock me."

She returned to the counter and jammed two slices of bread in the toaster, refusing to turn around despite his commanding presence behind her.

"I'm serious, Kate," he said quietly.

She almost believed him. God, she wanted to believe him. But she couldn't. Too many others had led her to believe otherwise.

Even her father. Though part of her knew better, the child in Kate always felt that if she'd been prettier, thinner, her father would have stayed instead of disappearing on his fruitless quest. She wasn't beautiful and never had been.

But Robin was a charmer. She had to remember that. And a very good charmer, too. "I don't want to talk about it."

Pulling the butter from the refrigerator, she kept her back to him. "We need to search for the will and circlet today. I'm running out of time."

Robin didn't reply. After several moments of silence, Kate

turned to look at him. His expression was serious, almost angry, his lips pressed together.

"Robin?" What had she done?

He nodded his head in a quick movement, a twinkle appearing in his gaze. "As you wish, sweet Kate. Sweet, *beautiful*, Kate."

His words sent a rush of pleasure through her. Okay, so he was a charmer. That didn't mean she couldn't enjoy his nonsense.

Still, she tried to keep as much distance as possible between them while they spent the bulk of that day and part of the next morning going through every room of the large house. They searched through drawers, in closets, in corners, lifted cushions, mattresses, tables, rugs, everything. And the result remained the same. Nothing. No will. No circlet.

Kate collapsed on the couch in the living room and laid her head back, despair creating an ache in her gut. "They're not here."

Robin paced the room. "The circlet is here. I know it."

"Then use your magic to find it." Weariness made Kate snap at him as she sat upright.

The surprise in Robin's gaze made her immediately regret them. "I wish it was that easy," he said quietly. "But I'm half-mortal. My magic is limited."

"I'm sorry." Kate rested her forehead on her palm. "I don't know what to do next."

"We'll rest, then search again."

Where else could they look? As much as Kate hated to admit defeat, she had to face her uncertain future. "I don't have time for that anymore."

"What do you mean?" Robin sank onto the cushion beside her, his closeness triggering a sudden rush of heat through her veins.

Kate inhaled deeply. She'd managed to keep away from him until now for fear of just this. He affected her in a way she didn't want to be affected, made her dream of things that could never be.

"I'm going to have to move." Speaking the words aloud

made them real, gave them weight, and brought a rush of tears to Kate's eyes. She hated to leave her home. "If I'm not out of here by Friday, Adam will throw me out."

"He won't do that." Robin touched her shoulder, his encouragement only making Kate feel worse. "He may not be the most pleasant man I've ever seen, but he's not that cold-hearted."

"He wasn't until he married money-hungry Cordelia. He intends to claim the house and sell it." Kate swallowed the lump in her throat. "His father always thought I was a free-loader and now Adam intends to get rid of me."

Robin's brief pause added silent agreement. "Where will you go?" he asked finally.

"To an apartment, I guess. Preferably furnished and cheap." With a sigh, she reached for the newspaper on the table and turned to the rentals section in the classifieds. There were several one-bedroom furnished apartments listed, but the ones in the better parts of town were far above her price range.

This was going to be more difficult than she'd thought. Robin peered over her shoulder as she circled some potential places. A knot formed in her stomach, growing tighter with each selection.

"Don't you want two bedrooms?"

Kate jerked around to look at Robin, realization dawning with a sense of dread. How could she live with him? Just two days in his company had her hormones ready to tango. "You can't stay with me."

"And I can't leave." His slight smile held a hint of wistfulness. "You're stuck with me until Titania removes her spell, and I don't dare approach her without the circlet."

He needed the circlet. She needed the will. Kate surveyed the vast room, praying for both items to reveal themselves. But there wasn't a place left they hadn't already searched.

Unable to stay still any longer, she jumped to her feet. "Let's go." She snared her purse from the bureau in the entry hall, then headed for the garage, Robin following.

"Are we going in one of those motor vehicles? A car?"

The excitement in his voice made Kate grin. "Such as it is."

His expression faded to surprise when he spotted Kate's car. Her pale yellow and cream hatchback had seen better years, but as long as it worked, she planned to keep it. "I know it's not much." She opened the front door and showed him how to get in. "But it still runs."

"I'd hoped it would be red." Disappointment tinged his voice.

She shook her head. "That's a guy thing, isn't it?"

He looked at her in confusion and she shook her head. How was she to explain red sports cars to a man who'd only seen them on TV?

His questions continued as she drove around town, comparing apartments and rental costs. If she hadn't already been convinced that he came from a distant time, his amazement at common things like street lights and billboards would've done so. However, he did have an amazing familiarity with fast food places, pointing out each one as they passed.

Kate grinned. Ah, the wonders of television.

Her amusement faded as she ruled out one apartment after another. Those she could afford weren't anything she wanted to live in and those she preferred exceeded her present ability to pay. Her savings account had dropped considerably after she'd settled Nana's bills. If she used her remaining money on an apartment, her dream of becoming a teacher would be delayed that much longer. But what choice did she have?

She was down to two possibilities, neither with a price listed, when she pulled in front of a small apartment complex. The exterior appealed to her at once.

The six apartments formed a row with the manager's larger dwelling at the end, creating an L-shape. The grounds were neatly kept, the bushes budding with spring greenery, and the grass trimmed. Metal stairs led up to the apartments. The rail lining the walkway in front of the apartments contained flower boxes blooming with daffodils and crocuses.

"This might not be too bad," she murmured to Robin as they approached the manager's door.

"It's better than most we've seen thus far."

The apartment was all she'd hoped to find, small but clean with sturdy furniture and a tiny den that could double as a spare bedroom, at least until Robin left. Kate watched him playing with the faucets in the kitchen and bit back a smile. He had to leave soon . . . before she found it too hard to let him go.

"I like this." Kate turned to Arlan McGrew, the manager. "But it's so nice I hate to ask how much it is."

"Seven-fifty a month, plus utilities." Her heart sank. "Plus three hundred damage deposit and the first month's rent in advance."

"I see." She turned away as disappointment swelled. There was no way she could scrape together that much and the rent would barely leave any money for other bills.

"Kate, what is it?" Robin left the kitchen and took her hands in his, his gaze concerned.

She shook her head in despair. "I can't afford it."

"You like this one, don't you?"

"Yes. It'll never be Nana's, but it's comfortable and close to work."

He squeezed her hands. "I'll talk to him."

His confidence eased her depression. "What are you going to do? Charm him out of it?"

Robin's reply was a wink and impish smile before he left her side and approached McGrew. "Excellent accommodations, sir. My friend is interested, but finds the cost a trifle steep."

The manager shrugged. "If she doesn't take it, there are others who will."

That was true. With the town's booming economy, affordable housing was becoming more and more scarce. What did Robin hope to accomplish? McGrew wasn't about to lose out on a hefty profit.

"But none of the others are Miss Carmichael. She is a tenant beyond compare with unblemished character and dependable finances." Robin flashed his warm smile. "Perhaps you could make an adjustment in her case?"

To Kate's surprise, McGrew didn't dismiss the idea out-right. In fact, he appeared to hang on Robin's words. "I . . ."

"Of course, the fee would have to be fair to you as well as her," Robin continued. He rested his hand on the man's shoulder. "But I can see you are a reasonable man. What amount would you suggest?"

This was insane. Robin could be as charming as he liked, but the manager wasn't about to change his mind. Kate held out her hand to stop him. Better he quit now before McGrew became angry.

McGrew hesitated, his gaze still locked on Robin. "I'm sorry, young man, but I can't possibly rent this place for less than three-fifty a month."

"I think that will be acceptable."

The blood drained from Kate's head. Surely she hadn't heard right. She sank toward the nearby couch and missed, landing in a heap on the floor.

Three

Once Kate regained her composure, her rental of the apartment moved quickly. When McGrew examined her completed paperwork, he beamed at her as if he'd just signed a princess instead of a school secretary, and waived her damage deposit, settling instead for just the first month's rent.

Giving Kate the keys to the apartment, he left her and Robin in the middle of the living room. Kate stared at the closed door for several moments before she turned to Robin. He watched her, arms crossed, his expression smug.

"What . . . what did you do to him?"

"Just a bit of glamour and charm. I told you I had powers of persuasion."

"But . . . but . . ." Kate couldn't find the words to express her unease. She'd seen nothing out of the ordinary, only Robin's usual good nature. "What if he changes his mind? How long will it last?"

"He believes he's made a good deal. It's worth a discount to have you for a tenant."

"But how? Why did he act like I was so important?"

"Because you *are* important."

She knew better than that and gave Robin a glance that told him so.

He grinned. "When you filled out the contract, I made him see what he wanted to see—the perfect tenant."

"But I didn't see anything." She'd been there the entire time, looking at the same sheet of paper.

"You wouldn't. You have the faerie sight. Otherwise you never would've seen my name on the portrait."

"There's no such thing as faerie sight." She turned away as an ache blossomed deep inside at the familiar words. "Now you sound like my father."

"And that's a bad thing, isn't it?" Robin's tone turned dangerously soft. "After all, you still haven't forgiven him for deserting you."

The ache swelled as she whirled on him. "You know nothing about it." What did he know about a girl who'd adored her father, who'd lived for each letter he sent, who'd died inside when the letters stopped and never resumed?

"Ah, but I do." Robin stepped closer. "You forget I saw you weeping. I heard your prayers to bring him home. He broke your heart, sweet Kate."

She thought she'd gotten over that pain, but it washed over her as fresh as the day when she'd realized her father must be dead. Tears threatened again and she turned her back on Robin, unwilling to let him see how easily he broached her defenses.

He placed his hands on her shoulders and brought her around to face him. "I hated seeing you hurt. I wanted to climb out of that portrait and hold you in my arms and make it all better."

Tremors shook Kate and though she tried to stop them, tears trickled down her cheeks. "Adam's father insisted Dad left me there to get rid of me. But he wouldn't have deserted me, Robin. He wouldn't."

"No." He cradled her face between his palms, his gaze intense. "No man could ever leave you."

She stared at him, confused. How could he say that?

Everyone had left her—her mother, her father, Nana. Even
Robin would leave as soon as he could.

He brushed the tears off her cheeks with his broad thumbs.
"I didn't see much of him, but your father loved you, Kate.
Don't ever doubt that. He loved you very much."

His words broke through her emotional barrier and Kate
buried her face in his chest as sobs racked her body. She'd
always kept her tears hidden from Nana, only allowing herself to cry when with her confidante—the man in the portrait
. . . Robin.

He wrapped his arms around her, allowing her to cry.
Slowly, the sobs eased, giving way to small hitches in her
breathing, but Kate didn't move. When was the last time
she'd been held with such tenderness, such caring?

It felt so right, so good to be in Robin's arms that she
didn't want to leave. But she had to. He was only being kind.

She pushed against his chest in an attempt to step away,
but his hold remained firm. Surprised, she looked up, then
caught her breath.

Fire blazed in his eyes, his gaze searching her face until
it rested on her mouth. Her lips softened in response and she
moistened them with the tip of her tongue.

His arms tensed around her. "Kate." Her name emerged
as more of a groan. He cradled the back of her head in one
hand as he drew nearer, his warm breath caressing her skin.

Anticipation created a different type of trembling and Kate
closed her eyes. Would this kiss be as devastating as the first?

"Ah, Kate." Instead of Robin's lips, Kate felt his forehead
rest against hers. He exhaled a shaky breath, then released
her and stepped back, not meeting her gaze. "Shouldn't we
return to the house?"

Kate couldn't stop the wave of disappointment that washed
over her as he turned for the door. What had she expected?
That she would actually attract someone like Robin? Yeah,
right.

He was her friend, nothing more. He only remained because he couldn't leave. She had to remember that. Otherwise she would find herself alone and hurt.

Again.

"I don't like this." Kate paused outside the elementary school where she worked and looked at Robin. "You can't hang around all day."

"I have no choice."

Though Robin had dressed in appropriate clothes for work, the casual brown shirt and pants enhancing his handsomeness, Kate had no idea what he'd do for an entire day in school. "I've lost my home. I can't afford to lose my job, too. Can't you make yourself invisible or something?"

"I'm afraid not." Impish lights danced in his eyes. "But it will work out. I promise."

"You can't charm an entire school."

He lifted one eyebrow. "Can't I?"

His cheerful confidence didn't diminish Kate's apprehension as they entered the school. How could she explain his presence all day, every day? The minute she started spouting tales of magic and men appearing from portraits, she'd be out of a job. Jenna Manderly, the principal, didn't mind some whimsy in the classroom, but she wasn't about to tolerate crazy stories from her secretary.

And Kate liked her job. Though she wasn't a teacher as she longed to be, she still had contact with children and felt as if she played some role in their lives, however small it might be.

Shannon Jones looked up from sorting her mail as Kate entered the main office. "So, how did it go Friday?"

It took Kate a moment to recall her last day of work. She'd left early to go to the lawyer's office. So much had happened that Friday seemed like years ago. "Not good. Nana's grandson inherits everything."

"I'm sorry." Shannon's expression reflected her dismay. "I know how much you love that house."

Kate forced a half-hearted smile. "I haven't given up yet."

From the way Shannon gazed past Kate, her jaw dropped and eyes wide enough to fill her face, it was apparent she hadn't heard Kate's reply. Only one person could cause that type of reaction.

Kate turned and motioned toward Robin. "Shannon, this is my friend, Robin Goodfellow. Robin, Shannon Jones. She may look like a student, but she's actually a first-grade teacher."

Nodding, he extended his hand, his devastating smile working its magic. How could any woman resist it? "It's a pleasure to make your acquaintance."

When Robin took her hand, Shannon came close to dissolving into a puddle on the floor, her gaze filled with adoration. The last time Kate had seen that look, Shannon had been eyeing a movie poster of Val Kilmer. "The pleasure is all mine."

An ugly spark of jealousy burned in Kate's gut and she pressed her lips together. She had no claim on Robin. And Shannon was cute, vivacious. Thin.

She breathed easier once Robin released Shannon's hand. To Kate's surprise, he glanced at her and shared a private wink, amusement dancing in his eyes.

Shannon gave him a thorough appraisal, her mail forgotten. "Are you new in town?"

"You could say that." Robin hugged Kate's shoulders. "I'm staying with Kate for a fortnight or so."

Shannon raised her eyebrows and grinned at Kate. "Lucky you." A bell rang and she gathered her papers. "Gotta go. I hope I see you again."

"I'm certain you will." Robin gave a slight bow that had Shannon glowing as she left.

Kate shook her head. "Maybe you *will* dazzle the entire school." Placing her purse behind her desk, she examined the day's schedule. Thank goodness, it promised to be a fairly normal day.

She glanced at Robin, who was studying the children's artwork posted around the office. Maybe normal wasn't the right word.

Mark Dewitte came in next, giving Kate a friendly grin. "Morning, Kate. Another Monday, eh?"

"They come too soon." When Mark's gaze landed on Robin, she introduced them. "Mark teaches fourth grade," she added. "His class is next door."

"And she never hesitates to let me know when we're getting too loud," Mark added.

"Next door?" Robin repeated.

Mark pointed toward the wall opposite Kate's desk. "Just on the other side of the wall."

"That will work."

Kate felt as confused as Mark looked. What was Robin up to now? Before she could ask, Robin spoke to Mark.

"I planned to spend some time here at the school and your class would be the best choice."

"Oh, a parent helper?" Mark asked.

"Not a parent." Robin's charming smile emerged. "But a helper."

Ah, that explained it. She'd told him about teacher's aides and parent helpers. If he could stay in Mark's classroom, he'd be within their allotted distance.

"I can always use help. How long can you stay?"

"All day, every day while I'm visiting Kate."

"You're a friend of Kate's?"

Robin deployed his irresistible grin. "I've known her for years."

"Works for me," Mark replied. "Come with me, Rob, and I'll show you the classroom."

Robin nodded and turned to follow the teacher. At the door, he hesitated and glanced back at Kate. His excitement shone from his face. "Don't go too far away."

She couldn't help but grin. "You either." She sat down, her spirits lifted. This might work out after all. Why had she ever doubted Robin? He gave the word "impossible" new meaning.

The morning passed quickly, filled with the usual events of forgotten homework, lost lunch money and ill children. Kate had just finished signing out a student to his mother when she turned to find Robin standing behind her, a sheepish grin on his face.

Hearing the noise from outside, she guessed the situation at once. "Don't tell me. Recess."

"They all went outside," he replied. "But I'm limited to the building."

"I need to stretch my legs. Come on." Taking his arm, she led him to the back door. "I can stay out for a couple minutes. Go on."

He squeezed her hand and ran to join Mark's class at the ball diamond, where Grant, the gym teacher, had students practicing their throwing and catching. Yep, it was definitely spring. Playground baseball was one of the sure signs.

Kate strolled onto the grass, careful to keep close to Robin, and watched him interact with the children. Whether it was his magic or his boyish enthusiasm, he had a natural talent with them. Already they formed tight circles around him, each demanding he watch them throw or hit or catch. He addressed each child as if he or she was the most important person in the world—a definite gift. Magic? Or just Robin's unique personality?

From the way he bounced around the ball field, darting first to one child, then another, Kate could tell he was having a great time, despite his inexperience with the sport. And that probably wouldn't last long. He listened as carefully as the children to Grant's directions. From the way he'd picked up American speech just watching television, she knew he was a quick study.

She stood there for several minutes before she motioned to him and started back for the building. It usually didn't take long for chaos to break out when she left her office.

Robin joined her as she stepped inside, his face flushed with excitement. "Thank you, Kate. I'm glad I could participate."

"You did a great job. The kids like you."

"I like them." His infectious grin caused a passing teacher to return it. "I've always enjoyed children. They're much more accepting of magic and things that everyone else says can't exist."

Sudden panic gripped Kate. "You're not going to tell them the truth?"

"No, no." He touched her shoulder. "Don't worry. I won't tell anyone you're sharing your house with an eight-hundred-year-old member of the Fae." Pausing at the door to her office, he ran his finger lightly down the bridge of her nose. "Anon, sweet Kate."

With that, he hurried toward the classroom as Kate heard the children returning from recess. Smiling, Kate went to her desk. Somehow, with Robin around, life appeared brighter.

She needed his cheerfulness that evening as they packed her few belongings in preparation for the move to her apartment. With each item she folded and placed in her suitcase, her depression deepened. Leaving this house would be the most difficult thing she'd ever done. But as when her father left her there twelve years ago, she had no choice.

After carrying one load to the front hallway, she entered the living room and turned on the radio. Maybe some music would help.

Robin dropped to his knees to examine the small stereo system. "How can you deny magic when you can do this?" he asked.

"It's not magic. It's technology."

His gaze questioned her and she shrugged. "I can't explain how it works—radio waves and towers and tubes and things like that. When put together the right way, they enable music and words from far away to reach many places at once."

"Amazing." He glanced at the TV. "This is the same principle as the picture box, is it not?"

"More or less." She ran her hand across her damp forehead. "I'm getting a Coke. Do you want one?"

"A Coke?" After following her into the kitchen, he brightened at seeing the red can she pulled out of the refrigerator. "Oh, 'the real thing.' "

Kate laughed. How could anyone remain depressed with

Robin around? "So they say." She handed him a can of regular, then took a diet soda for herself.

He drained his drink before they reached the second floor for the next load and claimed another can when they returned below.

"I guess you like it," Kate said.

"It's fascinating—bubbly, sweet and intoxicating." His impish grin appeared. "Like you."

When he downed the second can just as quickly, Kate wasn't sure she'd done the right thing in giving him one. At least, it didn't appear to harm him.

After their third trip downstairs, she gazed at her small pile of possessions—clothing, a boom box, a small TV, and a few personal items. Staring at the small pile, Kate bit her lip. It didn't look like much, but Nana had provided everything. And Kate wasn't about to take anything that would encourage Adam to call her a thief.

"I don't even have any dishes of my own," she murmured.

Robin squeezed her shoulders. "It'll be all right." Before she could reply, he released her and whirled into the living room where a Celtic tune played on the radio. "Ah, now *that's* music."

As Kate stared in amazement, he danced around the large room, his arms and feet following a pattern only he knew, a cross between Texas line dancing and the Irish River Dance.

"Are you all right?" she asked.

"Certainly." He continued to dance, whirling in circles, as he spoke again. "Tomorrow we move and the remaining days we clean this place. Is that correct?"

He spoke so quickly, Kate could barely understand him. She nodded with a puzzled frown. "Are you *really* all right?" He was usually energetic and enthused, but not like this.

"I . . ." He paused as if searching for the correct words. "I must move. I can't stay still."

Comprehension dawned and Kate groaned. "The Coke. Robin, I think you're high on caffeine and sugar."

"High?"

"Not quite down to earth."

He grinned. "I've never been down to earth." He whirled in front of her and extended his hand. "Join me, sweet Kate."

She shook her head. "I don't dance and I certainly don't know what it is you're doing."

"An old dance. Very old. One the Fae dance around the fire when the moon is full." He took her hands and pulled her with him into a lively jig. "Like this."

Left with no alternative, Kate studied his feet and found she learned the steps quickly. They only looked complicated because Robin performed them so fast. He kept hold of her hands as they whirled around the room, gaining speed with every pass.

"Isn't this grand?" he exclaimed. "Can anything be wrong with the world when we have this?"

Kate laughed. At that moment she couldn't think of a thing, except Robin's grin and the music pulsing through her veins. When was the last time she'd danced like this? At ten? Nine? A brief vision of her father whirling her around flashed through her mind. Then she'd laughed, too, but had she felt this same exhilaration? No, not like this.

When the song finally ended, Robin rested his hands on her shoulders, his mischievous smile still in place, his breathing rapid. "Ah, that was good. It's been too long." His gaze met hers. "For me *and* for you."

"Yes." It had been a long time. Too self-conscious, she'd never participated in any of the school dances and no one had asked her out in a long time. It felt so good to have blood rushing through her body, to feel alive, to be happy. "Thank you."

"We're not done yet."

The music changed to a slow tune, reminiscent of passion and undying love. Before Kate could move, Robin placed her hand on his shoulder, then took her other one, resting his other hand on her waist. "Shall we?"

"I don't—"

He didn't give her a chance to protest and guided her around the room again, keeping the pace slower this time, his movements more graceful, his gaze focused on her face.

The world around them dissolved into a blur as Kate's heart caught in her throat.

Unable to speak or look away, she allowed him to lead her in an elegant waltz. As her blood warmed, spread, then settled low in her belly, she could imagine herself in a fine ball gown, in an opulent ballroom full of men and women dressed in period clothing.

His gaze grew darker and slowly, so slowly she almost didn't realize it, he drew her closer until his hand rested in the small of her back, her breasts pressed against his chest. She closed her eyes, not fighting the emotions the music aroused—passion, desire, the unique sensation of being the most beautiful woman in the world.

As if.

Robin lifted his hand off her back briefly, then returned it even more securely. "Ah, Kate." His voice held a huskiness that added to the ache growing inside her. A tingling washed over her, changing the way her clothes rested upon her, loosening her braid. As if she'd undergone a transformation.

The sudden feel of Robin's hand against her bare skin brought Kate's eyes open in shock. She pulled away and stepped back, staring. He'd switched into the well-fitting pants and shirt he'd been wearing in the portrait, the shirt opened slightly to reveal the dark hair on his chest.

But he wasn't the only one who'd changed.

Her T-shirt and jeans were gone, replaced by an elegant floor-length gown that had to be made of silk by the way it glided over her skin. The back dipped dangerously low, stopping just above her buttocks, but the front caused her more concern. The dark green fabric barely concealed the tips of her breasts, leaving her ample cleavage open to view.

As she covered her breasts with one hand, she realized her hair was released from its usual braid, the unruly curls tumbling over her shoulders. She inhaled a deep breath before she could speak. "What have you done?"

"Only added to the magic of the moment. I can change it back." He lifted her hand from her breasts and kissed her fingertips, sending thrilling jolts of desire to her very core.

"What's wrong with dressing you like the beautiful woman you are?"

Kate could barely breathe with such passion sweeping through her. With an effort, she pulled her hand free. "Is that the secret, then? If I flaunt my breasts, men will pay attention to me?"

His heated gaze dropped to her revealing cleavage. Her nipples hardened as her breasts swelled in response. For a moment, Kate feared they would burst free of the tight, low-cut gown. She whirled around, covering herself with both hands this time.

"You're a beautiful, exciting woman, Kate." Robin came behind her to grasp her shoulders, his accented voice husky against her ear. "That you choose to disguise it is what keeps men away."

"Disguise it?" She turned to face him, achingly aware of his hands on her bare shoulders. "What do you mean?"

"You dress in clothes that hide every facet of your desirable figure. You keep men at a distance, never allowing them to get too close."

Anger added to the heat in her cheeks. "What do—"

"Because if one did get too close, you'd have to care again, sweet Kate, and you're still not ready to do that." When she opened her mouth to protest, he placed his thumb over her lips, the roughness of his skin creating a new awareness along her nerves. "Before you can care, you need to learn to accept who you are—your voluptuous figure, your beautiful hair, your powerful sensuality."

He touched her riot of curls, an impish smile framing his lips.

She trembled. If she didn't get away from him soon, she'd do something stupid like throw herself in his arms and beg for his kisses. Kate tried to step back, but Robin's gentle grip proved surprisingly strong.

"I . . . I know who I am." She straightened, unwilling to let him know how powerfully he affected her.

"No." He drew her close again and to her horror, she couldn't resist. "I don't think you do."

She started to protest, but his lips covered hers, sensuous, caressing, every bit as dangerous as his hands which gently roamed over her bare back. Resistance faded. Every coherent thought disappeared. Only the fire in her veins and the ache in her belly remained.

His kiss alone could seduce a woman, his lips as potent as any whiskey, his ability to awaken every sense to full awareness a talent in itself. After thoroughly claiming her mouth, he transferred his kisses to her throat, each touch acting as a brand that further stirred her need for this man.

Kate dropped her head back, her eyes closed, reveling in these new sensations claiming her body. She'd never felt like this before . . . aching, wanting, needing.

When Robin lowered his kisses to her breasts, she gasped. It was too much. It wasn't enough. How did a woman survive this?

His swollen erection pressed against her belly, intensifying her longing. She wanted him. Oh, God, she wanted him.

But did he want her? Really? Doubt filtered through her desire-induced haze. After two hundred years of abstinence, wouldn't any woman do?

He would make love to her. She didn't doubt that. But he would also leave her. She knew that as well. And she couldn't survive another loss. Not now.

With a cry of pain, she broke free and hurried for the stairs.

"Kate." He came after her.

She didn't dare look around. "I . . . I thought you were my friend."

He stopped abruptly, leaving a potent silence to fill the emptiness.

Halfway up the stairs, Kate finally peeked over her shoulder. His expression held remorse, though his eyes still glowed with an inner fire.

"I am," he said quietly. "I'm sorry."

"Just leave me alone. Please." Tears threatened . . . for

what might've been, for what couldn't be, for what she didn't dare experience. Choking back sobs, Kate fled to her room.

Robin sat on the edge of his bed. It was no use. He couldn't sleep. The ache in his loins refused to subside. Of course, the way he kept replaying the moments with Kate didn't help—the softness of her skin, the sweetness of her mouth, the desirability of her curves.

Stones, when had a woman last excited him so thoroughly? Enough to make him forget the vow he'd made previously? He was her friend. He wanted to remain her friend, a pleasant memory decades after he left this place.

And he was failing miserably.

She tempted him more than any woman he could recall and he didn't dare make love to her. Yet he couldn't allow her to think so little of herself either.

Needing to do something, he started downstairs for another of those interesting drinks . . . a Coke. Perhaps it would help clear this muddle in his head.

Before he touched the bottom step, he felt the tingling and groaned. Not again.

He appeared beside Kate's bed. She slept among disheveled covers, traces of tears still staining her cheeks. Robin clenched his fist. He'd hurt her. He hadn't intended to, but the end result remained the same.

He couldn't do this anymore.

But he had to do something. She needed to realize how wonderful she was, what she had to offer, how much passion she kept buried deep inside. Someone had to awaken her.

No, not someone. Himself.

No other man had the talent he possessed. He could make her aware of all that she was and still not make love to her.

Robin rubbed a strand of her hair between his fingers. Soft, silky, yet untamed. So like Kate. It would be agony not to pursue this wooing through to its natural conclusion, but he had to remember their friendship was more important.

He owed this to Kate. Closing his eyes briefly to blot out

Kate's enticing form, Robin turned back toward his room.
After he was gone, some man would be thankful for the
passionate woman who remained.

For some reason, that thought didn't appeal to him.

At all.

Four

"There has to be somewhere we haven't looked." Kate dropped her purse on her desk in the school office in discouragement. Hoping for an answer, she turned to face Robin.

"I don't know where." He leaned against the doorjamb, his expression as discouraged as she felt. "After two nights of cleaning and searching, there isn't a spot in that house we haven't touched."

Hearing him say it only confirmed her fears. If Nana wrote a will, it wasn't in the house. And her lawyer didn't have it either. "Then I'm going to lose my home." Kate sank onto her desktop, fighting the urge to cry.

Robin came to stand before her and took her hands in his. "Home is wherever you make it, sweet Kate. Even in that tiny apartment."

"Easy for you to say." She didn't meet his gaze, didn't want his optimism right now. "It's not your home."

He took her chin in his fingers and lifted her face so she had to look at him. "I've lost more homes than you'll ever have, including the one most important to me. You'll survive."

Kate immediately regretted her words. He'd endured more than she could imagine. "You're right." She forced a smile. "I'll survive." What choice did she have?

His answering grin made her spirits rise despite her determination to feel bad. "Right you are." He ran his finger down her nose. "Now I'm off to work, sweet, beautiful Kate."

Beautiful. Yeah, right. Kate shook her head as he departed the office. He could say it as many times as he wanted, she'd never believe it. Mirrors didn't lie.

Taking her chair, she started in on the ever-present stack of papers.

"Kate? Kate?"

She heard her name twice before it penetrated enough to capture her attention. Glancing up, she found Shannon beside the mail bins. "Hi, Shannon."

"Is Mr. Gorgeous still with you?" Shannon approached the desk with a smile.

"Robin? Yes, for now." Maybe forever at the rate they were finding things. The circlet hadn't turned up in any of their searches either.

Forever. That thought made Kate pause. How could she ever lead a normal life with someone like Robin around? Of course, after just a few days with him, she wasn't sure she really wanted a normal life, not if it meant he had to go.

"Are you . . . ?" Shannon hesitated, which caught Kate's attention. Her friend usually had more self-confidence than kids had homework excuses. "Are you involved with him?"

Involved? Kate grimaced. She was involved, all right, but not how Shannon meant it.

He *had* kissed her and insisted she was beautiful. But it wasn't like he was around any other women either.

"We're not dating or anything, if that's what you mean."

"Good." Shannon beamed a smile at Kate. " 'Cause that's one man I definitely want to know better."

"Feel free." Kate spoke casually, but her chest suddenly felt too small. Shannon was better for Robin than someone like Kate. Shannon was cute with a great figure, though Kate sometimes wondered how her friend had room for her internal organs with such a skinny waist. Maybe they were only the size of thimbles.

"You're sure?"

"He's just a friend." Kate smiled wryly. "Look at me. He's not likely to be interested in me."

"Great." Shannon spanked the desk top, then turned for the door. "Wish me luck."

Words stuck in Kate's throat. She couldn't wish her friend luck. Selfishly, Kate wanted Robin all to herself. Foolish girl. She had him all to herself until the spell was broken . . . for all the good it did her.

When the children escaped outside for recess, Kate accompanied Robin to the playground so he could participate. He gave her a cheerful grin, then dove into a small group of boys. In a short time, they were all running and laughing at a game he created.

He did have a way with kids—probably because he was more than part child himself. Kate shook her head at her whimsy. The man was several hundred years old. She watched him fall to the ground laughing as the boys piled on top of him and her stomach clenched at his handsomeness. For an old man, he certainly looked good.

Too good.

His passion and kisses still lingered in Kate's memory, sneaking out to bring a flush to her cheeks at the most inopportune moments. If she wasn't careful, she'd start to believe his silly flatteries.

And worse—she'd start to fall for him herself.

Shannon followed her class outside and directed her path toward Robin. Kate's breath caught. Maybe she'd already passed the starting-to-fall point.

If she were honest, she'd have to admit she enjoyed his kisses, his touch. In fact, she wanted more of them . . . she wanted . . . Kate forced back her crazy wishes and looked away as Shannon engaged Robin in conversation.

Be realistic. Robin was a fantasy in her life, a tornado who would whirl through, change everything, then leave. And he would leave. She needed to remember that most of all.

He was still talking to Shannon when the bell rang. Worse than that, he was laughing. Kate didn't wait for him to catch up with her but hurried into her office and the relative safety of her desk as if she could avoid what he might have to say.

"Are you all right?" Robin peered around her office doorway before she had time to sit down.

So much for that plan. Kate nodded at Robin's question. He must've been right on her heels. "It's just a crazy Friday, that's all."

He didn't respond at once, but studied her with that thoughtful expression that always made Kate uneasy. She waved at him.

"Get back to class or you'll be late."

He moved then, but paused at the door. "Anon, my lovely Kate."

Before she could brush off his nonsense, he vanished into the hallway. But she couldn't shake the feeling that their conversation wasn't yet finished.

Something was wrong with Kate. Robin knew her well after many years of observation and even better after their few days together. The *joie de vivre* that he enjoyed so much was missing.

True, they hadn't found the circlet or the will but this went beyond that. When they'd left Nana's house last night, she'd been more resigned than depressed.

He peeked inside the door to her office. She was still busy with a student. Not that she appeared to mind that. Her love for the children always shone through when she dealt with them.

"Hey, Mr. Goodfellow."

Looking around, he spotted two boys from Nick's class. "Josh, Danny." After just a few days in the classroom, Robin already knew each student's name. "Haven't you gone home yet?"

"We're going," Danny replied.

"We had soccer practice," Josh added.

"And you didn't invite me?" Robin raised his eyebrows.

Even if they had, he couldn't have gone—not unless Kate came as well.

"Next time." Both boys nodded to confirm the statement.

"I bet you can run circles around Coach Steve," Danny said.

Robin grinned. "I'd certainly try." Thus far, he'd enjoyed all the games he learned with the children. In fact, he enjoyed the children, too. Why hadn't he spent much time with them before?

Danny held up his hand in a motion Robin quickly recognized. Without hesitation, Robin slapped the boy's palm in a series of deft movements, not missing even one of the unusual ritual. Apparently, he did it correctly for Danny beamed.

"Cool, Mr. Goodfellow."

The term meant good. A slow warmth spread through Robin. His intense study of this series of slaps had been worth it.

"See ya next week," Josh said.

Robin watched the boys leave, enjoying the fellowship of their exchange. He should've tried this type of employment earlier.

Children came as close as any mortal could to the antics of the Fae. When he was with them, he forgot his imprisonment, his years of duty to Oberon in this world.

"Earth to Robin."

He knew that voice. Turning, Robin smiled at Shannon. She had bells in her tone. If he closed his eyes, he could believe he was listening to Liliana, the Fae musician he knew eons ago.

"Are you going home?" he asked.

"Finally. It's been a long week."

Maybe for her. For Robin, the days had flown by. Perhaps because of his new freedom from the portrait. "Do you have plans for the weekend?" He'd heard others ask that question as they left the building.

"Actually . . ." She touched his arm, her gaze meeting his. Her eyes were pretty—a deep sea blue. "There's a new art exhibit in Denver. Lots of Renaissance stuff. I wondered if you'd like to go with me."

An art exhibit. Robin paused. That could be useful. Would Kate enjoy it? "Kate and I—"

Shannon shook her head. "Not Kate. You."

As if he could go anywhere without Kate. As if he wanted to.

At a small sound beside him, he caught a glimpse of Kate standing just inside the doorway, her careful mask gone, revealing her emotions. She was hurting.

Realization slowly dawned as Robin glanced at Shannon. Because of her friend? Shannon was attractive in a waiflike way, but Robin preferred his sweet desirable Kate.

Which was his penitence as well as his pleasure. For he could never seduce the woman who was his one true friend.

"I'm sorry, Shannon," he replied. "My plans for the weekend include Kate."

Shannon's eyelashes flickered but her smile didn't fall. "Another time, maybe." She peered around him. "Have a good weekend, Kate."

"You, too." Kate came to stand even with Robin. Once Shannon pushed through the front doors, she faced him. "You should have gone. We could've worked something out."

How could she question his desire to be with her? He pressed a light kiss to the tip of her nose. "I wanted to be with you."

Wrapping his arm around her shoulders, he led her toward the door. "So, what are our plans?"

"I want to stop by Nana's again."

He admired her persistence, though it was misplaced in this instance. "There's nowhere left to look."

"There must be." After she opened the door to her car, she turned to look at him. "I have to find that will, Robin."

"It's not in the house."

"Where else could it be?"

He hesitated. There was one option . . . "What if she meant to write it, but never did?"

Kate didn't reply at once. "I've thought of that," she said finally. "But I can't believe she'd tell me I'd be taken care of if she hadn't already written it."

"She was elderly and ill. Maybe she thought she did." He'd seen too many mortals decline with the inevitability of old age. Thank the Stones he'd never experience that.

"She was ill but she never lost her mind. She was always sharp." Kate guided her car toward the large tree-lined streets where Nana's house stood. "The will does exist. I know it."

Robin didn't reply. They'd searched the entire house from top to bottom, looking inside drawers and boxes. The will was not there. And neither, unfortunately, was the circlet.

That bothered him still. He'd felt confident that the spell he'd cast to keep his portrait near the circlet had worked. Why else would he have come to America? Why else would he have stayed within this one family for so many years?

Maybe he needed to spin the spell again. He couldn't determine the exact location of the circlet, but he should be able to tell if it was near.

When Kate stopped her car in the rear driveway and headed for the house, Robin paused beneath the large ash tree shading the back lawn. Drawing strength from the energy of nature, he spread his arms wide and recited an incantation.

"*Winds that search the world freely, guide me to what I seek most dearly.*"

"What are you doing?"

He glanced toward Kate standing on the rear steps. Before he could reply, the pull swept over him, almost physically yanking him toward where she stood, toward the house.

Stones! It didn't make sense. The magic insisted the circlet was still here.

He grimaced. "Trying to find the circlet."

"And?"

Joining her, he shook his head. "It should be here."

"Then we have to look again." Kate stuck her key in the door lock, then frowned. "It won't fit." She jiggled the key, then tried another on her chain, but it didn't match the lock either. Confusion lit her gaze as she looked at Robin. "Something's wrong."

"Perhaps if you try the front entrance."

They quickly circled the house, but neither key fit the front door. Noticing fresh scars on the door's surface, Robin ran his finger over the lock. "This has been changed recently."

Kate bent to examine the keyhole. "You're right." Horror filled her expression. "Adam's changed the locks. I can't believe it."

Indignation rose in Robin. He'd watched Adam and Kate since they were children. At one time, they'd been friends. Still, Robin knew by now what mortals were capable of doing to each other. "And if you hadn't found another place to live by now?"

"I wouldn't have anything." Kate's voice trembled and dampness filled her eyes.

"He will pay for this." Robin spoke quietly. He'd been left among mortals for just this kind of vengeance—to teach a lesson to those who delighted in cruelty to others.

"No." Kate touched his arm. "Don't hurt him."

"He cannot be allowed to do this to you."

"The law says he can." Kate turned away and trudged to the back, her steps heavy, her vitality diminished.

"Then your law is wrong." What kind of people made laws to harm innocents? Among the Fae there was only one rule— a member of the Fae could not kill another of the Fae— which was why Titania had imprisoned him instead of destroying him as she preferred.

"Perhaps." Kate reached her car and buried her face in her arms on the roof. "The only thing that will help me now is the will."

No wonder she refused to give up her search. "I can find Adam and persuade him into giving you the house," he said impulsively. Such an action would have repercussions, but for Kate he'd do it.

Kate shook her head, not bothering to look up. "It wouldn't be right. Besides, I have no idea when he'll be here again."

Robin touched her shoulders, pulling her within the circle of his arms, her head nestled against his shoulder. She fit perfectly, her generous curves soft against him. Desire raged through his blood, fueling his next foolish promise. "We'll find the will, Kate. I swear it."

Kate couldn't shake her lethargy, despite Robin's efforts to cheer her. It was over. She knew it, but couldn't bear to say the words.

Despite Robin's rash promise, she held no hope of ever locating Nana's will. Not now.

Sitting on the couch, she stared at the blank TV screen, toying with the end of her braid. Her home was gone. Just like everyone . . . everything that mattered to her. Her mother, her father, Nana, and soon, Robin.

She glanced toward the kitchen where he hummed noisily while cleaning up after dinner. He'd insisted, though the clanging of the pots and dishes made her fear for what little dishware she'd obtained.

He'd come to be important in her life, whether she wanted him to or not. But he was trapped here. She had no doubts he'd be long gone if Titania's spell didn't keep him near.

With a sigh, she closed her eyes and laid her head on the back of the couch. What a mess.

Pressure throbbed at her temples and she reached up to rub them. Warm hands covered hers and she jerked her eyes open to see Robin peering down at her from behind the couch.

"Let me," he said softly. He placed her hands in her lap, then proceeded to massage her temples, his fingers gentle as they moved in small circles.

Her tension eased and she found her eyes drooping shut again. He was good at this. But then he was good at everything—adapting to a new life, working with children, handling modern conveniences, making her feel special.

She smiled slightly. Of course, he was magical.

"Better now?" he asked.

"Some." He removed his hands and she sat forward. "I'll just take some aspirin . . ."

"No." He came around to sit beside her. "Let me try something else first."

She eyed him warily. What did he intend now?

"This won't hurt a bit." He gave her a warm smile, then turned her back to face him. She jumped when she felt his hands on the end of her braid.

"What are you doing?"

"Trust me, Kate."

Trust him. Lord knew she wanted to. But if she did that, then her heart would soon follow, and she couldn't stand to lose anyone else.

He loosened her braid and ran his fingers through her hair, easing out the tangles. "Relax," he murmured.

It did feel good. He continued to comb her hair in long, gentle strokes. She closed her eyes, forcing the tight muscles in her neck to loosen. He definitely knew what he was doing. Already her headache was fading.

But an ache of another kind took its place. As his hands touched the unruly waves of her hair, she imagined them touching other places as well—her face, her shoulders, her breasts.

Her nipples stiffened in response as heat pooled low in her belly. Sensuality oozed from this man. His strokes grew slower, his fingers lingering on the strands.

"Your hair is so soft, so beautiful with gold among the copper." His voice took on a melodic quality, his accent adding to the tension growing within her. He paused, then lifted her hair with his hands and drew his fingers through it. "You should always wear it long," he continued. "The light dances over it, making a man ache to touch it."

She almost believed him. Her body throbbed in response, wanting more than his hands on her hair. When had she last wanted a man like this?

Never. No man ever made her skin flush with heat, her breasts swell in response or her core moist with desire by his words and simple touch.

He separated her hair into thin strands, caressing each one as if it were more precious than jewels. "Let me dress you for the next few days."

Dress her? At this moment she'd prefer it if he undressed her. His light strokes acted as a catalyst to the flame burning inside her. "Robin . . ." She couldn't say anything more, her throat tight with need.

Whatever he wanted.

He released her hair and guided her around to face him. She opened her eyes to find him staring at her, his expression intense. Her breath caught as the world ceased to spin.

For a moment, time itself stopped.

Catching her face between his palms, he leaned forward to kiss her nose, then her cheek. "You are beautiful." He whispered the words, then kissed her other cheek. "You are beautiful."

He dropped light kisses on her face, over her eyes. "Say it, sweet Kate."

She stared at him. Say it? A brilliant light blazed in his eyes . . . passion, desire, appreciation. For her.

He brought his mouth within a breath of hers. "Say it."

The thudding of her heart filled the silence. She longed to feel his lips on hers, his hands on her body. Seeing her reflection shine in his pupils, she did feel beautiful, as if she were the only woman on the face of the earth.

"I . . . I'm beautiful." Her voice was barely audible, wrenched from her unwillingly. She closed her eyes, ready to experience the headiness of his kiss.

"Kate, sweet Kate." His voice sounded husky, deeper, and his fingers tightened on her face as his warm breath played over her mouth.

She trembled with need. *Kiss me.* All she had to do was lean forward, just a little.

Abruptly, Robin's hands dropped away and he drew back. Kate lifted her lids in surprise. What had she done?

Robin jumped to his feet and paced the length of her tiny apartment. "We have to admit that the will and circlet are lost."

His change of subject, of attitude left her baffled. "Robin?" Was it all a game?

The gaze he turned on her was pained, dark, almost as . . . as if he regretted not kissing her. She knew that feeling. "And I can't continue to force myself into your life."

Cold realization dashed Kate's desire. He wanted to leave her. "I see." She could barely move her stiff lips. Maybe it was a different type of regret she saw on his face—regret that he was trapped with her.

"I need to go to Titania and ask her to remove the spell."

"I thought you needed the circlet to do that." Was he so anxious to get away from her that he didn't care anymore?

"It would help." He sank back onto the couch with a sigh. "But I don't dare wait any longer." He gave her a slight smile. "I can't locate your will, but Oberon will be able to."

A flutter of hope beat in Kate's chest. "He can?"

"If Titania doesn't put me back in the portrait right away."

The hope died as a sudden ache blossomed in its place. Robin back in the portrait? Kate couldn't bear to think of his vitality locked away again. "Then maybe you shouldn't be in a hurry."

He didn't answer right away. When he did, his words sounded as if they were dragged from him. "I'm sorry, Kate. I must leave."

Five

The grief-stricken look that flickered across Kate's face made Robin wish he could retract his words. He hated leaving her, but the more he was around her, the more he desired her. So much so that he found himself using every excuse to touch her. If he didn't want to lose her precious friendship, he needed to find some way to distance himself physically . . . soon.

Yet he still hadn't located Titania's circlet, despite his spell telling him it was at Nana's house. He had nothing to take to Titania. All he had left was his magical charm. Perhaps he could somehow convince the faerie queen to remove her spell.

He grimaced. That would be magic indeed.

"You can't just leave," Kate said, a waver in her voice. "You'll be pulled back."

"I know." Robin forced himself to meet her gaze. Her eyes were damp, but no tears fell. He stepped toward her, aching to gather her in his arms and kiss the hurt away, then stopped. He didn't dare.

He knew himself. Kisses would never be enough with Kate.

"You'll have to come with me to the land of the Fae." As he watched her face, Robin wished he could find another way. Mortals weren't welcome in the magical realm. But he was Oberon's son; he'd ensure Kate came to no harm.

"Go with you?" Panic mingled with excitement in her voice. "I can't do that."

"Yes, you can. Humans have visited the faerie realm since time began. How do you think your Will Shakespeare learned so much about us?"

Her eyes widened. "You knew William Shakespeare?"

"I tormented him, I'm afraid. But I had to stop him from revealing our entrance to others." Robin grinned at the memory. "In return, he portrayed me most unfairly in one of his plays."

A smile softened Kate's face, drawing Robin back to sit beside her. "If you're talking about *A Midsummer's Night Dream* then he did treat you most unfairly," she agreed. The mischievous light in her eyes tugged at his self-restraint. "But what I meant before is that I can't just up and leave my job."

He understood that. After only a week with the children, Robin found any thoughts of leaving them depressing. "It'll only be for a short time, a week perhaps." *I hope.* "And not right away."

"We do have spring break in another couple weeks." Kate caught her lower lip between her teeth, a movement that made Robin long to touch her seductive mouth. "Are you sure Titania will remove the spell?"

No.

He gave her his brightest smile. "Certainly."

"Very well. I'll go." Her expression suddenly sobered, her gaze staring beyond him.

"What is it?" He knelt before her, glancing into her face.

"I'll actually be visiting the one place my father spent his life trying to find." Her eyes misted. "Too bad he didn't know you were in the portrait. You could've shown him the way."

Robin glanced down for a moment. "No, I couldn't." When Kate lifted her eyebrows quizzically, he continued, "I don't know the way."

"What?"

"The entrance changes location randomly to make it difficult to find. The last time I was there was two hundred years ago. I'm certain it's moved since then."

"Then how do you find it?"

He winked. "There's always magic."

As he expected, doubt flitted over Kate's face. Despite her acceptance of him, she wasn't yet ready to fully welcome magic into her life. He needed to change that before he left.

Unfortunately, this wasn't the right time. "Don't worry, sweet Kate. Magic is the one method I dare not use in this case."

She frowned, obviously puzzled. "Why not?"

Her willingness to believe gave him hope. "If I send a magical call to the Fae, I'll learn the location of the entrance, but Titania will also learn I'm free from the portrait. I prefer she didn't discover that yet."

Much to Robin's relief, Kate nodded. "What else can you do?"

"I need to find someone I can trust." He hesitated. Who among the Fae was most likely to still be living among the mortals after all this time?

Recalling Shannon's earlier invitation, he grinned. "What say you we visit the art exhibit tomorrow?"

Kate blinked. "The one in Denver?"

"Yes, exactly." A rush of excitement coursed through Robin's veins to mingle with regret. Perhaps at the museum he could find an answer to the Fae's location.

And be one step closer to leaving Kate forever.

Kate frowned at the art exhibit's sign as they entered the Denver Museum—ART THROUGH THE AGES: FROM MEDIEVAL TIMES TO THE PRESENT. What was Robin expecting to find here? Or who? Shannon?

Jealousy reared its ugly head and Kate tried to smother it. She had no claims on Robin . . . other than the fact that he couldn't get farther than fifty feet away. As attractive as she found him, she didn't want Robin by her side because he was a prisoner.

Kate sighed. What other reason would there be for a man like him to be with her? Well, because she could bring him to an art museum for one.

As they reached the first hallway, Robin studied the direction signs for a moment, then headed directly for the Elizabethan area. Kate hurried to match his stride.

"Are you looking for something in particular?" she asked.

"Yes." Robin motioned her forward, then took her hand, his eyes lit with excitement. "Paintings by an artist named Nicholas Hilliard."

"Why?"

"I used to know him."

Kate still had difficulty accepting Robin's agelessness. He appeared to be only in his late twenties or early thirties. How could he be hundreds of years old? "How will that help you?"

"He's Fae."

"Excuse me?" A member of the Fae was a known artist? Kate frowned. Wasn't that cheating? Realizing the folly of her thoughts, she smiled. No doubt the Fae did whatever they pleased.

Robin paused before a set of carefully preserved miniatures and studied the biography of Nicholas Hilliard. Kate read it as well. Nothing in the information gave a hint that the artist was anything other than human.

"Are you sure?" she asked.

"Certain." Robin bestowed one of his devastating smiles on her, sending an extra tingle up her arm through their joined palms. "Nic loved art more than anything. He continually took on human identities in order to pursue it. He'd even change his appearance so that he aged while living in one identity."

"But why?"

"To appear mortal, of course."

"No, why did he take on human identities?"

"Painting is not given the same recognition among the Fae

as in the mortal realm. I've always enjoyed it. Besides Nic, many of my friends have been artists."

Kate examined the miniatures. The artwork was excellent with such minuteness of detail that the subjects seemed to come alive. One in particular caught her eye and she leaned forward to examine it more closely. The young man leaning against a tree looked familiar. More than familiar in fact. Yet different enough to make her wonder.

She read the title. *Youth Leaning Against a Tree Among Roses*. No hint of identity there.

Glancing back at Robin, she found him watching her with a twinkle in his eye and a smile on his lips. "Is that you?" she asked.

He nodded. "Not a bad likeness, is it?"

Unable to believe she'd heard right, Kate stared at the miniature. "You look young." The inane words emerged before she thought. Of course, her brain was having some trouble comprehending this. To know Robin was ageless was one thing. To see proof of it was another.

"I was younger then." Robin released her hand to touch her shoulder. "Are you all right?"

"I . . ." Kate glanced at him—handsome, alive, vibrant and very, very sexy. To imagine him as this man from four hundred years ago played havoc with her reason. He shouldn't be standing here. He . . .

Robin ran his hand over her cheek, then cupped her face. Her stomach knotted as she found herself caught in his gaze. "I'm me, Kate. I'm still the man you freed from the portrait. I'm still the man who finds you beautiful beyond compare, who wants to kiss you so badly I ache from it."

His words sent flashes of fire through Kate's veins even as her cheeks grew warm. They were in the middle of a museum. People were walking by. Yet Robin didn't acknowledge them. He appeared so sincere, sounded as if he meant it. She moistened her suddenly dry lips and his gaze followed her action, his eyes darkening.

"Just one kiss." His voice dropped to a whisper taking on a huskiness that created a yearning low in her belly. He pulled her gently toward him, his breath warm on her face. "A kiss between friends."

Friends.

Her desire went cold. That's all they could ever be. She was a fool to think he might see more in her than that. What was she thinking to even consider a kiss in a place like this? She drew back before his lips found hers and turned away. "What . . . what happened to your friend?"

Robin didn't answer and she risked a glance over her shoulder to find him frowning at her. Unnerved, she looked back at the miniature, but found no comfort there. The artist had managed to capture the hint of mischief in Robin's eyes and the beginning of a smile.

"He appeared to die, then took on another identity elsewhere." Robin finally spoke, a coolness in his tone that made Kate close her eyes against the sudden pain it caused. "We lost touch, though I'd sometimes see his work appear under a different name."

"And that's what you want to find here?" Kate now realized why Robin had insisted they come to the exhibit. "You want to find his current work?"

"Yes." The single curt word hung in the air for several long moments.

Slowly, Kate forced herself to face him. Now he'd hate her for certain. But she didn't dare kiss him, didn't dare allow herself to feel emotions that would never be returned.

Instead of anger, sadness lingered in his eyes and he shook his head. "Sweet Kate, you still don't believe in yourself, do you?"

She stiffened. "I believe in myself. I'm a good worker. I have friends."

"True." He stepped closer. "But as a woman? Do you see yourself as the desirable, beautiful woman you are?"

"I'm not—"

Before she could finish, he took her hand once again and pulled her after him with determined strides.

"Where are we going?" Why did he continue to insist she was beautiful when all society said differently?

"Look." He paused before a display of Peter Paul Rubens's work and pointed to each picture as he named it. *"The Four Quarters of the Globe, Union of Earth and Water, Cimone and Efigenia.* Are you going to deny that those women are exquisite?"

Kate had heard of Rubens's paintings of full-figured women, but she'd never seen one before. The women were beautiful, their generous curves giving them a softness and desirability she hadn't believed possible. "No." She spoke quietly but Robin heard her.

"Good." He caught her shoulders and turned her to face him. "When we get home, I want you to look at yourself in the same way. You're all a man could want."

"And more," she quipped, patting her full hips.

"And much more," Robin repeated, his husky voice giving a different meaning to the words.

A blush heated Kate's cheeks. Robin could convince an ostrich it could fly. But then, his magic was in his charm.

"Come." Grasping her elbow, he started for the modern art.

"Did you know Rubens too?"

"He was a good friend." Robin paused. "I learned a lot from him."

"About women?" Obviously, Rubens's artwork had made an impression on Robin. Had he watched the artist paint? Had Robin known the models?

He gave her a mischievous grin. "Especially about women."

His answer didn't help. Kate grimaced. What exactly about women? To appreciate them or make love to them?

Reaching the more modern display, he stopped. "If you see something that looks like Nic's work, let me know."

"I will." They split up there, each moving along a separate wall. Kate examined each painting critically, not sure she'd even recognize the earlier artist's style.

Until she came to the portrait of a young girl on a swing. Though full-sized, the detail and lighting reminded her of the earlier miniature of Robin. "Robin." She motioned him over and he joined her. "Is this him?"

"It is." He sounded so certain, she glanced at him quizzically. He pointed to the picture. "Look there, in the sky, can you read it? He puts his signature on every painting he does."

"Nic," she read. "Won't it give away his identity if he does that?"

Robin grinned. "Only those with faerie sight can read it. It's meant for members of the Fae."

Frowning, Kate looked from the obvious signature to Robin. "You mean no one else can see that?"

"A few mortals have the sight, sweet Kate, like you, but not enough to jeopardize Nic's repeating lifetimes." Robin read the display plate. "*Girl on a Swing* by Nic Stone. Now to find out where he lives."

"How?" Did he have some magical way to do that?

"I'll ask." Robin spotted one of the exhibit assistants and moved toward him. "Can you tell me more about Nic Stone?"

"Nic Stone." The assistant beamed. "He's a new, talented artist who's only recently gathered notice."

"Can you tell me where he lives?"

The man frowned. "I can't give out that information."

Robin's posture changed and he produced a smile that Kate spotted as being his charm at work. "But he's a good friend of mine. We lost touch and it's urgent I contact him."

The assistant stared at Robin. "The last I knew he was living somewhere in San Francisco. I don't know the address."

"Thank you. That's very helpful." Swinging his arm around Kate's shoulders, Robin led them toward the entrance. "It is helpful, isn't it?"

She nodded. "It could be."

"Then I think we should celebrate."

"Celebrate?" Kate eyed him warily. "Like how?"

"Let's pick up one of those party packs and take it home."

"Party packs?"

"You know, like on the TV. With the dog. Tacos and . . .

and crunchy things. Someone brings it home and there's a party."

Kate grinned. "I see. I know what you're talking about. Anything else?"

He paused on the street to look at her, a slow smile creasing his face. "Yes, there's one thing I'd really like."

Her heart skipped a beat. "Yes?"

"A Coke."

It was possible to have a party with only two people, Kate discovered after they returned to the apartment with a party package of tacos and a six-pack of cola. She set the food on the counter and turned to find Robin waiting behind her, his gaze on the soda.

"Only one can." Kate grabbed a can and held it out of Robin's reach as she wagged her finger at him.

"One?" A gleam appeared in his eyes and Kate took a step backward. He took a step forward. "What if I want more?"

Kate shook her head, laughter bubbling up. Robin was the only person she dared to play with like this and she enjoyed every moment. "It makes you silly." As she retreated across the small apartment, Robin pressed his advantage.

"And what's wrong with being silly?" He lunged for the can held high in her hand and knocked them both onto the couch, Robin lying atop of her. "You should try it sometime," he added, his voice low. His gaze met hers and he made no effort to move away.

His body aligned with hers perfectly, his male hardness meeting her curves in just the right places. Kate found it difficult to breathe, her pulse racing. She should tell him to move. She should.

But she didn't want to.

He watched her closely, his eyes darkening. Placing the Coke on the floor, he lifted his hand to trace the contours of her face, his fingers gentle, each touch sending a burst of heat through Kate's veins.

He brushed her eyelids, the slope of her nose, the curve

of her cheek, pausing as he ran his fingertip over her lips. "You are magnificent."

Never before had Kate been so aware of herself as a woman. Her skin tingled with sensation, every nerve alive, vibrantly attuned to this man. For a moment she could almost believe him.

Robin hesitated, then pressed his lips to her forehead, following with kisses to each cheek and the tip of her nose.

He exuded sensuality. How else could she explain the tightness in her breasts, the fire between her legs from his simple caresses?

Simple. Ha. Nothing was simple with Robin.

Pausing, he brought his lips near hers and Kate closed her eyes, wanting his kiss, aching for the ecstasy of his mouth on hers. Even if she was just deluding herself, she wanted this.

His warm breath played over her lips and for a brief moment she thought she felt the light brush of his touch, then abruptly he stood and strode away from her.

"Forgive me." His voice sounded rough. "I keep jeopardizing our friendship."

"That's all right." Though she said the words, she didn't quite believe them. She'd come so close to giving in to him, had wanted him to continue. And here she'd been the one to tell him to keep away. Kate sighed as she sat up, her body trembling. Robin wasn't the only one at fault now.

Releasing a shaky breath, she stood and turned toward the kitchen. "How about those tacos now?"

Once seated across from each other, they ate without talking, the only noise that of the crunchy shells. Kate took a bite and nearly choked, unable to swallow through her thick throat.

Why did she have to be so easily affected by Robin? Her weakness was going to ruin their friendship. As it was, she didn't dare look at him, but kept her gaze on her plate.

The sound of Robin chugging his Coke made her glance up and grimace. Now he'd not only be silly, but he'd burp every ten minutes.

Catching her gaze, Robin bit into another taco, then grinned. "Here, lizard, lizard."

His imitation of the old commercial made Kate giggle. Though new to this time, Robin had his commercials down pat. "Wouldn't you be shocked if Godzilla did show up?" she responded.

"Is it real?" Surprise filled his expression.

"No." Kate paused. "Though after meeting you, I shouldn't be so positive. Let's just say I've never heard of him really existing."

His smile lingered in his eyes. "You're learning."

He didn't elaborate so Kate focused on the question that had been nagging her since they left the museum. "How are you going to find this Nic Stone in San Francisco? It's a huge city and Stone is a common name."

"If I'm near him, I'll know."

"Maybe so, but it might not be that easy to get near him." She tried to think of a comparison he would recognize. "San Francisco is much larger than London was when you last saw it."

"I see." He finished a taco and picked at the meat that had fallen on his plate. "How does one find people in this time?"

"Through a local phone book or the Internet." Kate sat upright. "That's what we'll do. When we get to work on Monday, I'll search the net with the computer and see what I can find."

"Computer?" Robin frowned, then tapped his plate as awareness dawned. "Oh, 'affirmative, Captain. The Klingons are entering the neutral zone.' "

As he mimicked the Star Trek computer, Kate erupted into laughter. "I'm afraid that's a little ahead of our time." Rising, she took her plate to the sink. "I'll show you at school."

They cleaned the kitchen in amiable silence with Robin sneaking another soda from the fridge before he entered the main room. "I'm developing a tolerance," he said in reply to Kate's raised eyebrows.

She followed him, still smiling, when she caught sight of her reflection in the decorative mirror on the wall. Was that really her? Caught by her reflection, she stopped and stared in surprise. With her hair unbound and the smile on her face, she looked . . . well, pretty.

Robin came up behind her, his gaze meeting hers in the mirror. "Do you see it, sweet Kate? How beautiful you are?"

She responded automatically. "I'm not beautiful." But the face looking back at her, while familiar, appeared different somehow—more alive, more real. Was she changing?

"You *are* beautiful." He whispered in her ear as he ran his hands over her sides. "You have curves Venus would envy, hair so radiant it glows and so soft a man can't resist touching it." He pulled his hands gently through her hair, letting the strands slide between his fingers.

Watching herself, Kate noticed how a hot rush of blood colored her cheeks at his caress, how Robin's eyes glinted with promise.

"Your eyes hold vulnerability and passion, a lure that draws men in," he continued.

Kate smiled wryly. She'd never noticed men flocking to her side.

Placing his hands on her shoulders, Robin turned her to face him. His face was serious. "And your lips beg for kisses, promising a sweetness beyond compare."

"I think you must have been a poet at some time in your life," Kate said lightly, attempting to hide the yearning he brought to life.

"Charming always," he replied, sliding one hand behind her neck. "A poet never."

Their gazes caught and held, silence filling the room until Kate swore she could hear her heart pounding. When he eyed her mouth, her stomach clenched and she gripped the front of his shirt.

"Kiss me." The plea emerged on a breath. She hadn't intended to say it but if he didn't kiss her, she would die.

"Sweet Kate." With a groan, Robin drew her close and claimed her lips in a hungry kiss that sent lightning bolts to the tips of her toes.

A woman could lose consciousness from his kiss. The

world fell away as he caressed her mouth. As he ran his tongue over her lips, she opened to him and his tongue continuing his effortless seduction.

Kate's legs wobbled, her bones dissolving beneath the onslaught of desire ravaging her body. Only her hold on Robin's shirt kept her upright . . . and his arm wrapped tightly around her.

Her mind could barely reason, lost in the rapture of his kisses. He lifted his head briefly, then continued to work his magic along her neck.

"Robin." This was wonderful, heavenly, unbelievable. Soon she'd be past caring where this led, past caring that they had no future, past caring that he would leave.

Leave.

Reality jerked her to her senses and she turned away, hating the kisses to stop even as she hated herself for wanting them.

"Kate?" Robin didn't release her despite the question in his voice.

"This . . . this isn't wise." She didn't dare look at him. To do so would only make her long for more.

"I suppose not." He sounded disappointed.

She risked a glance back. "What will you do once you find Nic Stone?" She had to ask the question, had to hear the answer despite the pain.

Unease flitted across his face. "He'll tell me where to find the entrance to the magical realm and we'll go there."

As much as she wanted to see that place, she knew where it would end. "And you'll be free from me."

"If we're lucky, Titania will remove the spell."

"And I'll never see you again." Her chest ached at the thought. Already he'd become important to her.

An emotion glittered in his dark eyes. Pain? Regret? Or relief that he'd finally be free of her?

"Isn't that for the best, Kate? I should go soon before it's too hard on you." He spoke as if trying to convince himself as well.

"Yes, for the best." She repeated the words automatically

and eased out of his hold, heading for her bedroom.

Robin's departure was inevitable. She'd known that from the beginning, known he had to leave before her heart was broken again.

Only it was already too late for that.

Six

Kate glanced up from her computer screen to where Robin sat on the edge of her desk. This wasn't going to be as easy as she'd hoped. "There are seven Nic Stones in San Francisco, according to this."

"Seven?" Robin leaned forward to peer over her shoulder, his warm breath caressing her cheek. "Does this say where they live?"

"Yes, but most of them have phone numbers. Let me print this out and we can call them from the apartment. That'll help." She grinned at the amazed expression on Robin's face as he watched the pages emerge from the printer.

"And you say there is no magic," he said.

"That isn't magic. It's technology."

"The Fae can't make words appear on paper like this." He lifted a sheet and eyed it in awe. "I find this mortal magic most interesting."

"It's not magic," she repeated with more force. "It's just bits and bytes moving along a wire. I can get you books that show you how it works."

Robin didn't reply, his gaze still focused on the paper. Smothering a laugh, Kate turned back to the screen and logged off. What had she expected? After two hundred years, he was bound to find some things very different, despite his heavily commercialized TV education.

"Hi, Kate. Almost done?"

She looked up as Grant Coates, the gym teacher, entered the office. He was actually speaking to her?

"Almost," she replied slowly. She'd found Grant very handsome when he joined the school staff a year ago, but he'd barely noticed her. Now he was initiating a conversation?

He examined his mail slot, then came to stand before her desk. "Have a good weekend?"

"Very nice." Robin's kiss came to mind and she fought back a rising blush. "Robin and I went to the art exhibit in Denver."

"Robin?"

"I'm Robin Goodfellow. I'm a friend of Kate's." Robin slid off the desk, placing his hand on Kate's shoulder as he faced the man. She glanced at Robin in surprise. Did he realize what a proprietary gesture that was? Probably not. It was more likely just Robin being Robin.

"Robin Goodfellow?" Grant frowned. "Isn't that the same name of a goblin or something?"

"A member of the Fae," Robin said coolly. "King Oberon's son."

"I see." Grant paused and his smile appeared forced. "Well, I only wanted to mention how nice you look today, Kate. I like that dress." He nodded at them. "See you tomorrow."

"See you tomorrow," she echoed, too stunned to do anything more. She looked nice? When was the last time anyone had told her that? Besides Robin?

She glanced at him to see his smug smile. Despite her misgivings that morning, she'd given in and worn the sea-green form-fitting dress he'd found in her closet. It hugged her abundant curves too closely for her peace of mind, but Robin had insisted she looked great in it.

And now Grant had complimented her.

Maybe Robin was right after all. She felt vulnerable in the dress, preferring to wear loose-fitting clothes, but Grant had never even asked the time of day of her before. Obviously, Robin's charm was wearing off on her or else Grant needed glasses.

"Oust that thought right now," Robin ordered.

Kate glanced at him in surprise. "What?"

"I can tell what you're thinking. He gave you an honest compliment. Accept it as that." A hint of amusement entered his eyes. "Besides, it was the truth."

Kate had to smile. If he kept that up, she was going to believe him. Picking up her purse, she rose, unwilling to engage in this argument again. "Let's go. We have some phone calls to make."

But a few hours later, they still hadn't located the right Nic Stone. Kate hung up the phone and grimaced. She was getting tired of repeating the same convoluted story. No doubt all these Nic Stones thought she was crazy. "That's the last one with a phone number."

"Two remain on the list." Robin tapped the paper, pointing to the two lines not yet crossed out.

"True, but without phone numbers, how do we contact them?" Even as she asked the question, Kate knew the answer. Robin never did things halfway.

"We'll have to go there." He made the announcement as if saying the words made it so.

"I can't just go to California, Robin. I have responsibilities."

"But you have the weekend."

"And we need money to fly there."

"Fly?" He lifted his eyebrows. "As in 'Fly the friendly skies'?"

"Right." She smiled at his analogy. "It's too far to drive in a weekend."

"Is that wise?"

"What? Flying?"

He looked dubious as he nodded. "Most of the ones I saw in the picture box were in trouble of some kind."

She grinned. "It's a TV, Robin. Sounds like the movie of the week to me. Don't worry. Airplanes are very safe. But, we still have to buy the tickets and I doubt if that's cheap."

"I can get the tickets."

His certainty was incredible. "You can't charm people out of tickets. They cost hundreds of dollars."

Her words didn't faze him at all. "That remains to be seen."

Kate shook her head, but lifted the phone to place the call. Before she could dial, he pushed the receiver back into place.

"Not with that. I need to see the person." Mischief danced in his eyes as he linked his arm through hers. "Take me to a place where we can get tickets."

She hesitated, then reached for her purse. What the heck. The airport was open all night. "You won't be able to do this," she said as they left the apartment. Robin had an amazing ability, but she couldn't picture any agent charmed into just giving away plane tickets.

His smile sent sensuous shivers dancing along her spine. "I love a challenge."

In less than an hour, they emerged from the airport. Kate still couldn't believe it. Robin had charmed them tickets to San Francisco. Not free, but two round-trip tickets for under a hundred dollars was miracle enough for her.

She suspected the female clerk at the ticket counter had made up the fare just to please Robin. He'd had her practically drooling. Not that Kate could blame the agent. Kate found it difficult to reason when Robin turned his smile on her as well. And she knew about his charm.

"So, we go to San Francisco this weekend?" he asked. Self-satisfaction mingled with amusement in his expression.

Kate stared at the tickets in his hand. "I guess we will."

"And we will find Nic there." He started for the car, but she paused for a moment before following him.

Robin's magic continued to surprise her. Nervous anticipation produced tap-dancing butterflies in her stomach. What kind of surprise would this weekend hold?

●   ●   ●

"So, now what?" Kate glanced at Robin in frustration as they left the residence of the last known Nic Stone in San Francisco.

They paused at the street. Robin's expression held none of the discouragement Kate felt. They'd come all this way for nothing. Both of the Nic Stones they hadn't been able to contact by phone had turned out to be the wrong man.

"We must return to the beginning," Robin said.

"What?"

"We learned of Nic first at an art display. This city should have something similar." Robin gestured to encompass the horizon filled with hills and houses.

Kate nodded, even as another thought occurred to her. "The library. We can probably find some information there." In fact, she should've thought of that a long time ago.

It was Robin's fault. His potent presence created memory lapses. When he was around, she had difficulty remembering her name.

"The library. Yes." Robin smiled and a tingle danced over her skin.

The man's charm could be lethal if he chose. Thank goodness he didn't use it on her. His presence alone was enough to melt her bones.

She turned toward their rental car, unwilling to pursue that thought any further. "Let's go."

After locating a nearby library, they settled before a computer terminal where Kate initiated a search on the artist's name.

Several references came up in reply and Robin squeezed her shoulder. "That's good, isn't it?"

"It depends." Kate skimmed the dates. Most of the articles were over a year old. She wanted the most current information.

There. That one was only three months ago. Kate brought the magazine article up on the screen and Robin read it aloud from behind her.

" 'Artist Nic Stone opens gallery in Dallas.' " Robin paused. "Where's Dallas?"

"Texas." Kate continued reading. " 'In order to give other young artists a chance to showcase their work, Stone created the Artisan's Gallery. Located in Dallas's Olla Podrida, the gallery offers budding artists space to exhibit their artwork in hopes of being discovered as Stone himself was five years ago while selling his paintings on the wharf in San Francisco.' "

"Where's Texas?"

Kate glanced at Robin and found a familiar glow in his eyes. "Far from here." They were not running off to Dallas until she'd checked and double-checked that Nic was actually there.

The corner of his mouth lifted. "That means we're not going there today?"

"Exactly. I want to know more first." Kate printed a copy of the article, then pushed her chair back. "We can call when we get back to the apartment. One wild-goose chase is enough."

Robin grinned. "No more chasing geese?" he teased

Kate couldn't help but respond in kind with a smile. "Not today, anyhow." As they emerged outside, she glanced toward the horizon where the ocean blended into the sky. The enticing view tugged at her. "Let's go the beach instead. I'm not about to come this far and not wade in the ocean."

He followed her gaze. "I'd like that."

She drove for a while before she found a stretch of beach where she could park nearby. As they stepped onto the sand, she paused to remove her shoes, eager to feel the sand on her bare feet. The sand shifted beneath her as she took a step and she curled her toes in deeper, finding it cooler beneath the surface.

Closing her eyes, she wiggled her toes. Why hadn't she noticed what a sensuous experience playing in sand could be? It caressed her toes and sent tingling awareness over her skin.

Hearing Robin laugh, she turned to see him running to where the waves lapped at the sand. His shoes sat beside her.

"Oh no you don't," she called. He wasn't going to beat her to the water.

She dropped her shoes and ran after him, the wind catching her hair and whipping it in her face. The heady sense of freedom surrounded her as if for this moment in time she could release her worries about the house, her father, and Robin.

They reached the shore together and paused. Robin tugged playfully at her hair. "A good idea, my sweet Kate."

"This is wonderful." Kate turned to look out to sea. Though not the sea of a Hawaiian postcard, she found the waves soothing. Gray skies reflected onto gray water and the approaching sunset wove its red and purple colors between the clouds. "It's almost enough to make a person believe in magic." She glanced at Robin over her shoulder and gave him a teasing smile.

"Almost?" He stood upright, then scooped his hand into the water, emerging with a perfect shell in his palm. "Believe, my lady." He presented it to her with a precise bow.

If she hadn't known better, Kate would've thought the shell glowed. She accepted the palm-sized gift with a curtsey, then ran her finger over the curves. "It's beautiful."

"As are you." His voice was husky.

Kate looked up and found Robin's gaze dark and intense. Her heart skipped a beat as her throat went dry. She could almost believe him when he looked at her like that . . . as if she was the only woman for him.

A gull screeched overhead and Robin blinked. He stepped back, then whirled around to run along the packed sand. "Come on," he called.

Kate's breathing was too erratic for her to follow him. Instead, she slid the shell into her pocket, then rolled up her jeans and eased into the surf. She gasped. "Cold." Somehow she thought the water would be warmer in California.

Well, maybe not in April.

She adjusted to the temperature and waded deeper until the water lapped at the hem of her jeans. Now this was worth the trip. Peace washed over her . . . a peace wrapped in sensuality. Even the feel of the water caressing her toes made Kate think of Robin.

Where was he?

As she turned to look for him, he suddenly appeared in front of her. Caught off guard, she yipped and toppled backward into the water, sending up a fine spray that showered over her. She shook her head as she caught Robin's expression. He would hurt himself if he didn't let that laugh out.

"Went too far, didn't you?" she asked, a giggle mingling with her words.

"Afraid so." He extended his hand to help her up.

Kate took it . . . and pulled. His eyes widened as he teetered for a moment, then fell to his knees beside her. She gave him a mischievous grin. "It seemed only fair."

His laughter escaped, a deep sound, full of fun and so infectious that Kate couldn't help but join him. It felt good. How long had it been since she'd laughed this hard? Had it been since her father went away? As long ago as that?

When they paused to catch their breath, Robin stood first and offered his hand again with a teasing smile. This time, Kate took it and he pulled her up in one swift movement so that she fell against him. His arms came around her as if to steady her, but remained even after she found her footing.

He pushed her damp tendrils back over her shoulders with gentle fingers. "My sweet Kate." Fire blazed in his eyes, a fire that bathed her in warmth despite the coolness of the wind. "Kate." His voice grew rough as he palmed the curve of her cheek.

"Robin." His name emerged from her constricted throat. Nothing else seemed important.

He bent toward her and anticipation soared through Kate's veins. Though good sense said she shouldn't want his kisses, every other part of her wanted them with an intensity that bordered on painful.

His lips touched hers, greeted, soothed, promised.

"Well, if it isn't Robin Goodfellow."

Kate jumped at the odd quavering voice, reminiscent of someone speaking under water, and they broke apart, each of them turning to find the source. No one was near.

Then who'd said that?

Kate inched closer to Robin and he wrapped his arm around her shoulders, his gaze focused beyond her to the undulating waves. As she watched, the water appeared to rise up in a pillar, then took shape as a . . . a person. The water glistened as if alive, then fell to the sea, leaving a man with a chest that would do Kevin Sorbo proud, clad in nothing more than a piece of cloth around his hips.

She swallowed. Who . . . what was that? He looked human yet displayed definite differences. His long dark hair flowed down his back, strands of seaweed mixed among the strands. His ears made her think of Mr. Spock, rising to a point beside his head. And his eyes . . . his eyes sent shivers over her skin. A pale green, they appeared luminescent.

The man waded toward them and Robin tensed, dropping his arm from her shoulders as he stepped forward. "Callum. I did not expect to see you here."

Callum shrugged, his massive shoulders exaggerating the gesture. "Time passes and there is much to see." He paused before Robin. "It has been—what?—two hundreds years since I last saw ye."

"As you said, time passes."

Robin's icy tone sent a chill over Kate, adding to that already created by the increasing wind and wet clothes.

"The tale I heard said Titania had locked ye in a portrait." Callum gave Robin an unpleasant smile. "Yet here ye are, walking around."

"Yes, here I am."

Callum walked past Robin toward Kate and she stepped back even before Robin shot his arm out in front of her in a protective gesture. "And who's this, Robin? Another lady love?"

"No." Robin sounded indignant and Kate grimaced. He couldn't have made his true feelings any clearer. "She's my friend."

"Friend?" The uninvited visitor laughed without mirth. "A man like you doesn't have women as friends, only as lovers."

"Kate's different." Robin moved closer as Kate tried to hide her despair.

Oh, yeah, she was different. She'd probably be the only woman Robin never slept with. But she *was* his friend. She mentally shook herself. And that was important. Right now, he needed a friend more than a lover.

"What do you want?" she asked. Maybe they could give this Callum what he wanted and he'd leave.

"Why, only to exchange greetings with my old acquaintance." Callum studied her until Kate shifted nervously from one foot to the other. He looked at Robin. "She knows about ye."

"As I said, she's my friend." Robin's tone held menace and Kate shivered. She'd never seen this side of him.

Robin glanced at her, concern replacing the iciness. "Cold?" When she nodded, he wrapped his arm around her shoulders once more. "We need to go. Good-bye, Callum."

"Good-bye, Robin. 'Twas good to see ye again."

Robin didn't answer, but hurried Kate across the beach toward the car. When he paused to scoop up their shoes, she risked glancing back. Callum was gone.

"Who was he?" she asked, barely raising her voice above a whisper. Who was to say Callum wouldn't appear from nowhere again?

"One of the Fae." Robin looked in Callum's direction and scowled.

The Fae? Somehow, Kate had always imagined them as prettier, nicer. "But he—"

"Not all Fae match the images in your books, sweet Kate." Robin propelled her forward. "Callum likes to spend time with the sharks and sea serpents and it shows."

"Sea serpents?" Kate settled into the car and closed her eyes. This was too much. Water faeries and sea serpents and . . .

At the sound of the car engine, she bolted upright. Robin sat in the driver's seat. "You don't know how to drive." She reached for the steering wheel, but he thrust the gears into drive and the vehicle jumped.

"I've watched you enough." Robin's impish smile reappeared. "I learn fast."

"But there's more to it than—"

He dove into traffic and Kate swallowed the rest of her sentence, digging her fingernails into the armrest. "Robin, I really think I—"

"Trust me, Kate."

She tried, but her muscles refused to relax until Robin pulled safely into the parking lot of the cheap motel where they'd reserved a room for the night. Her heart still hammered from the journey. Amazingly, every stoplight he'd encountered had turned green and every time she'd closed her eyes, certain he would hit another car, she'd opened them to find the other car mysteriously gone.

"We're here." His chest swelled as he came around to open her door. Obviously he thought he'd driven well.

"Uh huh." Her legs weren't completely steady as she entered the small room.

It contained two single beds, but she still wished they could've afforded two rooms. Even Robin's charm had failed there, simply because the motel was full. No other room was available.

Kate dropped onto the nearest bed and flopped back, throwing her arm over her eyes. Her head still whirled. Though she knew Robin was different, meeting another member of the Fae unnerved her. Fae, sea serpents. These were things of fantasy, not reality. Maybe this whole thing with Robin was nothing more than an elaborate dream. Was she losing touch with reality? Was that what happened to her father when he left on his fatal journey to find faerie gold?

"Are you all right?" He sat beside her and Kate peeked out at him from beneath her arm.

If it was a dream, she'd just as soon not wake up.

"Just a headache," she murmured.

"Let me help." He removed her arm and gently maneuvered her until her head rested in his lap. Easing her hair away from her face, he massaged her temples with a light touch that tantalized even as it soothed.

Headache? What headache?

It vanished as more pressing sensations made themselves known—the heat in her blood, the tightening in her belly, the ache in her breasts. Dear Lord, if he kept this up, she'd soon be putty.

Move, Kate. Her body resisted. *Get up, Kate.*

Something else rose instead, a hard ridge beneath her head. *Now, Kate!*

She jumped to her feet, very aware of her nipples pressing against her damp T-shirt. "I . . . I need to change." Grabbing her small travel bag, she hurried into the bathroom and locked the door.

Staring at her reflection in the mirror, she noticed her flushed cheeks and wide eyes and overly red lips. What had she been thinking to agree to coming here? She ran the cold water and splashed it over her face in hope of cooling her inner fire.

As she removed her jeans, she found the shell in the pocket and stared at it. Its elegant beauty touched her, rekindling memories of Robin's expression when he gave it to her. Her heart ached.

It was going to be a long night.

He would never make it through the night. Robin stared at the closed bathroom door. He wanted her—wanted her more than he could recall desiring any woman. With Kate, his longing went deeper than satisfying the body. It delved into his soul.

Bloody hell. Robin stood and paced the small room. This was madness. He had to remember that Kate was a friend, a very special friend. He could not make love to her, then leave her—despite the intense urgings of his lust. He had to focus, to think about something else.

He needed to concentrate on what they'd learned that day. Nic was in Dallas, a city far away. Once he found his friend, he'd learn how to enter the magical realm and free himself from Titania's curse.

And he'd never see Kate again.

Which was as it should be. He was immortal. She was not.

Robin paused by the window and gazed into the falling darkness. He'd always used that rationale when leaving women in the past and never found fault with it. Why, now, did it bother him?

The sound of a door clicking open brought him around and he watched Kate emerge, clad in a shapeless, long gown that she no doubt thought hid her voluptuous figure. If so, she was mistaken. He had no difficulty locating the curves of her breasts or the roundness of her buttocks.

"I think I'll just go to bed ... to sleep," she amended quickly. Twin spots of color heightened her cheekbones.

"Are you not hungry?" They'd eaten the noon meal many hours ago.

"No, not really." She climbed into the bed and drew the blankets up around her.

A barrier to ward him off. Robin nodded. At least one of them was thinking. "Sweet dreams, my lovely Kate."

"Good night." She rested her head on the pillow but he could sense her tension.

Robin couldn't relax either. He ached with want for her.

"I'll change, too." He strode into the bathroom, closed the door, then braced his hands on the sink. He would take a cold shower. Maybe that would help—it was one modern convenience he'd used a lot lately.

When he finally felt more in control, he emerged to find Kate sound asleep, her palm relaxed in sleep, the blankets bunched around her waist. Her magnificent hair sprawled across the pillow and Robin barely managed to stop himself from touching it, from touching her.

He stood over her bed as the all-too-familiar yearning grew within him. She was beautiful, intelligent, caring, and passionate. He knew instinctively the passion was there. Each day she came closer to realizing it, to believing in herself.

He would see that before he left. He had to see it.

Robin forced himself to turn away and went to stand outside the room where the cool breeze could ease his ardor. Soon Kate would become the woman he knew she was, able to share her passion with a man, to give freely without reservation.

A sudden pain spiked through him. He'd known from the beginning it wouldn't be him, shouldn't be him. And yet he wished very much that it could be him.

Seven

Kate sighed with relief when the plane touched down at the Colorado Springs Airport. She desperately needed to put some distance between herself and Robin before she went into severe lust overdrive. Granted, she couldn't get far away with their fifty-foot limit, but even going into a different room was better than being by his side almost constantly for the past two days.

Damn him for being practically perfect—handsome, intelligent, fun to be with and very, very charming. How was a woman supposed to remain detached around someone like him?

"I can't wait to get home," Robin said as they disembarked and headed for the baggage return.

Home. Nana's house still appeared in Kate's mind when she thought of home. Would she ever get over the pain of losing it?

She nodded in response, but her face must've reflected her sense of loss for Robin paused and squeezed her shoulder. No words were necessary and that alarmed Kate even more. This man was becoming too important even as they were searching for a way for him to leave.

After retrieving their bags, they stepped outside into a steady rain. Kate grimaced. "Didn't we just leave this weather?"

Robin grinned. "It'll make the flowers grow."

"Optimist."

After stowing their luggage in her car, they headed for the apartment. After they arrived, Kate eyed the glistening outside steps to the second floor with resignation. The rain still fell with no signs of letting up. Well, it wasn't as if she wasn't already wet. All she wanted right now was to get inside and collapse.

Robin grabbed the bags and followed her. Kate had almost reached the top of the steps when abruptly her foot slid out from under her, throwing her off-balance.

Trying to grab the rail, she cried out. She was going to break her neck.

As she tumbled backward, Robin grabbed her waist and yanked her hard against him. Their bags tumbled down the metal steps instead, spilling open as they reached the bottom.

Kate clung to Robin, then wrapped her arms around his neck when she finally found steady footing again. He kept his hold snug around her and she nestled her head against his shoulder.

His heart beat as rapidly as hers. "Are you all right?" he asked.

A large lump blocked her throat, making speech impossible so she nodded. With Robin, she felt safe, cared for.

"Did you slip on the water?"

She swallowed hard and glanced up at the shimmery step. "I guess. It felt like ice." In fact, she would've sworn it was ice.

"That's impossible. It's not cold enough." Robin hugged her tighter. "At least you're safe."

He had to be right. It wasn't cold enough for ice, yet . . . He ran his hand over her hair, then lifted her chin so her gaze met his and Kate forgot about everything except Robin and the feel of his arms around her. His eyes were uncommonly dark and concern etched his features. "You scared me out of a hundred years, my sweet Kate."

She gave him a wan smile and tried to keep her tone light despite her hammering pulse and trembling knees. "What's a hundred years when you're immortal?"

To her surprise, he didn't return her smile. Instead, he searched her face as if looking for something. What? He leaned forward and her stomach clenched in anticipation, her breath catching in her chest.

He placed a gentle kiss on the tip of her nose, then softly—so softly she wasn't sure she hadn't imagined it—he brushed his lips over hers and drew back. "Let's pick up our stuff and get inside."

His voice sounded rough as if speaking had been difficult, but he turned, keeping his arms firmly around her shoulders, and led her back down. Upon reaching the bottom, Kate eyed their clothing scattered over the wet pavement.

"Great," she muttered, bending to pick up a shirt. Now it was not only dirty from wear but adorned with mud.

Robin lifted a pair of her white cotton underpants and grinned, mischievously. "This will never do, Kate."

As she stared at him in surprise, he shook the panties and transformed them into red silk edged with lace. They spoke of sex—hot, fiery sex. Heat flooded Kate's cheeks and spread through her body. She'd never worn anything like that. What if she did? She had no difficulty imagining Robin removing that garment from her. In fact, she longed for him to do just that.

Robin located her bra and changed it to match the panties. As he held up the items, he looked at Kate, fire blazing in his eyes. "I'd like to see you in these," he said huskily.

Her breasts swelled and Kate drew in a deep breath. "That's not me."

"Yes, it is." He tossed the underwear into the open suitcase. "You just don't know it yet."

Tremors shook Kate, whether from the longing in her veins or an aftermath of her fall she didn't know. Possibly both. Scooping up the remainder of their clothing, she dumped it into the suitcases and snapped them shut. "Come on."

Upon reaching her apartment, Kate discovered her hand was still shaking as she tried to open the door. Robin eased the key from her grasp, turned the lock, then guided her inside. Leaving the bags by the door, he disappeared into her bedroom, then emerged carrying her favorite quilt.

He wrapped it around her and Kate closed her eyes as warmth filtered into the cold pockets of her soul. "You're still in shock," Robin said. "You could've been hurt." Before Kate realized his intention, he swung her into his arms and carried her over to the couch.

"What are you doing?" Was he trying to give himself a hernia?

He sank onto the sofa, pulling her onto his lap, wrapping his arms around the blanket to hold her close. "I'm keeping you warm."

Oh, she was warm all right. In fact, the longer she sat this close to him, the warmer she became. Didn't he realize the effect he had on her? "I . . . I'm fine."

"Just relax." He shifted so that her head rested against his shoulder. "You're safe now."

Safe? From harm perhaps, but not from her traitorous yearnings.

"Thanks to you." She drew away so she could look into his eyes. "You saved me, Robin. I owe you now."

"You don't owe me anything." His words said one thing, but the way his gaze darted to her mouth said another. Heat exploded inside Kate's belly and without thinking she pulled his mouth down to hers.

He didn't resist, but neither did he respond as she touched his lips. Had she offended him? She broke the contact and stared at him, aware of the tension in his muscles.

"This isn't a good idea," he said, his voice choked.

"I know." But she couldn't move, couldn't look away from his mesmerizing gaze. She was a fool to want him, to ache for his touch.

With a groan, Robin cradled her head and kissed her, passion searing her lips.

Kate opened to him, mating with his tongue in an erotic dance that sent fire through her veins. Oh, God, it was wonderful to be foolish.

She ran her palm over the firmness of his chest, pausing as his nipples grew taut beneath her fingers. Were his nipples as sensitive as hers? She brushed a nub and was rewarded with a moan from deep inside him.

His kiss grew more intense, promising fulfillment of the need swelling inside Kate. And she wanted that fulfillment. He reached up to cup her breast, running his thumb over her already swollen peak, and she arched upwards, wanting more, yet not sure she could stand it.

"Kate, sweet Kate." He left her mouth to place kisses along her chin, down her neck, to suck on her earlobe. She'd never considered that an erogenous zone before, but the ache between her legs convinced her otherwise.

"Robin, I—" She stopped, stunned by the words that leapt involuntarily to her lips. Realization acted as a tray of ice down her back. No, she couldn't love him. That was crazy. It had to be her lust talking.

Robin obviously sensed the change in her, for he pulled back. "Kate?"

"This . . . this is a mistake," she said before she could change her mind.

He blew out a slow breath. "My body disagrees with that, but what little mind I have left says you're right." He released his hold and Kate climbed unsteadily to her feet.

Her blood still pulsed with fire, her body still yearned for him to continue. She didn't dare look at him. "I'll get the laundry together."

She hurried to her bedroom, feeling his scorching gaze on her during each step of the short journey. Closing the door, she leaned against it, allowing relief to wash over her. But another emotion claimed prominence.

Regret.

● ● ●

Kate prepared for work slowly the next morning. Her dreams had made sleep almost impossible. In them, Robin made love to her, touching her, kissing her. Her body responded with passion. This was all she wanted, needed.

Then, in the midst of her climax, he was gone. She called for him, searched for him, but in her heart she knew she'd never find him.

And again, she was alone.

Kate shook her head to clear away the clinging wisps of the dream. It didn't tell her anything she didn't already know. As much as she wanted Robin, he'd soon be gone. Forever.

Snatching at her watch on the dresser, she only succeeded in knocking it behind the furniture. "Damn."

With a sigh, she grabbed the corner of the heavy wood dresser and tugged it away from the wall, just enough so she could slide her hand in. She found the watch but also felt something else . . . paper. Closing her fingers around them, she pulled both items out.

The paper turned out to be an envelope, the address on the front clearly that of the apartment. Obviously it belonged to a previous tenant. She'd drop it off with the landlord and see if he could forward it.

After tossing the envelope on the bed, she finished getting ready for a day at school. Thanks to the weekend's whirlwind trip, Friday felt like a lifetime ago. Emotionally, it had been. Each day she found it more difficult to resist Robin's magical charm. Or was it just his magic?

No, he was kind, supportive, and fun to be with on top of his devastating charm and good looks. She didn't need magic to find him irresistible.

She needed magic to resist him.

Enough of this. She had to get to work.

As she grabbed the envelope off the bed, she paused, staring at it, then glanced back at the dresser. How long had this letter been hidden there between the furniture and wall? The postmark was unreadable.

Kate's heart skipped a beat. What if Nana had accidentally

lost her revised will behind a piece of furniture? Kate hadn't looked there during her frantic searching.

She needed to do so.

Now.

Seizing her keys and purse off the table by the door, Kate hurried from the apartment toward her car. Abruptly, she ran into a man's solid chest.

Robin's chest.

Robin's *bare* chest.

Drops of water clung to his skin and Kate gasped, realizing he'd been yanked to her as he stepped from his shower. She dropped her gaze to his hips as he wrapped a towel around them. But not before she caught a glimpse of his impressive maleness. He put her one previous lover to shame.

Glancing up to find amusement dancing in his eyes, Kate shut her jaw with a snap. "I . . . I'm sorry."

"In a hurry?" For a man standing half-naked on the front porch of an apartment complex, he appeared much too relaxed.

But Kate wasn't. She struggled to keep her gaze focused on his face and not his muscular torso covered with a sprinkle of dark hair. A sudden longing to run her hands over his chest swept over her, making it difficult to concentrate. "I . . . I . . . Nana's will. It could be stuck behind a dresser or something."

"It could." With a grin, Robin turned her toward their apartment and pushed her in front of him. "But you're not going there now."

"I have to." Though reluctant, Kate allowed him to guide her back. It was her fault he was out here like this. He needed to get inside.

What if someone saw him?

Kate gave a wry smile. A woman would probably start drooling, too. Why didn't Robin produce clothing for himself? She knew he had that ability, yet she wasn't about to complain. His body was magnificent, godlike . . .

They stopped inside the door and he pushed it closed before coming to face her.

She feasted her gaze on his chest.

Struggling against the impulse to touch him, she clenched her fists and took a shaky breath. "Why don't you get dressed so we can go?"

"You have to be at work soon." Robin continued to grin as he turned toward the bathroom. "We can go to the house later."

"But—"

"If the will's there now, it'll be there later."

Kate found herself staring at the muscles in his thighs and the tightness of his buttocks against the towel as he walked. Thoughts of the will disappeared as her belly knotted with a sudden rush of desire. The man was sexiness personified.

He turned at the doorway to catch her staring and a flush warmed her cheeks. To her chagrin, he winked at her. Then, entering the bathroom, he pulled off the towel, giving her one final glance of his bare butt—the most magnificent buns she'd ever seen.

"Oh, my." Kate sank onto the couch as heat suffused her body. Nothing in her imagination could equal that.

Maybe it was a good thing Robin was planning to leave. The way her willpower was fading, she wouldn't be able to resist him much longer.

And worse—she wasn't entirely certain she wanted to.

The FOR SALE sign in front of Nana's house made Kate's heart sink as she drove past to the back driveway. Adam wasn't wasting any time. If only she had the money to buy it. If only she . . .

Kate shook her head. Life was full of if only's. If only she could find Nana's will, the house would be hers. Then she'd at least have one thing she loved in her life.

After she parked the car, Robin came around to join her in examining the house. "The locks were changed," he said.

She hadn't forgotten. "There is another way in—a window that doesn't latch."

Before she could move to the side window, he caught her shoulders, holding her in place until she met his probing gaze. As always, her unease grew under his scrutiny. He seemed to see into her soul, into her heart.

She dropped her eyelids as her heart gave a sudden lurch.

"Kate, the will may not be there. Is it worth this?" Though his voice was gentle, she caught a strange tone. Was he accusing her of something?

Lifting her chin in defiance, she looked at him. "My mother's dead, my father's dead, Nana is dead and you're going away. This house is the only thing I have left. Do you want me to give that up, too?"

Sadness entered his expression and he stroked her cheek. "No. If I could, I'd change all those things for you. I only want you to realize you have enough right now."

"Enough?" She couldn't keep the derision from her voice. She had a tiny apartment with furniture that wasn't even hers and a job that was a distant second to what she really loved. Maybe she was being selfish, but she wanted more than that.

"You're a beautiful woman, Kate. You're intelligent, personable, sexy—"

She whirled away from him with a sigh of exasperation. "I'm tired of hearing that bull. I'm going in. You can stay out here or not."

"You know I go where you go." He sounded tired and Kate winced at the sudden flash of guilt that wrapped around her.

Was she really asking so much to look more one time?

As she expected, the window opened easily and she climbed inside the house, Robin following. Once he joined her, she motioned toward the staircase. "Let's start in her bedroom and sunroom."

They'd already searched it thoroughly, but this time Kate concentrated on pulling the dressers and tables away from the wall. She discovered one of Nana's missing pearl earrings, but nothing resembling a will.

"It has to be here." A note of desperation colored her words and she glanced at Robin, wanting him to agree.

Instead, he gave her an encouraging smile and moved to the doorway. "Then we'll look in the other rooms."

But Kate found only disappointment. And no will.

By the time they went downstairs, she wanted to scream. Why had Nana said Kate would be taken care of? Why raise her hopes if a revised will didn't exist?

"She wouldn't lie to me," she murmured.

"Not intentionally." Robin paused by the staircase. "But it's not here, Kate. We've looked everywhere."

"I know." She closed her eyes to hold back the threatening tears. This was the end. Her home was lost to her forever.

Robin wrapped his arms around her and she nestled against his solidness. If only she could stay here and never have to move.

He ran his hand over her hair. "It'll be all right."

Glancing up, she had to smile. Flowers would bloom in winter for Robin. "If you say so."

"I know so." He trailed his finger lightly over the bridge of her nose, then released her. "Let's go."

Kate nodded, but didn't move, her gaze caught by the majestic oak chest in the front hallway. "I wonder if Adam is going to sell that, too. Nana said it's been in their family for decades."

A sudden alertness swept over Robin and he stepped forward. "For decades?"

"What is it?" The energy in the room had changed.

"Perhaps the circlet is there."

"I doubt it. We only used it to hold purses or mail." Kate inhaled sharply. "Mail."

They approached the bureau together, then froze as the front door swung open and a light flashed in their faces.

"Hold it. Don't move."

Kate blinked in surprise until she could focus on the man behind the flashlight. A policeman.

"It's all right, Officer." She smiled at him. "I used to live here and—"

"How'd you get in?" The officer glanced around the room, though his flashlight didn't move away from Robin and Kate.

"Through a window. The locks—"

"Breaking and entering." The man located a switch and

flicked on the entryway lights. As he did, Kate noticed the gun in his other hand and gulped. Surely she could make him understand.

"I'm just looking for something I left here. It's not what you think." Her heart pounded heavily in her chest.

"And what do I think?" His ominous gaze didn't give her much hope.

"That we're thieves. And we're not. You can search us. We don't have anything." She held out her arms and hands to illustrate her point.

Robin followed her example and stepped forward. "It's just as she says." His tone changed, his charm going into action. "We've done nothing."

"I . . ." For the first time, the policeman's stern demeanor weakened. He lowered the gun.

"I suggest you let us go." Robin moved even closer. "And forget you even saw us here."

"You used to live here?"

He turned toward Kate and she nodded, holding her breath. Would this work?

"Perhaps—" Before he could finish, the front door opened again and Adam stepped inside.

"Thanks for coming so quickly," he said to the officer. "I didn't want to come inside once I saw the lights moving around."

Kate released her breath. Adam would explain things. "Adam, when did you get back in town?" She beamed at him. "Would you tell this officer who I am?"

"You're in my grandmother's house after you were told to leave."

Kate blinked in surprise and reached for him. "But—"

"And you're a thief."

"What?" She'd never stolen anything in her life. Even Adam knew that.

He seized her hand and held it up to the light so the gold band around her ring finger glistened. "That ring is a family heirloom. You stole it."

"No, I didn't." How dare he accuse her of that. She'd worn

this ring for years. He had to have seen it before. Kate glanced at Robin for assistance only to find him staring at her ring. "Nana gave it to me on my twenty-first birthday."

"Hardly likely." Adam turned to the officer. "Arrest her at once."

"Adam." She wanted to grab him, force him to see reason.

To her horror, the policeman detached a pair of handcuffs from his belt and reached for her. "You have the right to remain silent . . ."

Eight

By the time she reached the police station, Kate's stomach churned relentlessly, adding nausea to her throbbing headache. This couldn't be happening. She'd never done a dishonest thing in her life.

How the hell could Adam do this? Didn't he know her at all? She grimaced. Obviously, *she* didn't know *him*.

The only bright spot—if there was one—was that Robin had been arrested with her. It would've been interesting if he'd suddenly appeared beside her in the police cruiser.

Upon entering the station, the officers separated Kate from Robin and led her into a small interrogation room. With luck, they'd put Robin close by or else he'd soon be joining her. And how would they explain that? She was in enough trouble without him popping in.

With a sigh, Kate waived the right to an attorney and sank into a chair before a small table. This was ridiculous. And a little excessive. She hadn't done anything wrong, no matter what Adam said.

The door opened, admitting two officers, their faces impassive, devoid of any emotion, and her stomach gave another fierce twist. Maybe she shouldn't have waived the attorney.

One of the men settled in a chair opposite her while the other stood to the side, his arms crossed, his gaze pinning her in place like a moth in an insect collection. Kate swallowed. Why did she suddenly feel guilty when she knew she was innocent?

The seated officer leaned toward her. "Why were you in Adam St. John's house?"

"It used to be my home." Though she tried, she couldn't keep the defensiveness from her voice. "I went back to find something I'd left behind when I moved out."

"Or did you return to steal Mrs. St. John's ring?"

"I didn't steal it." Kate clenched her fists. What happened to the presumed innocent part of the law? "Nana gave me that ring on my twenty-first birthday." She massaged the bare spot on her finger where the ring had rested for the past four years.

"And why would she give you a family heirloom?"

"Maybe because I was more family to her than her own flesh and blood." Anger crept in now. "Ask Adam how often he came to see his grandmother."

"Mr. St. John is not the one under suspicion here." The other officer spoke, his tone holding a veiled threat.

A chill crept over Kate. What would it take to make them believe her?

"Did anyone witness Mrs. St. John giving you the ring?" the first officer asked.

Kate paused, recalling the event, then smiled slightly. Let them argue with this. "Yes, Mary Woodburn."

The officer obviously recognized the name for he lifted his eyebrows. "*The* Mary Woodburn?"

Kate nodded. "She was a good friend of Nana's. I'm sure if you ask Mary, she'll verify what I'm telling you."

The officers exchanged glances, a hint of doubt in their expressions. Good. Mary Woodburn was an icon in Colorado Springs, known to everyone, well-respected and well-liked. They'd believe *her*.

"If you'll excuse us." The men left and Kate released a long breath. With luck, Mary would soon set things straight.

Glancing around the stark room, Kate kept expecting to see Robin appear. Where was he? What questions were they asking him? What was he saying? Was he trying to charm the entire police station into releasing them?

Unfortunately, she didn't see him succeeding.

Kate sighed. If she hadn't insisted on going back to Nana's house today they wouldn't be in this mess. Adam would've never missed his grandmother's ring if he hadn't spotted it on her hand. Worst of all, her search hadn't found the will.

Closing her eyes, Kate brought her palms up to cradle her head. Stupid, stupid, stupid. She wanted Nana's house badly but was it worth this? The sterile, cold atmosphere of the jail seeped into her bones, chilling her from head to toe.

How much longer was this going to take? What if Mary wasn't home? Kate's stomach sent out another painful reminder of its unsettled state. Mary liked to travel when she could.

Dear Lord, don't let her be in Europe.

Though time seemed to drag, Kate didn't think it had been more than half an hour before she heard Mary's Southern drawl through the closed door. Within moments, the tiny woman burst inside and enveloped Kate in a bear hug.

"Are you all right? I can't believe they brought you here." She didn't give Kate a chance to answer before she whirled on the two officers and Adam who'd followed her in. Though she only reached Kate's shoulder, the white-haired woman radiated a vibrant energy. "I do hope you're all going to apologize to this young lady. Bringing her here was entirely unnecessary. You should have called me immediately."

"Ma'am, we didn't realize—"

Mary didn't let the officer finish. She wagged her finger at Adam. "I have no idea why you did something like this, Adam St. John. I know you were raised better. Your grandmother adored Kate and if she wanted to give her this ring, you have no business questioning it. You'll never find a more honest soul than Kate."

"It's a family heirloom. It could be worth a lot of money. Grandmother—"

"Zelma gave it to Kate because she loved her. Kate took care of her when she got sick, used her own money to keep that place going when Zelma couldn't function anymore. Where were you during that time, young man? And how do you repay Kate? By kicking her out." Mary shook her head. "Shame on you."

Adam actually flushed, a dark red stain creeping up his neck. Kate couldn't resist sending a vindictive glance in his direction. They wouldn't get her the house, but Mary's words warmed her.

Mary shifted her attention from Adam back to the officers. "I'm sure you intend to let Kate go now." Her voice softened as she gave them a brilliant smile.

Kate smothered a grin. Before meeting Robin, she'd always thought Mary the most charming person she'd ever met. Though she appeared soft and grandmotherly, Mary was a true steel magnolia—intelligent, elegant, and very, very persuasive. A wise person didn't get on her bad side. Already, the officers were shifting like naughty boys caught with their hands in the cookie jar.

"Yes, Mrs. Woodburn. Now that you've verified her story," an officer said.

"And if Mr. St. John doesn't wish to press charges for breaking and entering," added the other.

Mary gave Adam a glance that dared him to try. To Kate's surprise, he dropped his gaze. "No, let her go." He looked up long enough to eye Kate. "But stay away from the house."

Kate nodded reluctantly. The will wasn't there. Robin had to be right. Nana had never actually written it. Her dream was gone . . . lost forever.

"Then you're free to go, Miss Carmichael."

"And my friend?" Kate wasn't about to leave without Robin. As if she could.

The officers glanced at Adam, who grimaced and shrugged.

"We'll get him." The men left, Adam following, and Kate hugged Mary again.

"Thank you, Mary. They wouldn't believe me."

"Foolish men." Mary drew back and studied Kate. "Are you doing all right?"

"Well enough." Kate had a job, food on the table, and a roof over her head, which was more than some people had. "I miss Nana."

"Me, too." Mary sighed. "She did care about you, my dear."

"I know." Kate had never doubted that, but no matter how hard she'd tried to help, Nana had still died.

"Kate." Robin preceded the officers into the room and came over to wrap her in a warm hug. "Are you all right?"

"I'm okay." She gave him a slight smile. "You?"

"Worried about you."

"And who is this?" Mary's accent grew even thicker.

Kate grinned and stepped back so they could face each other. "Mary, this is my friend, Robin Goodfellow. Robin, Mary Woodburn."

"Ah, yes." Robin took Mary's hand and bent low over it, his English accent stronger as well. "One of Zelma's closest friends."

Mary blinked. "Have we met?"

"Not in the usual sense." Robin's grin held a hint of mischief and Mary's eyes twinkled, subtracting years from her appearance.

Tilting her head, she looked at Robin again. "You do look familiar but I can't recall meeting you." She tapped her chin. "I'm sure I'd remember it."

"We were never introduced."

Kate swallowed a laugh. It would've been hard to introduce Mary to a portrait.

Turning from Robin, Mary gave Kate another quick but fierce hug. "Definitely a keeper, dear."

"Your ring, Miss Carmichael." One of the officers held out the gold band.

"Thank you." Kate slipped it on her finger. She was never taking it off again. Not for any reason.

Mary gazed at the police officers, her bright blue eyes alert and on target. For a moment, Kate could swear they paled. "Are we settled now?" Mary asked.

"Yes, ma'am."

"Oh, do call me Mary." Mary turned up the charm to maximum as she linked her arms through theirs and led them from the room. "Have either of you thought about helping in the schools during our upcoming celebration?"

They were goners now—no one turned down Mary in full persuasive mode.

"Thank goodness for Mary." Kate waited until Mary's voice faded away before she turned to Robin. His smile had dimmed and he watched her, his expression serious. She touched his arm, concerned. Had the police done something to him? "Are you all right?"

He nodded. "Let's go home."

Kate's trepidation rose during the drive home. Robin had never been this quiet before. What was wrong? "What's going on?" She glanced at him as they entered her apartment.

He hesitated and Kate's heart skipped a beat. Something was definitely wrong. "We need to talk," he said finally.

She swallowed the sudden lump in her throat. Did he intend to lecture her on her stupidity? "I know we shouldn't have gone to the house. But I never thought Adam would have me arrested."

"It's not about that." Robin took her hand and led her to the couch. Instead of releasing her palm, he continued to stroke her fingers. Encountering her ring, he turned it gently around.

"Then what is this about?" The tremors that danced along her arm came as much from nerves as Robin's touch.

"How long did Zelma have this ring?"

His change of subject surprised her. "Always. Her mother gave it to her." Remembering when Nana bestowed the heirloom on her, Kate's eyes misted. "Nana said I was more family than Adam's wife, that I should pass it on."

"I see." For several long moments, Robin didn't say anything. He looked up, his gaze dark. "We did achieve some success today."

"We did?" She hadn't seen any sign of that. As far as she was concerned the day had been horrible and the experience in jail one she never wanted to repeat. But at least she was able to keep Nana's ring, the only thing of value left in her life.

"I found Titania's circlet."

"You did?" Why wasn't he leaping for joy? "Where is it?"

He drew a slow breath. "You have it."

"Me?" Certainly she'd know if she had a queen's circlet. Kate studied Robin's face. Was he joking? He didn't look like it.

Robin looked down and turned her ring again. Kate followed his gaze and frowned.

"My ring?"

"Titania's circlet."

"That's impossible. A circlet is a crown. This is a ring." He had to be mistaken. Kate stared at Nana's ring. It didn't resemble anything a queen would wear. The band was gold with a single twisting line etched around it and a Celtic knot at the top. Wouldn't a crown be different? More pointy?

"The Fae are actually much smaller than mortals." He returned to caressing her fingers. "The circlet doesn't change size outside of the magical realm like we do."

Sudden dread sent a chill through Kate's blood. She knew what was coming next and couldn't face it. Not after all she'd been through already today.

"Believe me when I say this ring, this circlet will fit Titania perfectly." He started to ease the ring off her finger, but Kate impulsively snatched her hand away and cradled it to her chest.

"No." Irrational panic filled her veins.

"Kate, I have to have it." Robin didn't reach for her, but Kate could sense his restraint. "It's the only chance I have of convincing Titania to remove the spell."

"It's all I have left." Kate rose to her feet, knowing she

was being childish, yet unable to give Robin what he so desperately needed. Too many memories claimed her tonight, too many disappointments. "I've lost my mother, my father, my home. I can't let this go, too."

Another loss flickered across her tumultuous thoughts. If Robin did have the ring, he would leave. Now. And the pain of his departure would be worse than giving up her heirloom.

Robin stood. When he opened his mouth to speak, she leapt in. "You already said you'd face Titania without it."

"And I fully expected her to put me back in the portrait. She hates me, Kate. I was only going so you'd be free of me."

"What if I don't want you to go?" Kate gasped as she spoke without thinking. He didn't need to know that.

"Kate." His voice gentled as he reached for her.

She stepped back, tears filling her eyes. "No. Please, Robin. Don't ask this of me tonight. Not now." Maybe she was being too emotional, but damn it, this had been an emotional day. Maybe tomorrow when she could think rationally, she could give up her last link to Nana, but not tonight.

Whirling around, she dashed into her bedroom and shut the door firmly. She couldn't face this now. To give up this ring would be to give away her heart and soul and Robin. Could she do that?

A single tear slid down her cheek. Damn. Robin needed the circlet, not her. If he had it, he'd leave.

Once again, she wasn't enough.

Would she ever be?

Robin frowned as the door shut behind Kate with a firm click. Bloody hell. He'd known she wouldn't be happy about giving up the circlet, but he'd fully expected that she would do so anyway. Wasn't she his friend? Didn't she want to help him?

Given a choice of facing Titania with the circlet or without, he'd prefer with. He definitely didn't want to end up in the portrait again—this time perhaps forever.

Robin stepped toward her room, then paused. He couldn't

force Kate to give the circlet to him. But he could talk to her, explain how much he needed it.

He ran his fingers through his hair. Her reaction bothered him. She obviously suffered from more than giving up the circlet. But what? Should he approach her now when she was upset or wait until morning when they were both calmer?

What if by waiting he lost all chance to get the circlet?

Not giving himself a chance to think about his actions, he rapped on Kate's door.

"Go away." Her reply was muffled.

"Kate, this is important." His life hung in the balance.

"To me, too."

He softened his voice, her distress tugging at him. "Please, Kate, open the door."

The door inched open until Kate appeared. Her eyes were red-rimmed, her expression desolate. For a moment, Robin faltered, until thoughts of eternity in a portrait steadied his resolve.

He touched her cheek. "Kate, you know how much I need that circlet."

"I know." She hesitated. "But it's all I have left of Nana."

"I'll get you another ring." The thought of finding a ring appropriate for Kate, of sliding it on her finger brought an ache to his chest. Suddenly he wanted to do just that.

"That's not the point," she said sadly.

He cupped her face between his palms, meeting her weary gaze. This wasn't the time for talk, not when he could comfort her, ease her pain.

"Dear Kate." He leaned forward to claim her lips, to taste the unique sweetness that was Kate. Her response followed, shy passion that hinted at the smoldering desire beneath.

Robin drew her into his arms, making love to her mouth, reveling in the softness of her lips, the heat of her body. Who was he fooling? He wanted this for him. With a groan, he deepened his kiss. He wanted her . . . all of her.

This woman affected him like no other. True, he'd desired others, made love to others, but none had created this ache in his chest, this fire in his veins that threatened to consume him. Only Kate. His sweet Kate.

Her mouth moved under his—sweet, soft, seductive. A mouth that made a man want more. And he did. Fates help him, he did.

He nibbled on her full lower lip, drawing forth a moan from Kate as she wrapped her arms around his neck. His groin tightened. Seizing the opportunity, he found her parted lips and sought the inner heat of her mouth. Her response was tentative, but soon they imitated the sensual dance of love.

He wanted this woman, needed this woman. He ached to bury himself in her welcoming softness.

Moving his hand between them, he cupped her breast, finding the pebbled tip with his thumb. Kate gasped and Robin left her mouth to taste the silky skin along her throat, behind her ear. Her breath quickened, matching his rapid pulse.

He continued to caress her breast, savoring her small moans of pleasure. This was only the beginning. She would know ultimate gratification before he finished. Her nipple was rock hard when he found her breast with his mouth and suckled through her blouse. Kate dug her fingers into his shoulders with a cry, arching back to allow him better access.

Sweet. Wonderful. But not enough.

Guiding her back toward the bed, he ran his hands over her blouse, then her bra, removing both with a thought—literally. He caressed her swollen breast. Kate gasped as he lowered them to the bed.

She didn't resist, but ran her fingers through his hair, holding him close. He teased her other nipple with his hand as he used his tongue to torment the one in his mouth. She stiffened, her head thrown back, her breathing ragged.

Her breasts were wonderful, filling his hands, the peaks pink and hard. He concentrated on them with his lips and hands, reveling in Kate's cries, in the responsive movement of her hips . . . a movement that begged an answer from him.

Soon. But not yet.

Her body was made for loving and love it he would. He caressed her skin and planted kisses on the soft underside of her full breasts, then brought both hands up to caress the tips.

"Robin." His name emerged as a cry of half-pleasure, half-pain. "I . . . I . . ."

He found her lips again and drew encouragement from her eager response. Her tentativeness was gone now, her hands roaming over his torso, her tongue meeting his. Nestling his male hardness against the juncture of her thighs, he pressed against her, aching to possess her.

Soon they would be joined.

But she would know one pleasure first.

Gently he eased his hand along her belly and beneath her jeans. She was damp, hot, ready for him. Finding her swollen nub, he concentrated his touch there until he gained the reward he sought. Her body stiffened and rose off the bed, a loud cry sounding from deep within her. Robin studied her in the throes of her release. Bright pink color stained her chest and neck. Her head arced back, her eyes closed, her fingers grasping the bedspread.

As her breathing slowed, she raised her hands to touch his face. "I never . . . I . . ."

Robin smiled. She would soon know how much more wonderful it could be.

But as she lowered her hands, the gleam of the circlet caught his eye. He hesitated. Would she be more willing to give it to him now? Did he have the right to ask?

"May I have the circlet, Kate?"

"I . . . I . . ." She bit her lip, but nodded, giving him her hand.

Working the circlet free, Robin stared at it in the palm of his hand. So small, so plain, yet possibly the key to his freedom.

Kate stroked his cheek, returning Robin's attention to her. Her gaze met his, blazing with passion and more. Enchantment.

Stones. His charm was at work. Had his passion triggered

it? Her response, her giving up the circlet—both were a result of his magic. He'd never intended this.

Disgust slammed into Robin. This wasn't what he wanted from her. Damn the ring. Damn his magic. "I can't do this."

He returned Kate's clothes to her body, then dropped the circlet on her shirt. Swinging off the bed in a fluid movement, he fled to the living room, not daring to look at her. He couldn't bear to see the dismay and confusion of her expression.

Dropping onto the couch, he buried his face in his hands, waiting for the physical ache of unfulfillment to subside. The emotional ache would take much longer. Kate was special, the one woman he'd found himself caring about. How could he for even an instant think the circlet meant more than she did?

Now he'd ruined their friendship. Most people never knew they'd been charmed. In fact, they usually assumed the ideas he guided them to were their own. But Kate had the sight. Once the magic wore off, she would know, she'd realize what he'd done.

Robin groaned. He deserved to be sentenced to eternity imprisoned in a portrait. As much as he desired Kate—still desired her—he had no right to pursue her with magic. He wanted her passion given freely.

"Damn you to hell!"

A book ricocheted off Robin's shoulder and he turned to see Kate standing in the bedroom doorway, her eyes blazing, her cheeks flushed an angry red. Magnificent.

His chest tightened. He rose to face her. "Kate, I—"

Tears shimmered in her eyes. "How dare you. Thank God you'll be gone soon because I want you out of my life. Forever."

Before he could respond, she whirled around, back into her room and slammed the door behind her.

Robin sank back onto the furniture and closed his eyes. *Oh, hell.*

Nine

She couldn't very well hide in here all day. Kate faced her reflection in the mirror. Damn it, her face reflected her sleepless night. It wasn't fair. Now Robin would know how he'd affected her, how her body had ached for the remainder of the night, longing for his touch.

Did the blasted circlet mean so much that he'd seduce her to get it? That he'd use his charm to befuddle her mind?

And here, for an instant, she'd thought—actually dared to hope—that he'd honestly wanted her. She should know better. As much as Robin called her beautiful and praised her ample curves, he didn't mean it.

Damn him.

In a burst of anger, Kate bolted from the bedroom and grabbed her purse and keys off the table by the front door. The sound of clanking in the kitchen gave away Robin's location.

She didn't call to him, didn't wait for him, but stalked from the apartment and down the hallway to the parking lot. She couldn't avoid him forever, much as she liked to. Sooner or later she'd have to deal with him. Especially once she exceeded their distance limit. If only it could be later.

But she had to get to work, had to escape to the one world where she felt she had a small measure of control.

Robin appeared by her side just before she reached the parking lot. He looked as haggard she felt. Good.

Now if only she could stop the blush from staining her cheeks or the sudden leap in her pulse. It wasn't fair.

"Kate, I . . ." He paused to clear his throat. "I made breakfast."

"I'm not hungry."

He reached out as if to touch her shoulder and she drew back. He'd done all the touching she was going to allow.

Dropping his hand, he tightened his jaw. "Then I need to go back and turn off the stove."

"Fine." Kate turned on her heel and stormed back to the apartment, then leaned against the outside wall. "I'll wait here."

When Robin appeared a few minutes later, neither of them spoke. They entered the car in silence and remained that way throughout most of the drive to school.

Finally Robin turned his gaze on her. "I'm sorry, Kate. I never meant to use my charm. If you won't give me the circlet willingly, I don't want it."

That wasn't all she'd almost given him. Memories of his mouth on her breast, of his hand sending ripples of pleasure through her body sent heat into Kate's cheeks. "You used me like a cheap whore. I guess you figured if I had good sex, I'd give you anything." She didn't try to contain her bitterness. He knew how lost she felt right now and obviously intended to use that to his advantage.

"No, I didn't intend . . . I only wanted . . ." Robin trailed off, obviously at a loss for words. That was a first. "I'm sorry. It'll never happen again. I swear by the Stones."

"You're right." She looked away from the traffic long enough to glare at him. "It'll never happen again."

She'd allowed herself to be foolish long enough. The only reason Robin showed any interest in her was because she was the only female around. Evidently he needed sex and wasn't choosy where he found it. What else could she expect from a man after he'd spent two hundred years locked away?

Robin needed to return to the Fae, to his own kind. The longer he stayed, the more she convinced herself that he wouldn't leave. But he would. They all did.

Better she should help him do so.

Kate spent her lunch hour searching the Internet for more information on Nic Stone. Everything she found indicated he still resided in Dallas. In fact, his gallery was a resounding success, introducing new talent to the artistic world as well as additional paintings by Nic.

But she couldn't find a phone number for him. No doubt he kept it unlisted. She did, however, locate a number for his gallery. Maybe they could reach Nic there.

When Robin stopped by her office on the way to recess, Kate handed him the slip of paper without a word.

"What's this?" he asked.

"Nic's gallery's phone number." She didn't bother looking up. Seeing Robin's apologetic expression would only make her feel sorry for him and he didn't deserve her pity.

"Shouldn't it be five hundred and five instead of three hundred and sixty one?"

"What?" That brought her around to face him.

"The phone number. Shouldn't it be five hundred and fifty five?"

For once, his TV-fostered misconception didn't spark her smile. "No, that's only for fictional numbers. Like on TV."

"I see." Robin stuffed the paper in his pocket, then sat on the edge of her desk. "Kate, how many times do I have to tell you I'm sorry?"

"I don't think you'll live long enough." Even for an immortal. She turned her back on him again, trying to type at her computer. If only she could find the right keys.

He sighed. "If I didn't care about you, I wouldn't have stopped."

A group of students rushed into the office with the grace of wild horses as Kate swung around to face Robin, her heart in her throat. He sounded as if he meant it.

"Mr. Goodfellow, you promised to show us that new game," Ian said.

The other students chimed in their agreement. "Do I get to be the goal tender?" Jessica asked.

Steven glared at her. "I already asked."

Robin slid from Kate's desk with a rueful smile. "I'll be right there. Just let me finish here."

"Oooo, Mr. Goodfellow likes Miss Carmichael," Jason crowed. Giggling, the children tumbled out of the office.

The silence felt even thicker upon their departure. Robin gently cupped Kate's cheek. "He's right, you know."

He left and Kate sat frozen, her fingers on the keyboard. His sincerity wrapped around her frozen aching heart and warmed it back to life. He had stopped his sensual assault as soon as she'd given him the ring. And left her more frustrated, more hungry for a man to fill her than she could ever remember. Still, he had given her pleasure—an internal explosion that she'd never experienced before.

"Oh, Robin." Why couldn't it have been because he wanted *her* instead of the circlet, wanted *her* instead of any willing body?

Yet he had left the ring even after she'd given it to him. She recalled that moment and the sense of loss as he removed the ring from her finger. But the waves of pleasure still vibrating through her body had seemed a fair trade at the time.

Damn him.

"Rough day, Kate?"

She glanced at Shannon as her friend entered the office to check her mail.

"I've had better," Kate replied.

"Something's wrong with Robin, too." Shannon paused before Kate's desk. "Usually he's so cheerful and bouncy I want to strangle him, but he's barely said two words today."

"Yeah." Kate wasn't about to share their disagreement. Shannon might be a good friend, but some things were too personal. Especially when they involved Kate making a fool of herself.

Concern entered Shannon's gaze. "I hope he'll be all right."

A sudden realization focused Kate's attention. Shannon cared about Robin. She was pretty and vivacious—an excellent counterpart to his handsomeness and charm. Kate knew Robin liked Shannon and Shannon made no effort to hide her attraction to Robin. In fact, she used every opportunity to corner him in the hall for conversation.

No doubt the only reason Robin started to make love to Kate was because of her availability. What if another woman was around? Would that help? Would that slake his lust and keep him from fueling Kate's hopeless dreams?

"I think Robin's down because he wants to date other women yet he's hesitant to leave me out since he's visiting." Kate spoke as the thought took root. "Why don't you come over for dinner on Friday?"

"Me?" Excitement flared to life in Shannon's eyes.

"Sure. It'll be fun. Come about six."

Shannon's smile lit up the room. "Great. I'll be there. Can I bring anything?"

"Just yourself." That's all Robin would need.

Shannon left the office, a bounce in her step, and Kate drew in a shuddering breath to ease the ache in her chest. This was the right thing to do. Robin would be happier for it and maybe they could regain their special friendship.

Unfortunately, she had the horrible feeling it would never be the same again.

"I'll be there in a few minutes." Robin waved at Kate from within the group of boys surrounding him. They only gave him a minute to respond to her before assaulting him with questions.

He certainly responded well to the kids. Kate had heard more than one student telling another about the "cool Mr. Goodfellow." Of course, the fact that Robin acted half-child himself probably helped. Still, he listened to them and gave value to their words. That alone endeared him to many children.

"I'll start the car." She hurried for the exit door while mentally figuring the distance between Robin's current position and where she'd parked. Maybe she wouldn't start the car. The kids might be more willing to accept the impossible, but Robin's position would be at risk if he disappeared in front of them.

Of course, if they were able to contact Nic Stone, Robin might not have to work here much longer. He'd be back among the Fae and Kate would be alone . . . again.

Why couldn't she be enough? Or it was because she was more than enough. Her generous curves might equal those of Rubens' models, but they weren't the accepted figure for today. And she would never be as thin as the women adorning the TV and movie screens. Hell, she'd have to be dead a year first and even then she doubted it.

Her stomach twisted but she only walked faster as if she could outrun the pain. Emerging from the building, she paused at the top of the three stone steps leading from the front door. The wind had picked up during the day, bringing with it cooler temperatures and dark clouds. Ah, Spring in the Rockies.

A wild gust shook the trees and pummeled Kate, blowing her hair into her eyes. As she pulled it back, another gust smashed into her, this one feeling like a push against her back.

A hard push.

So hard, it knocked her off-balance and down the steps. She cried out and grabbed at the railing as she fell, half catching herself, but still ended up with a bloody knee and wrenched ankle.

Damn, who pushed her?

She glanced behind her, but no one was there. Who would want to push her anyhow? She probably just tripped.

Frowning, she sat on the step to examine her knee through the hole in her pants. Not too bad. Some skin had rubbed off but she'd survive. Good thing there weren't more stairs.

She tried to get up, then dropped back to the ground as her ankle refused to support her. Damn. Her ankle throbbed and she pulled off her shoe to look at it. The outward appearance gave no sign of the pain within. Shouldn't it be black and blue or swollen?

As she gripped the railing to pull herself up, Robin dashed out to join her. "Are you all right?" He wrapped his arm firmly around her waist, forcing her to lean on him for support.

"Just bruised. I fell down the steps."

Robin followed her gaze toward the front stairs and frowned. "You're not usually clumsy."

She might argue that. Around Robin, she always felt like a klutz. Though that undoubtedly had more to do with the way her pulse increased in his presence. "Nothing's seriously hurt. I just turned my ankle."

"Then you shouldn't be walking on it."

Before Kate could protest, he lifted her off her feet and into his arms. In a reflexive movement, she flung her arms around his neck. He'd hurt himself if he didn't put her down. "I can walk." At least, she thought she could walk.

"Let me help you."

He didn't appear to be straining from the load, yet she would've found it easier to accept his help if his close proximity didn't awaken every memory of the previous evening. The warmth of his body and his familiar masculine scent triggered her hormones at once.

Her breasts swelled, the nipples pebbling. Her insides clenched, aching to be filled. Her blood caught fire, sending the heat through her body. She didn't dare look at him.

He headed for the passenger side of the car and she thumped his chest. "I can drive." She wasn't about to experience the adventure of his driving again.

Reaching the driver's side, Robin lowered her to her feet, but kept one arm around her as he opened the door.

"Thank you." Kate glanced at him as she spoke, then immediately wished she hadn't. His dark eyes caught and held hers, promising . . . promising what?

Had he moved closer? Had his mouth dipped toward hers?

Kate blinked and drew back. "I can manage from here."

"Of course." Robin waited for her to settle into her seat, then shut the door and walked around to the passenger side. "Can I help in some other way?"

Several things sprang to mind, but none that Kate dared to mention. "I'll just soak my foot when I get home. I don't think it's too bad." She gave him a reassuring smile. "You can help me up the stairs."

He smiled in return, his gaze warm. "Have you forgiven me then, sweet Kate?"

Apparently so. She couldn't stay angry with him. "Yes," she admitted. "What happened was my fault, too." She'd wanted him to kiss her, to touch her. He hadn't needed his charm for that.

"Thank you." The huskiness of his voice resonated within her, triggering tiny chills of longing.

Upon reaching their complex, Robin assisted her up the steps and into their apartment. He guided Kate to the couch, then knelt before her to examine her ankle. She winced as he probed with gentle fingers.

Well, she'd wondered about it not being black and blue and swelling. Now she had all three. "What is it for swelling?" she asked. "Ice?"

Robin started to speak, then stopped and nodded. "I'll get it." He returned from the kitchen with some ice wrapped in a towel, which he applied to her ankle.

Kate inhaled sharply. Cold. But it helped numb the ache.

Pulling a chair over, Robin cradled her foot on his lap and lightly massaged her ankle. New heat mixed with the cold to catch Kate's breath. "I . . . I don't think you have to do that."

"It should help," he replied as he continued his motions.

Oh, it helped all right . . . helped send her pulse into the stratosphere. He worked magic with those fingers . . . a magic designed to drive her crazy. Funny, she never would've expected an injured ankle to become an erogenous zone, yet every touch of Robin's fingers added to the pressure building inside her.

She had to stop this, had to fight her crazy desire before she grabbed Robin and forced him to make love to her. That thought brought a wry grin. As if she had the courage.

"Feeling better?" he asked.

Surprisingly enough, her ankle did feel better. The throbbing had ceased, though likely that was a result of the ice. She turned her foot expecting the ache to return, but received only a sense of stiffness. The pain was gone.

She eyed Robin with sudden suspicion. "Did you do something?"

Mischief danced in his eyes. "I massaged it." In fact, he continued to rub her ankle, his hands sliding further up her leg with each stroke.

And with each stroke, the knot low in Kate's belly drew tighter. Was he aware of his effect on her?

"Robin . . ." She started to speak, then forgot what she intended to say as he traced the entire length of her leg with his fingers, pausing near the top of her thighs before running them down again.

Oh, Lord, she was going to climax right here.

With a burst of panic, she tried to rise, but Robin gently pushed her back down. "I . . . I need to make dinner," she said.

"I'll do it. Rest that ankle." With a final stroke to her calves, he stood and headed for the kitchen.

Kate closed her eyes and drew in a ragged breath. Somehow she had to keep Robin from touching her, no matter how much she liked it. Truth was, she liked it too much and each encounter left her that much less resistant to his sensual nature.

Maybe after he spent the evening with Shannon, he wouldn't be so prone to touch her. Kate frowned. That thought didn't make her feel better.

Resting her head on the couch back, she debated on mentioning that she'd invited Shannon for dinner, then discarded the idea. She'd do it later.

Friday evening was a little later than she'd planned. As Kate bustled in the kitchen preparing a special dinner, she glanced again at the clock. Shannon would be here soon. She had to tell him. Now.

For some reason, she felt reluctant to do so. How would he react to her matchmaking scheme? Would he understand why she was doing this?

Robin returned to the kitchen. "There. I set the table. Anything else?"

Kate snatched two candlesticks off the counter and handed them to him. "Put these on, too."

"Candlesticks?" He raised his eyebrows, a slow smile appearing. "Is this to be a candlelight dinner?"

"Well, yes."

His smile broadened.

"But I won't be here."

"What?" Robin's grin disappeared. "What do you mean?"

"I . . . I invited Shannon for dinner. After the other night, I realized you needed female companionship. Someone besides me. Otherwise you wouldn't have . . . you wouldn't have . . ." Assailed by sudden memories of their encounter, she released a shuddering breath. "Anyhow, I asked Shannon over. You like her. I'm sure you'll have fun."

"Did you ever consider asking me what I wanted?" His frown made her pause. Was he worried about her being around?

"I know I can't leave, but I'll go to my room and you won't even know I'm here. Tell her I had something to do."

"Kate—" His voice held a warning note.

"I think it's a great idea." She turned away to check on the potatoes, unwilling to meet his gaze. "Shannon likes you and she's very pretty."

"So?"

"And she's a lot of fun to be with. I'm sure you two will hit it off right away." She rambled nervously, keeping busy.

"Kate . . ." He set the candlesticks back on the counter and stepped toward her. "Do you think the other night happened because I was desperate?"

"I'm not blaming you." She was afraid to look at him. "I know it's been two hundred years and a woman is a woman, but this way you don't have to put up with me."

"By the Stones, Kate." He seized her shoulders, forcing her to face him. Anger blazed in his eyes. He started to speak but the doorbell rang, blotting out his words.

"There she is." Kate eased free, grabbed the candlesticks and headed for the dining area. "Everything's ready. Have fun." She set the candles on the table, then darted into her bedroom, her heart hammering in her chest.

She stood beside the door, listening. Would Robin let Shannon in? Did he see the logic in her plan? His anger surprised her. For a moment she wished she'd heard his explanation.

Not that it would've changed anything. As much as she wanted it otherwise, they had no future together.

The quiet murmur of voices reached her. The front door closed. The voices continued. Good, he'd let her in.

So why did she feel so miserable?

Robin closed the door reluctantly after Shannon entered. His first instinct had been to send her away, then throttle Kate and kiss her until neither of them could breathe. What was she thinking? He was desperate, but not in the manner she thought.

"Where's Kate?" Shannon paused in the main room to glance back at him.

He hesitated. "She had other business tonight. I guess it's just the two of us."

Shannon gave him a slow smile that he'd learned to recognize over the years. She would not push him away if he kissed her. In fact, she'd gladly lie with him and ease the ache of need in his body.

Sitting on the couch, she crossed her shapely legs, raising her already short skirt even higher. "Come have a seat." She patted the cushion beside her.

Returning her smile, Robin sat. She was comely and he liked her well enough, yet for some reason he lacked the desire to take advantage of what she offered. He'd never found it a problem with all the women in his past. He'd willingly sampled their charms, then went on his way.

All women until Kate.

But Kate was his friend. He'd come dangerously close to losing that friendship. Despite his apologies and her apparent forgiveness, tension remained high between them.

And now he knew why. She thought he'd only kissed her because she was available. Foolish woman.

"Have you known Kate long?" Shannon kept her gaze on his as she ran her finger along his arm.

"Most of her life." From the time she'd first arrived in Zelma St. John's home. He'd seen her happiness, her pain, her caring. He'd watched her blossom from a gangly child into a stunning beauty. His breath caught in his throat. He didn't dare think of that now.

Or he'd be with her instead of entertaining the company she'd invited.

"But enough about Kate," he said. He shifted so Shannon's hand fell from his arm. "Tell me about you."

"What's there to tell?" A teasing glint entered her eyes. "I teach first grade at Mountainside Elementary. I'm single. I like fast cars and dancing all night." She glanced at him from beneath lowered lashes. "And I want you."

He knew this game, could play it well even though he hadn't played it in centuries. Yet he didn't move, didn't pursue the opening she gave him.

"I thought when you turned down my invitation for the art show that you and Kate . . ."

Kate. He didn't dare think of her. "We're friends." That word didn't sum up the feelings she created within him, the desire to be one with her. Though he tried to steer his thoughts away, they came back to her. "Have you known her long?"

"Since she came to work at the school. We hit it off." As she spoke, Shannon inched closer to his side. "I'm pleased she thinks you and I are right for each other. I've thought so from the first day I met you."

Robin eyed her warily. Away from school, she became more aggressive than he would've expected. "I believe dinner is ready."

He put out his arm to touch Shannon's shoulder, to hold her back, but she obviously thought he meant something different for she wrapped her arms around his neck and molded her body to his.

"I'm not hungry." The gleam in her eyes promised a night of passion. "For dinner."

"Ah, Shannon . . ." As much as Kate wanted him to find pleasure with her friend, he couldn't do it. The passion that rose so easily when Kate looked at him stayed dormant even with Shannon's small breasts branding his chest.

"But dessert sounds good," she added. Before he could respond, she lowered her mouth to his and kissed him.

Ten

They were talking. Kate could hear the murmur of voices through her bedroom door, but couldn't distinguish any words. Were they whispering? What was happening? Her imagination provided vivid details. Was Robin already charming Shannon?

Not that he'd need magic to do that. Shannon had told Kate often enough about her attraction to Robin.

"Enough about Kate." Those words came through clearly in Robin's voice and the air escaped her lungs in a whoosh. A blow to the gut wouldn't hurt as much. Obviously, he wasn't having any problem in relating to Shannon.

Whirling around, Kate threw herself face down on her bed, tears welling. This was what she wanted, wasn't it? After all, she'd arranged it.

She heard nothing now from the other room and her mind quickly supplied the mental picture of Robin holding Shannon, kissing her, making love to her. With a sob, Kate pulled her pillow over her head and allowed the tears to flow.

This *wasn't* what she wanted. *Be honest, Kate*. She wanted Robin for herself. Even knowing anything between them was impossible, she desired him. His kisses and touches only made her crave more. No one had ever come close to arousing the feelings he did.

And her feelings weren't due to his magic. She'd known that even when he was using it on her. Perhaps his magical charm overcame her initial mental barrier, but the rest of her had been happy to give in.

Robin was special. He took time for her, made her feel beautiful, treated her like the only woman in the world. His humor, his kindness, his passion made her appreciate him completely. Even after he left, she'd always remember him.

Kate choked on another sob. She couldn't deny it any longer. She loved him . . . loved him in a way she hadn't thought possible.

She loved him.

And he would leave.

Just like everyone and everything she'd ever allowed herself to care about.

But at least with Robin she'd known all along he meant to leave. He'd never hidden that from her. He hadn't tried to make her fall in love with him.

Now he would have his fling with Shannon, find his friend Nic and return to the land of the Fae.

All because Kate wasn't enough of a woman to make him stay. Even as a child she wondered if she'd been less plump or more outgoing if her father would've stayed instead of venturing on a useless quest. She was no different now and just as unable to keep the man she loved with her.

Kate drew her knees up to her chest in an attempt to withstand the pain that ebbed into every pore, a pain no medicine could cure. If only Robin hadn't stopped the other night. Then she'd have that memory after he was gone.

Or would it make her hurt worse?

Her body shook from her sobs. Could the sorrow be any more painful?

Abruptly, the pillow was yanked away and she looked up to see Robin standing beside the bed. Swiping at her damp cheeks, she rolled into a sitting position.

"What are you doing here?" She glanced at the doorway,

half-expecting to see Shannon standing there, but it was empty. In fact, the apartment was silent. "Where's Shannon?"

He dropped the pillow to the floor. "She left." His dark gaze met Kate's. "I . . . she . . . we both realized we were making a mistake."

"Mistake?" Kate hardly dared hope. What kind of mistake? Was he saying what she thought he was saying? He didn't have sex with her friend? Didn't he like Shannon? How could he not? "What happened?"

Robin continued to gaze at Kate, his expression clearly pained, his hands linked behind his back. "I've never had this happen before. Charming women has always been a part of me. I take advantage of what they're willing to give and move on. But I couldn't. Not this time."

"Because you . . . you like Shannon?" Kate had assumed Shannon wanted sex with Robin. She'd certainly dropped enough hints around Kate. Had Kate been wrong? Had Shannon been offended when Robin made his move?

"No." He paused and started to bring his hands forward, then stopped and linked them behind him again. "Because I like you."

Kate's pulse skipped a beat. "Me?" Couldn't she do anything more intelligent than echo his words? His statement was simple but it impacted her with the force of a bullet. She knew he liked her. They were friends after all, but this sounded as if he meant something more than that.

"For the first time I've met a woman I can be friends with, who I know as a person and not just a beautiful body." His voice grew husky. "I can't make love to Shannon or anyone else."

Anyone else? A lump caught in Kate's throat. All right, maybe they were just friends. What did she expect? That he would declare he wanted only her? Such was the stuff of fantasies. She could only stare at him, waiting.

"Because the only woman I want is you, Kate."

She hadn't heard right. Couldn't have heard right. Had he said the words she'd just imagined? Or was she dreaming? Her lungs refused to breathe. Her pulse entered an erratic pattern closer to an earthquake than any regular heartbeat. "You want me?"

"You and only you, sweet Kate." The deep roughness of his tone surrounded her, bringing goosebumps to her skin. "But I won't take advantage of you. I used you badly the other night and I—"

She didn't give him a chance to finish, didn't give herself a chance to question the wisdom of her actions. Her dream had come true and she wasn't about to turn away. Jumping from the bed, she wrapped her arms around his neck and kissed him.

His lips parted as he enveloped her in a tight hug and she molded her body against his. Her breasts swelled against his firm chest. Hot desire rushed through her veins.

Gasping for air, she looked at him, her gaze the only steady part of her at the moment. Could she do this? She had to. She might never have another chance. "I want you, Robin."

Anticipation danced in his eyes, shadowed by concern. "Are you sure?"

She ran her hands through the black curls on his head. "Very sure." Aching for the feel of his skin against hers, she pressed closer to him. "Make love to me, Robin."

"Kate." With a groan, he seized her mouth, passion filling his kiss, his teeth tugging gently at her lower lip. When she gasped, he made love to her mouth—teasing, seducing, promising more.

Need for more, for him warmed her blood, centering low in her belly. This time she wouldn't let him stop. She kissed him back, learning from him, mimicking his sensual movements.

He ran his hands along her sides, down her back, then cupped her buttocks to pull her snugly against his hard bulge. The ache for him to fill her wrenched a groan from low in her throat. She clutched his shoulders, inviting him closer.

Instead he held her away and ran his hands lightly along her spine and bottom. A sudden cool sensation alerted Kate that her clothing had disappeared. Unnerved, she started to cover herself with her hands, but Robin caught them and held her arms out to her side.

"Don't hide such beauty." He kissed her thoroughly, then bent to place kisses on the path left by his hands as he slid them over every inch of her exposed skin. Her inhibitions faded. Each kiss edged Kate's internal temperature higher as her breathing grew shallower.

By the time, Robin reached her breasts, the tips were hard nubs aching for his touch. He didn't disappoint her. Cupping her heavy breasts in his hands, he loved each one generously, slowly, until Kate wondered she could breathe at all. She'd always thought her full chest a nuisance, but now . . . now she reveled in the sensations coursing through her.

"Robin," she gasped, unable to say more. She didn't think she could take much more, yet she couldn't ask him to stop either. Her knees threatened to buckle as desire turned her bones to pudding. She clenched his shoulders, trying to make him stand even as he bent lower.

"You're wonderful," he murmured and she believed him. The way he touched her, kissed her made her feel priceless.

He continued his slow exploration of her body, dropping gentle kisses across her belly, eventually reaching the juncture of her thighs. Ignoring that part of her that yearned most for his attention, he nibbled his way down the inside of one leg and up the other.

Her legs were truly useless now. Unable to hold onto his shoulders, she clutched the bed's headboard. "Robin, I . . ."

He darted his tongue into her cleft and she gasped as an arrow of heat shot from her core. No man had ever done that to her. For a moment, the room wavered. Was she going to faint?

Rising slowly, he brushed his body along hers until he reached her lips again. Heat rose from between them. Kate was surprised she couldn't see it rise like waves off hot pavement. She ran her hands over his chest. Maybe she couldn't see the heat, but she felt it.

His skin was smooth beneath her palms and she realized

his clothing had vanished as well. "That must be a nice talent to have," she murmured with a smile.

He gave her a lascivious grin. "It has its uses." He suddenly scooped her into his arms, then dropped her on the bed, rolling to lie beside her, his arm holding her close, his body pressed along hers.

Her entire body tingled with awareness beneath his gaze. He looked at her as if she were beautiful. "I want to worship you, touch all of you," he murmured.

"I think you've already done that." For once, her bare body didn't embarrass her. Beneath Robin's heated gaze, she was every bit the equal to Rubens's models. Except she couldn't display the nonchalance they displayed in his paintings. The knot in her belly was so tight now, she felt like a jack-in-the-box ready to burst free. "I want you."

"Not yet." Though his firm erection pressed against her thigh, he continued to admire her, using his finger to trace her cheekbone, the line of her throat, and patterns on her chest, touching everywhere except where she wanted him the most.

When he finally brushed her nipple, Kate could've sworn electricity bolted through her body. She arched against the bed, a moan escaping, but he continued, bending to suckle the swollen tip, then pausing to blow on it.

"You're . . . you're trying to kill me," she gasped.

"No." He gave her a slow smile that added to her internal agony. "Only *la petite morte*."

She didn't understand, but neither did she care as his hands and mouth covered her skin with sensual ease. She'd never been so aware of her body before, so lost in sensation. Desire coiled tighter, every muscle responding in kind.

Unable to keep from touching him, she caressed whatever she could reach—his back, his muscular arms, his solid chest. She longed to grasp that part of him pulsing against her leg, but his wonderful assault on her senses made that impossible.

He ran his hand between her legs, his finger delving into her dampness. She lifted her pelvis, aching for him to fill her. Instead, he parted her thighs and found her with his mouth, his tongue tormenting her most sensitive spot.

The tension within her erupted with the force of Mount St. Helen's. Kate cried out, her body bowing as it shuddered with the force of her climax. Yet Robin continued to use his mouth on her, drawing out her contractions until she collapsed, exhausted.

"My God, Robin," she said when she finally found some air. No wonder women flocked to him. "That was incredible."

He chuckled against her belly, creating a ticklish sensation along her sensitive nerves. "It's only the beginning, my sweet Kate."

"Beginning?" Before she could fully comprehend his meaning, he put his hands and mouth to work again, teasing every part of her until desire once again fed the pulsing ache inside her. Only now it was hotter, more intense.

She seized his shoulders, trying to pull him atop of her, but he lavished his attention to her breasts. Every touch of his hand, every stroke of his mouth sent fiery arrows through her blood. "Robin."

A pleading quality filled her voice but she didn't care. She needed him. Now.

Raising his head, he smoothed her hair away from her face and bent to kiss her, slowly, as if he had all the time in existence. Maybe he did, but she didn't.

She grabbed his shoulders. "I'm going to die here."

"I don't think so." Amusement lingered under his husky tone. When she tried to protest, he claimed her mouth, his lips working a magic all of their own.

They were lethal weapons. Tension spiraled until her heart could barely beat. Her groan held all her frustration. "This is cruel and unusual punishment," she whispered. She grasped his firm buttocks and squeezed.

This time Robin thrust forward, entering her with one smooth movement. Kate gasped. He filled her completely and her inner muscles clenched around him. Finally.

He didn't move. "All right?" he murmured against her lips.

"Very." She'd never been so all right in her entire life. In response, she moved against him and he joined in the rhythm, his slow, deep thrusts driving her need even higher.

Wrapping her legs around his hips, she met each movement with equal passion. Nothing had ever been like this. She ran her hands over his firm back, holding him to her, inhaling his unique male scent mingled with the muskiness of sex.

Every muscle drew tight, her blood growing hotter with each thrust. Her sensitive nipples hardened further as the dark hair of his chest scratched over them. The pressure low in her belly built to a demanding ache.

The entire man was a lethal weapon.

And she loved him. She arched back her head, her breath coming in gasps, her hands stroking his hair and shoulders, and Robin found her throat, his lips leaving soft, sensuous kisses along the skin until he reached her ear. As he nipped gently at her earlobe, she found release once more.

She screamed his name as her body dissolved into a series of passionate explosions, each as intense as the previous. Robin suddenly groaned, erupting inside Kate with a force equal to her own.

After several long moments, they collapsed against the bed, their breathing shallow, and Robin encircled Kate in his arms. "Dear, sweet Kate." He kissed her softly. "You are beyond compare."

"Me?" She met his gaze, pleased at the dark passion that simmered there. "I've never experienced anything like that. It was magic."

"No." He placed a kiss on the tip of her nose. "It was you."

"And you." Sex couldn't possibly be like that with anyone else. She ran her hand over his chest, then snuggled closer to his heated form.

To her surprise, a yawn escaped and she clamped her hand over her mouth. How could she possibly be tired now?

Robin grinned and tightened his hold. "That's all right. Rest now."

"Will you stay?" She hated to think of him leaving her

bed after what they'd shared. Hell, she hated to think of him leaving at all.

"They'd have to pry me away." He kissed her forehead, then ran his hand over her hair. "Sleep, sweet Kate. I fear I wore you out."

"You he-man, you." Kate closed her eyes as commanded, but still smiled. Though exhausted, she'd never felt this good in her entire life.

Kate woke abruptly, an unfamiliar weight pressing upon her. As she blinked to awareness, she realized it was Robin's arm and leg thrown over her as he slept.

He lay on his side facing her and Kate rose up on one elbow to study him. Asleep, with his black curls tousled, he looked even younger than awake. Hard to believe he was eight hundred years old.

Yet he radiated sex appeal as if he bathed in it. And he certainly knew what he was doing in the lovemaking department.

Kate stretched to ease the kinks. Her body still simmered with the heat of their union. Their awesome, incredible union.

She would still have to let him go. She knew that. An immortal, magical man didn't stay with a very mortal, very unmagical woman. But she had no regrets. To be loved so thoroughly, so completely was more than she'd ever expected to find in her entire life.

No regrets. She'd known what she was doing. What she still wanted to do. Before Robin went, she wanted to experience many more nights like tonight.

Taking advantage of his stillness, she ran her hand over his chest, tracing the outline of his muscles, then over his hip, pushing down the sheet as she went. Even flaccid, he was impressive.

A small knot of desire sprang to life inside her, and she reached out to wrap her fingers around his penis. The skin was soft, smooth, warm. As she stroked him, he hardened, the softness giving away to a firmness that filled her palm.

Robin's breathing changed, coming faster now. "Kate?" His sleep-laden voice held a note of huskiness.

She smiled. He'd driven her to distraction before. Why not take advantage of her curiosity to return the favor?

Lifting his arm off her, she pushed him onto his back, then bent to kiss him, trying to employ the same techniques he'd used so satisfactorily before. His lips responded and she pursued her advantage, making love to his mouth even as she ran her hands over his solid chest and lower to the part of him that was now fully awake.

His quiet moan filled her mouth and she broke off the kiss to nibble her way across his chest, to lick at his nipples. His skin warmed. Or was it hers?

She made her way lower, across his flat stomach, along the line of dark hair, surprised at how his groans of pleasure added to her excitement. Straddling his thighs, she admired his erection, then bent to take him in her mouth, to torment him as he had her.

The way his hands gripped the sheets and his body stiffened proved she was succeeding. Using her hands and tongue, she teased him until he released a sharp cry.

"Keep that up and I won't be responsible for the consequences," he gasped.

Kate sat up and caressed his chest again, enjoying the rough feel of his dark hair. She would never tire of touching him. "What's the matter?" she teased. "Can't take it?"

He reached for her shoulders, but she rose up, then settled herself on his erection. They both moaned as he filled her. It was good, so good.

Clenching him tightly, she began to move, using slow, precise strokes just as he had previously. Each new plunge inched her tension higher. She closed her eyes, her head thrown back, her pulse rapid and blood hot.

Robin surprised her by finding her breasts and rolling the tips between his thumb and finger. Kate gasped and moved faster. The room grew warm. To heck with that—the room was hot. She was hot. Flashes of color danced behind her eyelids.

They peaked together, their cries mingling.

Kate gasped for breath. None of her fantasies could equal this. This feeling was more than satisfaction, more than great sex. It was . . . completion.

Robin touched her face and she opened her eyes to find his expression as dopey as she felt. "Are you all right?" he asked.

"No." She grinned as his eyes widened and she leaned forward to kiss him. "I'm fantastic."

A mischievous glimmer appeared in his eyes. Grabbing Kate's waist, he rolled her onto her back with him atop her in a movement so swift and smooth they stayed joined.

She gasped, but before she could speak, he kissed her thoroughly.

"Thank you, my sweet Kate."

"What for?" She should be thanking him.

"For taking time to pleasure me." He smoothed back her hair. "No one has done that before."

Her cheeks warmed as she recalled her boldness. "I didn't know I could."

"I did." His smile warmed her. "I knew you were a passionate woman, Kate, and you've proven me right."

Only with you. With him, she discovered new freedom, a side to herself she hadn't known existed. "I don't think I'd be like this with anyone else."

His expression grew thoughtful and he looked away. Instead of replying, he took a strand of her hair and teased her breasts with it. The peaks, which had just relaxed, tightened at once. A sudden flash of heat streaked to her core.

"Are you trying to start something?" She couldn't want him again already. Could she?

"Perhaps." He gave her an enigmatic smile. "I like touching you. Your body is magnificent."

Magnificent. Kate had never thought of herself in connection with that word, but with Robin looking at her, touching her, she didn't dismiss it. Maybe a few round curves weren't such a bad thing after all. He certainly appeared to appreciate them.

She reached out to stroke his thighs. Magnificent worked best when applied to him, though. Michelangelo's *David* paled in comparison to Robin, though the way muscles defined his arms, legs and torso, Robin could've been sculpted. He was strength and masculine sex appeal rolled into one.

And he was here with her.

He brushed her nipples with his finger and her inner muscles clenched around him. To her surprise, he hardened in response.

Kate stared at him. "You can't possibly do it again." Though she lacked experience, everything she'd heard indicated men didn't . . . couldn't . . .

Grinning, he lifted one eyebrow. "Would you care to make a wager on that?"

She gave him a smug smile. "You're on."

She lost.

Eleven

He shouldn't have done it. Robin gazed down at Kate as she slept. But even knowing that didn't make him feel guilty. She had been all that he'd expected and more. Making love with Kate had been more than exchanging physical pleasure. He'd experienced a binding deep in his soul. Had knowing a woman well made so much difference?

Yes.

Shifting, Kate snuggled deeper under the blankets and Robin drew her tighter to his side. He didn't want to let her go. Not now. Not ever.

Insane.

He'd never found it difficult to leave a woman before. In fact, he rarely gave them a second thought once their mating was over. But none of those women had been Kate.

Besides a body made for loving, her spirit held passion and giving. When she'd touched him, driven him nearly to distraction, his chest had ached with a feeling so deep he couldn't give it words.

They'd made love through most of the night—an accomplishment even for him. But when he thought himself sated, she had only to smile or touch him and he was as randy as a spring goat.

Robin softly smoothed her hair away from her face, memorizing the gentle curve of her cheek, the slope of her nose, the meant-to-be-kissed full lips. For once, he wasn't filled with the urge to move on. He wanted to stay . . . with Kate.

Why not? He didn't have to find Nic right away. Why not spend as many days . . . nights as he could? Time wasn't a problem. Then he could hold her, love her, and laugh with her for years to come.

And watch her grow old.

A sudden chill swept over him. He had nothing against elderly mortals, but to watch someone he cared for age filled him with panic. His mother had grown older, weaker, white-haired as he remained young until one morning when she'd stayed asleep—lost to the mortal's eternal sleep. The agony of her loss stayed with him for years, a constant reminder to keep his distance from mortals.

Then he'd later encountered a former lover at the end of her years. The change from the lovely young woman he'd known to the bitter, hunched hag disgusted him. He hadn't been able to flee her fast enough.

To watch Kate grow old—no. Robin's gut clenched. He couldn't do that. The horror of that image tightened his chest. He didn't want that as his final picture of Kate. He wouldn't experience that devastating loss again.

He would stay for now, for a while longer, then he would leave. A mortal and a member of the Fae didn't belong together for anything more than a brief interlude. That was the way it had always been and would remain.

If only it could be possible without hurting Kate in the end. Her feelings mattered. If he were wise, he'd leave right away, but when it came to Kate, his wisdom disappeared.

Kate moaned, rolled onto her back, and blinked her eyes, meeting his gaze with surprise before a slow smile curved her lips. "Good morning," she murmured, her voice still drugged with slumber.

The husky note instantly wiped away Robin's chill, replacing it with heat that soared to his loins. "Good morning."

He bent to kiss her. Her response nudged his internal heat into flame. Yes, he would stay for a little longer.

But he would still have to go.

"Turn there. On that dirt road." Robin pointed without thinking to the turn-off barely visible between the trees lining the road. Instinctively, he knew he'd find the perfect spot along the road.

Kate complied, then glanced over at him from behind the steering wheel. "Do you know where we're going?"

"No." He grinned, feeling more lighthearted than he had in centuries. "We're on an adventure."

Her laughter raised his spirits even more. "My life has been an adventure since I met you."

"Is that a bad thing?" He probably knew her answer, but his gut clenched, waiting.

Her soft smile eased his tension. "No, not at all."

Spotting a good site, Robin pointed. "Pull over there."

After Kate parked, he climbed out of the car, then turned to throw his jacket back inside. The day had started out cool—typical of spring—but now the sun warmed the air, banishing the chill back onto the snow-capped peaks.

"This is beautiful." Kate paused beside him, her gaze focused on the surrounding scenery.

Distant mountains towered above the aspens and pines, forming a half-circle around the grove. Colorful primrose flowers dotted the new grass, braving the inconstant weather. In the distance, water poured over rocks on its journey down the slope.

It was the perfect spot to share with Kate, a place where they could be alone and unite with nature. To make love to Kate here among the majestic glory would only heighten the experience. Robin grinned. Maybe he ought to rethink that plan. Making love to her was a heady enough experience in itself. Heightening that might kill him.

But he wouldn't complain.

"A picnic in the mountains was a great idea." Kate lifted a basket from the car. "How did you know this place was here?"

"I didn't." Robin grabbed the blanket and followed her to a spot near the stream. But some part of him had known, had wanted to share this beauty with her. He shook his head with a smile. He could no more explain how the Fae were at one with nature than he could find words to express the desire that rose within him when he looked at Kate.

Even now. She set down the basket, then turned to admire the mountains, her figure in profile. She wore her hair free and the wind blew the strands away from her face while it hugged her sweater closer to her full breasts.

Robin's chest grew tight. Though lovely, Kate was more than her outward beauty. Her caring and intelligence combined with her playful sense of humor continually piqued his interest. He'd never taken time to know a woman before. Now any woman he met would be compared to Kate.

"You're beautiful." He spoke without realizing it, his voice unexpectedly husky.

For once she didn't deny it. Instead she faced him, her eyes dark with passion, and waited.

She didn't wait long. He crossed to her in two long strides, pulled her in his arms and claimed her mouth as if it had been years instead of mere hours since he'd last held her. Would he ever tire of touching her, wanting her? Her unrestrained response burrowed deep inside him, awakening more than his desire.

"We'll never get lunch at this rate," she murmured against his lips, her laughter barely smothered.

"I'd rather have you." He drew several slow kisses from her lips.

"It's already mid-afternoon." Though she protested, Kate didn't remove her arms from around his neck. "And we missed breakfast."

"Are you trying to make a point?" The way she pressed her body along his only added to his growing need. He didn't want food . . . only Kate.

"I need to keep up my strength." Humor glinted in her eyes.

"Aye, that you do." But he was reluctant to release her. "Very well. We'll eat, *then* I'll ravish you."

"If you insist." She slipped from his grasp. "I'm going to wash my hands."

She cast him a grin over her shoulder and he smiled in response. He'd been smiling a lot lately. Not that he minded.

As she knelt beside the swift-rushing water, he paused to admire how her jeans hugged her rounded bottom. No, he didn't mind at all.

"It's freezing," she called.

He stepped toward her, then froze. Something was wrong. The forest had gone silent, the wind still. An icy finger traced his spine. He turned his head slowly, searching the surrounding area.

Bushes, trees, nothing amiss. Wait . . . there.

Had something moved on the other side of the stream? He stared at the spot, but saw nothing more. Releasing his breath, Robin tried to ease the tension from his shoulders. What did he have to be worried about?

Kate's scream answered him as she tumbled into the swift-moving stream. Robin ran toward the bank only to see the current tossing her against the rocks as it carried her away.

His heart filled his throat and panic dashed through his veins. What had happened?

"Kate!" He sprinted along the bank, trying to keep up with her. She tried to swim, but the current—the result of the melting snowpack—held too much power. When she disappeared beneath the surface, his heart skipped a beat. "No."

By the Stones, why wasn't his magic more powerful? If fully Fae, he could pull her from the water with a single thought. Now he had only his mortal abilities to save her.

She reappeared almost instantly and he pushed himself even faster. He had to get ahead of her, stop her somehow. A fallen tree jutted out over the stream and he rushed toward it. Grabbing the trunk with one hand, he jumped into the water.

Icy needles dug into his skin, stealing his breath. He ignored it, edging to the middle, his gaze never leaving Kate. Just before she reached him, she vanished once more. Robin lunged forward, almost losing his hold on the tree, and snared the back of her sweater, yanking her to him.

The current fought him, threatening to pull her free of his already numb grip. "By the Stones, give me strength." He muttered the plea as he struggled to hold onto both Kate and the tree. If he let go, she'd be lost.

Not Kate. He couldn't lose Kate.

With a final surge of energy, he managed to stagger to the shore, where he collapsed, hugging Kate close to him. Relief turned his limbs to water. He'd saved her. Even without his magic.

Or had he? Robin glanced at her pale face. "Kate?"

She didn't move and he sat up, new terror shooting through his veins. "Kate?"

She was limp, pale, her lips blue. "Kate?" He cradled her against him, seeking her pulse in the tender skin of her throat.

Her heart still beat, weakly, but it beat. He pushed back her wet hair and leaned close to hear her faint breathing. Alive. She lived, but her skin was so cold.

He was shivering, too. If he didn't do something soon, they'd both freeze.

With a brush of his hand, he removed their clothes, then carried Kate to the blanket. Cradling her in his lap, he wrapped the warm material around them. Would it be enough? He could start a fire, but didn't want to release her to do so.

His shivering ceased, but Kate continued to shudder, her teeth chattering. He pulled her closer, willing what little body heat he had left into hers. "Kate, sweet Kate."

He couldn't lose her. That thought overshadowed even the fear of returning to the portrait. Without Kate, he'd miss a vital part of himself. She'd done more to make him appreciate life than anything or anyone else in the past eight centuries.

What had happened? One moment she'd been kneeling beside the stream, the next in it.

He kissed her gently. Her lips had lost their blue color. Good. Her eyelashes fluttered and the tight bands around his chest eased. "Kate?"

"Why . . . ?" She drew in a ragged breath, then looked up at him, confusion in her eyes. "Why did you push me?"

"Push you?" Robin stared at her, stunned. "I didn't. I was here by the basket."

She rested her head back on his shoulder as if that effort had been too much. "Well, somebody did."

"There's no one else here." Or was there? Recalling the sudden change in the atmosphere, Robin frowned. Had some-one been in the bushes? Someone who'd pushed Kate, then vanished?

No, Robin would've seen him. And why push Kate? What purpose would that serve? "You must have slipped."

She didn't answer.

"Are you all right?" he asked, rubbing her smooth shoulder.

"I think so." She shifted, then gave him a wan smile. "You're undressing me again."

"I had to get you out of those wet clothes." Relief, pure and simple, flooded his veins. If she could joke, she was all right.

"One-track mind," she murmured. "The car has a heater in it, you know."

"Oh." That idea hadn't occurred to him. Cars were still too much an unknown.

He'd removed their clothes to get them warm, but Robin was suddenly aware of her body pressed close to his. In fact, he preferred this method of heating her. "Warmer?" *His* body temperature had become very warm.

"Some." She placed her hand against his chest. "Where are *your* clothes?" She raised her eyebrows, humor lighting her eyes.

"They were wet, too." The words barely emerged from his thickening throat. The more he tried not to think of their nudity, the hotter his desire rose. Not now. Kate didn't deserve that now.

In desperation he reached into the picnic basket and pulled out one of the chocolate eclairs they'd purchased for dessert. "Lunch?"

Wait, she'd nearly died. Food probably wasn't a good thing. "Maybe you shouldn't." He lowered the pastry, but Kate caught his arm.

"A taste," she murmured.

He held it up to Kate's lips and she took a bite, her tongue darting out to remove the traces of chocolate from around her mouth. Robin bit back a groan. This wasn't helping.

He bit into the pastry, barely tasting the flaky crust and sweet pudding as his hormones fought to take control. As he raised it again for Kate, she gasped. "What?" he asked.

Following her glance, he smiled. Pudding had dripped from the éclair to land on the slope of her breast. "Sorry." He met her gaze, unwilling to proceed without her approval. "I should clean that up."

"Yes, you should." She sounded breathless, very much like he felt.

Dipping his head, he lapped at the creamy substance, managing to brush her nipple as he did. The peak rose to attention at once. "I think I got it all." He raised his head to see the rose color back in Kate's cheeks.

"Are you sure?" A familiar gleam appeared in her eyes. Heat rocketed to his loins.

"Let me check." He lowered his head again and drew her swollen crest into his mouth to love it thoroughly before transferring his attention to her other breast.

Kate's moan urged him on.

"Warmer?" he asked.

"Oh, much warmer."

He lowered her to the blanket and covered her with his body, trying to touch all of her with his hands and mouth. His Kate. His beautiful sweet Kate.

She ran her hands into his hair, pulling him closer. "In fact . . ." She paused to inhale. "In fact, I'm downright hot."

Meeting her gaze, Robin gave her his best wicked grin. "Good."

"You're glowing."

Kate looked at Shannon in surprise. "What?"

"Your face is actually glowing." Shannon came to stand before Kate's desk. "It's Robin, right?"

Kate hesitated. Did her happiness show? The last thing she wanted to do was hurt her friend's feelings.

"I'm right." Shannon smiled. "Don't worry. I knew when I left on Friday it wasn't me he was interested in."

"I'm sorry, Shannon. I thought he'd like you." Though, truthfully, Kate wasn't sorry Robin had spurned Shannon's advances.

"He does." Her friend gave her a quick hug. "He just likes you better."

"I can't remember when I've been this happy." In fact, Kate had to work to keep a silly grin off her face.

"Good. You deserve some happiness." Shannon grabbed her mail from the slot and turned for the door. "Go for it, Kate."

"Oh, I intend to." Kate enjoyed every moment with Robin, acutely aware their time together was limited. Sooner or later, he'd return to the Fae. However, he had put off the idea of contacting Nic when she'd mentioned it. And she certainly hadn't argued with him.

Maybe he'd changed his mind about leaving. Giddy butterflies fluttered in her stomach at the thought and she tried to dismiss them. Robin had to leave. She couldn't expect him to remain tied to her for the rest of his life.

She paused. No, the rest of *her* life. The butterflies turned into a rock. She'd grow old but he'd remain young and handsome. How could they possibly stay together then? She found it amazing enough that he wanted to be with her now, but when she was old and gray? Not likely.

With a sigh, she turned toward her desk. Today was enough. In fact, the only way it could be any better would be to find Nana's will. Maybe . . . She shook her head to dismiss that fleeting idea. Her last experience in trying to find it had resulted in a visit to the police station. She wasn't anxious to repeat the experience.

"Good morning, Kate." Grant strolled into the office and paused by his mail box.

"Morning." She forced a smile and sank into her chair to pick up a stack of papers. Maybe work would take her mind off her dark thoughts.

"Um, Kate?"

Glancing up, she found Grant approaching her desk. "Yes? Do you need something?"

"Well, actually I was wondering if you'd like to catch that new movie on Friday."

Kate blinked. "With you?"

"Yes, of course."

Hot damn, he was asking her for a date. Her levity returned. "Thanks, Grant. That would be nice, but I'm seeing someone right now." How strange it felt to say that—how strange and how wonderful.

"Oh, um, I see." He backed away. "Well, keep it in mind."

"I will." Kate stood, her smile returning. Grant Coates had finally asked her out. Didn't it figure? Now that she'd met Robin, no one else could begin to compare.

"Kate." As if she'd conjured him up, Robin burst into the office, nearly knocking Grant over as the man left.

"What?" He appeared rushed, excited. Had something happened?

"I was thinking of you." Before she could respond, he pulled her close and claimed her lips in a fervent kiss that made her toes curl. When he finally lifted his head, he grinned, the usual mischievous gleam in his eyes. "There. I should make it now."

He dashed out as quickly as he'd arrived and Kate laughed. Okay, no more worrying about the future. She had to take each moment as it came. Life was too short to do otherwise.

At least, for her.

By Friday, she was still in a good mood. The nights with

Robin were glorious, filled with passion and laughter. And the days were broken up by those times when she knew she'd see him—like this afternoon at the school's spring social.

The kids echoed her excitement. Besides the social, this was the last day before their week-long break started. No one sat quietly today.

Especially Kate. She loved the games and goodies of the social. Plus it was one day she could wear jeans to work. Tidying the mail table for the third time, she jumped when Jenna spoke her name behind her.

She looked around with a sheepish grin. Jenna shook her head. "You're as bad as the kids."

"Can I help you?"

"Actually, I wanted to speak with Robin. Would you mind sending him to my office?"

"No, of course not." Kate frowned as she headed for the next-door classroom. What could Jenna want with Robin? Had he done something? Given away who . . . *what* he was?

What if she insisted that he leave right away? He couldn't unless Kate left, too. What then? Could Kate give up her job for Robin? Especially when this position meant so much to her? It was almost like being a teacher, and with her present situation, she wasn't likely to get her teaching degree any time soon.

She poked her head inside the room and motioned for him to join her. Emerging into the hallway, he grabbed her hand and squeezed it.

"Your hand is ice cold." His expression grew concerned. "Something wrong?"

"I don't know." She couldn't shake the feeling that something was going on. "Jenna wants to talk to you." She met his gaze. "Did you do something?"

"Nothing that would get me sent to the principal's office." Robin's warm smile didn't ease her tension. "Don't worry."

"But what if she says you can't help out in the classroom anymore?"

Robin was surprised by the sudden sense of loss. Not help out anymore? Lose his contact with the kids? He knew them now, liked them. What with spending his days working with the children and his nights loving Kate, he was content for the first time in centuries.

Maybe he wasn't doing exactly as his father would've wanted, but he was doing what *he* wanted.

"Why would she do that?" What *would* he do if he had to leave the school?

Kate looked so despondent that he kissed her lightly. "Don't worry." He hadn't revealed his magic to anyone—he knew that for sure. Jenna obviously wanted to talk to him about something else. "Maybe she wants to discuss the games this afternoon."

He didn't really believe that and judging from Kate's dubious expression, she didn't either. Reaching Jenna's office door, Robin squeezed Kate's hand again. He would find out soon enough.

Jenna looked up from a stack of papers before her and waved him to a seat beside the desk. "Thanks for coming, Robin."

Lowering himself into the chair, Robin sat, but didn't relax. Calm. He needed to remain calm. Odd, few situations made him nervous. After all, he had his charm.

But could he use it on Jenna? Should he? After his experience with Kate, he was reluctant to use his magic on people he knew.

"Is this about the games this afternoon?" he blurted when she didn't speak right away.

"Oh, no. I'm sure you and Mark have that well in hand." Her face didn't give anything away. Robin waited.

"I have something else I need to discuss with you. It has to do with your position here at Mountainside Elementary."

Robin clenched his fist. Bloody hell, Kate was right. Jenna intended to kick him out.

Twelve

Robin swallowed and sat straight. *Let her be done with it then.* "Very well."

"You get along well with the children. Mark's mentioned it and I've noticed how you interact myself."

"I enjoy them." Robin watched Jenna closely, confused. This didn't sound like a prelude to dismissal.

"And they enjoy you." Jenna looked down at her desk, then back at him with a smile. "I've been able to get a full-time aide slot approved for next year and the first person we all thought of was you. Is this something you'd be interested in?"

For a moment, Robin didn't breathe. A full-time position? At the school? For him? Excitement sparked along his nerves. "Very interested," he said before he thought.

Reality followed in equal measure. How could he accept a position under his present circumstances? Forced to remain close to Kate, he'd been fortunate to escape notice this long. "But I . . . I'm not sure if I'll be here next year."

Jenna's expression clouded. "Oh, I thought you'd decided to stay in the Springs."

How could she know? He'd only just decided that himself

a few days ago. If only he could free himself of Titania's spell . . . "Could I think about it?"

"Of course. Why don't you let me know after spring break?"

Robin nodded and stood, aware of the anticipation coiled within him. "Thank you."

"Thank *you*." Jenna rose and offered her hand. "Mark's very pleased with you. And spoiled. I don't know if he'll be able to work without a classroom assistant now." Humor danced in her eyes.

"I'm sure he'll manage." Robin shook her hand, then exited the office, barely managing to keep from dancing. This was wonderful . . . more than wonderful. He'd worked several odd jobs through the years but interacting with children had provided complete satisfaction. He wanted to do this.

But how? It was impossible as long as he remained under Titania's spell.

Kate sat at her desk and instantly met his gaze, her expression questioning and worried. "What happened?"

Keeping his face blank, Robin went to her. "It was as you suspected. She wanted to discuss my position here."

"Oh, no." Kate stood, her eyes clouded.

"She wants me to take a full-time assistant position next year." Robin took a breath and waited.

He didn't wait long.

Kate punched his shoulder. "You beast. How dare you lead me on like that?" She came around the desk to hug him and he pulled her into his arms without resistance. Any excuse to touch her would do. "A full-time position is great."

"Not under my present circumstances." He nuzzled her hair, soft and scented with lavender.

"Oh." Realization dawned and Kate drew back. "Oh."

Robin kept his arms around her. "I asked for time to think it over."

"What are you going to do?" she whispered as if afraid to speak aloud.

"I don't know." There was only one way to break the spell

and that was to face Titania—something he now wanted to put off for much longer.

"I don't want you to leave."

He heard her pain, felt it deep inside himself. "I don't want to go."

"But—"

He laid his finger over her lips. "We'll talk about it later. I need to get ready for the games. Want to come?"

"I'll be there as soon as I can." She stepped out of his hold and turned back to her desk. "Don't go too far."

That wasn't likely.

He paused to tell Mark of his plans, then waited for Kate to join him before he headed for the gymnasium and equipment for the games. Balls, a net, flags, cones . . . he had everything he needed.

"You're going to run those kids ragged," Kate said, her arms full.

"But they'll love it." And they would. Robin felt an affinity with these children, as if he knew instinctively what they would like. "One of the races is a coordination challenge around the cones you're carrying."

Kate shook her head, but Robin sensed her smile. "Just so long as I don't have to run it, we're fine."

He faced her, lifting an eyebrow. "You're not running?" He exaggerated his incredulity.

Not bothering to answer, Kate nudged him with her elbow and they resumed walking. Once outside, they worked together to set up the different relays and games he'd arranged. Robin couldn't wait to see how the children responded to them. After all, he'd actually planned this—a first for someone who usually acted on impulse.

But he wasn't the same man he'd been two hundred years ago. Whether it was his long imprisonment or Kate's influence, he didn't know, but he saw things differently now. Before Titania thrust him into the portrait, he'd wanted only to return to his kind, to learn if he'd done as his father wanted. Mortals were useful, but he'd always been reluctant to know any one person well. After all, they grew old—he shuddered—and died. His mother had shown him that.

Odd, but in the time he'd been with Kate, he hadn't felt that constant nagging guilt that he was letting Oberon down, that he didn't measure up to the mission of disciplining or helping mortals that his father had given him so many years ago. Of course, Kate had kept his hormones—and his emotions—in constant chaos since he'd obtained his partial freedom.

He watched her now as she cordoned off a square for the shoe relay, her shapely rear facing him as she bent to place another marker. The well-worn jeans caressed her curves much as Robin longed to do. Desire shot to his groin and he bit back a groan. This wasn't the time for that, but later . . . He smiled.

Returning to their small apartment always filled him with anticipation and a healthy lust that even a week of making love to Kate hadn't dimmed. Strange, that. In the past, he never spent more than a couple of days with a woman. Never wanted anything more.

But with Kate, it was never enough.

Kate turned toward him, her face reflecting the same excitement as most of the school's children, and his chest grew tight. When she looked like that, he wanted to sweep her into his arms and kiss her until neither of them could breathe.

Not a bad thought. He stepped closer, then froze as the school doors burst open and children poured out, their loud voices frightening away the birds that perched nearby.

Turning to greet them, Robin grinned. Good. He needed a distraction.

"Mr. Goodfellow! Mr. Goodfellow!" Matt and Jack joined him first. "Are we doing the peanut relay?"

"That's one of them," Robin said. "How about you boys help me get everyone into two teams?"

They were eager to assist, but it still took several minutes for Robin to quiet the children long enough to explain the current relay race. Yet their overexcited energy fed his as well.

He wasn't as sure about that an hour later when he guided

some third graders through the somersault race. Though their antics kept him amused, he hadn't seen or spoken to Kate since their arrival. No doubt she was as busy as he.

A gong announced the arrival of juice and cookies. Children flocked to the table near the lunchroom door and Robin ran his fingers through his hair. What had he planned next? More important, where was Kate?

Glancing up, he located her near the fence surrounding the school playground. Her gaze was fixed across the busy street and he turned to see what caught her interest. A tree?

He started toward her and she came to meet him. "You're going to think I'm nuts," she said.

He lifted his eyebrow and gave her a mischievous smile. "And?"

Wrinkling her nose, she continued, "I could've sworn I saw that . . . that thing from San Francisco, from the beach. What was his name? Oh, yeah. Callum."

Ice shot through Robin's veins and he jerked around to scan the opposite sidewalk carefully. Callum would have no reason to be here, yet Robin couldn't shake the tension that tugged at his muscles. "I don't see him."

Kate shook her head. "Maybe I'm seeing things. I mean, he has to stay in water, doesn't he?"

"No." Robin spoke slowly. "He prefers water, lives in water, but he can go anywhere he likes."

"Oh." She searched the street, trepidation in her gaze.

"But it's not likely he followed us here." Robin wrapped his arm around her shoulders. "Why would he want to?" Unless he was watching Robin. Callum hated him almost as much as Titania did. In fact, Callum belonged to a small portion of the Fae who believed Robin had no right to claim the magical realm as his home simply because he'd been born of a mortal.

The odd prickle of awareness Robin experienced at the river returned to tighten the muscles in neck. The river. Had Callum been in the bushes? Had he pushed Kate into the water? A cold fist squeezed Robin's heart. It didn't make sense. Callum had no reason to harm Kate.

He didn't want to think about that now, couldn't think about it, not with children racing toward him. "Come on." Robin drew her further into the playground. "Next is the shoe relay. I need your help."

The event went well, as well as this activity could after ten children threw their shoes into a pile, then raced to find them and put them on, tying laces in such a hurry that sometimes they laced two shoes together. Kate laughed so hard she doubled over and almost fell, but he was no help, being helpless with laughter himself.

Their gazes met as they straightened and again a strange sensation punched his gut, pushing the air from his lungs. He could laugh with Kate, enjoyed teasing her. Had he ever done that with a woman before? Had he ever felt it necessary?

Turning to lead the children into the next game, he lost track of Kate until he heard her raised voice containing a note of panic that brought him around at once. She was running toward the outer sidewalk.

"Timmy!" she cried again.

There. A small boy ran ahead of her, already through the small opening in the fence, dashing toward the street. Traffic had slowed slightly to allow a break between vehicles, but cars approached from both directions.

Fear propelled Robin forward, his throat tight. What was going on?

"Timmy, stop!" Kate rushed after the boy, through the fence, toward the street.

Why was the boy running? What did he see? The way Timmy concentrated on the street he obviously saw something. But nothing was there.

Or was there?

Robin's stomach knotted and he focused on the opening in the traffic, the area where Timmy was headed. Nothing, but . . . A glimmer rose above the pavement that triggered Robin's inner alarms. Glamour. Someone was using magic on the boy.

"There's a puppy," Timmy cried.

Robin barely heard him as the lad rushed into the street, Kate on his heels. And a large automobile only a short distance away.

Kate scooped up the boy and turned toward the sidewalk, tossing Timmy at Robin. "Catch him!" she ordered.

Robin did, swooping low to capture the lad in a firm hold. As he straightened, the squeal of brakes drove terror through his heart. Kate flew across the pavement to land unmoving at the edge of the road, blood pouring from her head.

"No!" Anguish filled Robin's cry. He handed Timmy to one of the teachers who'd joined him on the sidewalk and rushed to Kate's side. *Let her be alive. She* has *to be alive.*

Locating a thready pulse did nothing to ease his panic. "Kate." He could barely speak. Blood flowed freely from a gash on her forehead and he placed his hand over it, focusing all his healing energies on her.

By the time Jenna reached his side, he'd stopped the bleeding, but what if Kate had more serious injuries? If he was fully Fae, he could heal her completely in minutes, no matter what the injury. As it was, his magic was limited to slight injuries, such as her sprained ankle, or broken bones. If she'd damaged her internal vitals . . .

"An ambulance will be here soon." Jenna knelt by him. "She'll be all right."

She tried to sound confident, but her voice wavered. Robin met her gaze. "She has to be." To his surprise, his eyes grew damp.

Taking Kate's hand, he struggled to focus, to think of some way, any way he could help. He couldn't lose this woman.

Sirens pierced the air. He looked up and inhaled sharply. Callum stood at the edge of the road, his face twisted in a mocking grin. As their gazes locked, he gave Robin a jaunty salute and vanished into the crowd.

By the Stones. This had been no accident.

The ambulance arrived and Robin stepped back, his senses numb, to let the emergency personnel assist Kate. His mind reviewed the sequence of events with an odd sense of unreality.

Timmy had seen an invisible puppy in the road and raced to save it. Kate had raced to save him. Only Kate hadn't been saved.

A horror like none Robin ever experienced before enveloped him. Callum wanted Kate dead.

Robin clenched his fists, his pulse racing.

But why?

Robin forced the emergency attendants to let him ride with Kate. He wasn't about to let her out of his sight and rely on the pull of the spell to reunite them. While the attendants fussed over her, he held her hand, willing her to respond, to open her eyes and smile at him.

She remained still. Too still.

Their arrival at the emergency room didn't match what he'd seen in the picture box . . . TV at all. The place was quiet with people sitting in chairs, their expressions bored. Where were the doctors, the people rushing in and out, the excitement?

At this point he didn't care, his concern was focused on Kate. If the quiet meant she'd get better attention faster, he welcomed it.

A nurse greeted the emergency personnel and directed them down the hall. "Put her in room three. I'll page Dr. Castle."

Robin started to follow the gurney to a smaller room, but she stopped him. "You'll have to wait here."

"But—" He *had* to stay with Kate. He didn't have medical knowledge, but he had magic.

"I'm sorry, sir." She gave him a sympathetic smile. "We'll be sure to let you know what's happening."

He stood frozen, watching until he could no longer see Kate. If they went too far, he'd soon be there. In fact, he hoped the tingling would start that signaled Kate's pull.

No such luck.

When nothing happened, he resorted to pacing the waiting

area. How badly was Kate injured? Could the doctor help her? Robin had managed to lessen her head wound, but was it enough? His magic could heal some injuries but if Kate suffered much internal damage, he was useless. Blast his mortal blood.

Weariness swept over him and he sank onto a beige plastic seat, reliving every long moment of Kate's dash after Timmy. Why would Callum want to harm Kate?

To hurt Robin? Had Callum realized how much Robin cared about her during their brief meeting on the beach?

No, it had to be more than that. For Callum to leave his watery world, he needed more than his dislike of Robin.

Robin dropped his head onto his hands. Yet Kate had started having accidents soon after their trip to San Francisco. It was unlike Callum to act so quickly and so viciously. Now if it was Titania . . .

By the Stones, it *was* Titania.

Panic shot along Robin's nerves. Callum must've notified the Fae queen of Robin's freedom soon after their meeting. No doubt, she was the one trying to harm Kate.

But why Kate? Why not come after Robin?

He jumped to his feet, unable to sit still as realization dawned. If Kate died—his gut clenched at the thought—he suspected he'd be thrust back into the portrait. After all, the spell had transferred to her when she released him. Without Kate's life force to maintain the spell, it would undoubtedly revert to its original focus—the portrait.

That had to be it. Titania wanted Robin back in his eternal prison.

And once back in the portrait, Robin would have little hope of obtaining freedom again. Few mortals had the sight anymore.

Thus, Callum had come to Colorado to do Titania's bidding.

"No." Robin smashed his fist against a wall only to draw everyone's gazes toward him in surprise. With a grimace, he resumed pacing.

What was he to do?

"Sir? Sir?"

He needed a second call to realize the nurse spoke to him. "Yes?"

"I thought you'd like to know—the young woman you brought in is going to be fine. She has some broken ribs and a concussion. We're going to keep her overnight for observation, but she should be able to go home in the morning."

Relief melted the icy fear in Robin's veins. "Can I see her?"

"Soon. They're taking her to a room." She turned toward a counter. "You need to fill out some papers with the clerk."

Robin took a step then felt the familiar tingling. "Later," he said before he found himself beside the gurney carrying Kate down a hallway.

The young man pushing it pulled back in surprise. "Where did you come from?"

"I was waiting for you." Robin didn't waste time thinking of a clever excuse. Going to Kate's side, he stared down at her. She was still unconscious, still pale. "Are you sure she's all right?"

"Yeah." The man resumed his path along the hallway. "Doc just wants to watch her for a while."

Reaching a room, he pushed the gurney inside and lowered the side. Before the man could move Kate, Robin lifted her gently and laid her in the small bed.

"Hey, I'm supposed to do that!" the young man exclaimed.

Robin shot him a warning glance. "I can do it." Tucking Kate beneath the sheet, he found her hand and clasped it tightly.

"Yeah, right." The man's voice was dry. "Good thing you didn't drop her. She's not a lightweight, you know."

"I would never drop her." Robin gazed at her, hearing the gurney leave, but not turning to verify it. Her lashes looked long against her white cheeks, her lips drained of color. Where was his laughing, smiling Kate?

"Kate, sweet Kate." He brushed his hand against her cheek. "Come back to me."

To his surprise, she stirred, her eyelids fluttering several times before she opened them. "Robin?"

"I'm here." He squeezed her hand even more firmly.

"My head hurts." She tried to lift her arm, then dropped it again. "My side hurts."

"You'll be all right." Now that Robin knew where to concentrate his magic, he could speed her healing process. Fortunately, the injuries were limited enough. But he wouldn't completely heal her until she was home. The doctors would never understand if she were miraculously better. For now, he'd dim the pain, see to her comfort. "Sleep now."

He brushed her hair back from the white bandage on her forehead, then rested his hand over it as he concentrated on relieving the worst of the ache. When Kate sighed and closed her eyes again, he ran his hand along the curve of her cheek. "Better now?"

"Hmmm." She snuggled deeper beneath the sheet, slipping back into slumber.

Robin watched her for several minutes longer, then replaced her hand on the bed and went to stand before the window. It offered the worst of views, overlooking the gray parking lot beside the hospital. But he wasn't interested in the view right now.

He had to do something to ensure this never happened again.

Now, when he wanted to remain longer among the mortals, his choice had been made for him.

He had to face Titania.

Before she succeeded in killing Kate.

Thirteen

"I'm fine. Really." Kate gave Robin a reassuring smile as he tucked the comforter around her the next morning. "Just a little sore." More than a little sore actually, but she was alive and that was better than she thought she'd be when she hit the pavement. And she was home in her own bed, which helped a lot, especially with Robin to take care of her.

Better yet, Timmy hadn't been harmed. Though why he had run into the street like that still puzzled her.

"Can I get you anything? Juice?" Robin hovered over her like a faithful nursemaid and Kate reached out to take his hand. He looked haggard, as if he hadn't slept all night. Of course, he had stayed in the hospital chair beside her bed, which couldn't have been comfortable.

"You brought me home. That's enough."

"Actually Shannon drove," he said.

Which Kate appreciated, but Robin was the one who'd kept his arm around her for the entire ride, cushioning the bumps and corners, assisting her up the steps into the apartment.

Kate smiled. "I'm thankful to both of you." She shifted

against the pillows and winced at the stabbing pain in her side.

"I can help with that." Robin sank to the edge of the bed.

"It's not time for another pain pill." She grimaced. "Part of it is these bandages. They're so tight I can hardly breathe."

"No, not a pain pill." Robin touched her face and she met his gaze. "No more bandages either."

Disbelief hit her first. He could heal? She stared at him. Well, why not? He was magical after all.

She pressed a kiss into his palm, then held out her arms like a scarecrow and grinned. "Okay, make me well." The constant pain, not only in her ribs and head, but her entire body was no fun. If Robin could make it go away, she wasn't about to refuse.

"You believe I can do it?" He sounded surprised.

"You've forced me to become a believer." Though she injected lightness into her reply, she couldn't deny the truth of the statement. After knowing Robin, how could she deny that magic existed?

Robin leaned forward and kissed her gently, his lips tender, making Kate long for more despite her constant aches. But he pulled back and placed his hands over the bandages around her ribs. "Believe in yourself, Kate. Believe that you can be healed."

Warmth blossomed beneath his touch—a different warmth than he usually ignited. Kate closed her eyes and tried to imagine her ribs knitting the breaks together. The heat increased, growing to the point of discomfort. Her heart caught in her throat. Was it supposed to feel this way?

She opened her eyes as a sharp bolt of lightning seared through her. Gasping, she sat upright and grabbed Robin's shoulders. "What was that?"

"That's the worst of it." He removed his hands. "Your ribs are better now."

Broken ribs? All healed? Just like that?

Though dubious, Kate tried bending slightly, wincing in anticipation of the brutal pain. Instead, she only felt the tightness of the bandage around her. No agony. None. He'd actually done it.

She looked at Robin and he grinned. "Okay?"

"I think so." Swinging around, she sat on the edge of the bed only to catch sight of the bandage at her temple. "What about my head?"

"I took care of that at the hospital. You can remove the bandage."

No wonder her head hadn't hurt when she'd awakened. Peeling back the white tape, Kate stared at her reflection. Would there be a scar?

No scar. No stitches. Not even a bruise surrounded the area where she'd gashed her head.

"Boy, you're good."

"That's what they all say." Laughter danced in Robin's voice and Kate swung around to punch his arm. Then she flung her arms around his neck and kissed him.

To her shock, he resisted at first, but as she moved her lips over his, he responded, dropping to the bed and pulling her onto his lap, his mouth caressing. Desire flared at once. She'd never thought of herself as passionate but Robin had only to touch her and she wanted him with a force that stunned her.

He brought his hand up to cup her breast, then froze when he encountered her bandage. Dropping his hand, he drew back.

His withdrawal left her cold. She was fine. Why was he stopping? "Robin?"

"I can't do this." His words were choked.

"It's okay. I don't hurt anywhere, thanks to you." She ran her hand over his chest. "Well, maybe I still have one ache left. I want you."

He closed his eyes briefly. "Kate." He placed her on the bed, then stood and paced across the room. "I can't make love to you anymore."

A pain worse than any from her injuries sliced through Kate and she wrapped her arms around herself. He didn't want her. "I see."

"No, you don't see." He came to stand before her. "It's not you, Kate. It's me."

She remained silent. Wasn't that what they all said?

"Kate." He dropped into a crouch so he could see her face. His expression held anguish. "We have to talk."

"So talk." She blinked to keep back the threatening tears. She would *not* cry despite her breaking heart. Somehow she had to keep him from knowing the depth of her feelings. After all, it wasn't as if he hadn't warned her long ago.

She'd always known he would leave her. She just hadn't expected it to be so soon.

"I have to face Titania. Now."

"Why?" He'd agreed to wait a little longer before returning. Why now?

His expression reflected a mixture of sorrow and concern. "Timmy ran into the street because he saw a puppy there."

She shook her head. "There was no puppy."

"I know that. You know that. But Timmy doesn't have the faerie sight."

Frowning, Kate tried to make sense of his words. "You mean, someone made him see a puppy?"

"Callum." Robin's contempt was evident in his tone.

"Then I did see him. But why? Why would he want to hurt Timmy?"

"He didn't want to hurt Timmy." Robin drew in a deep breath. "He wanted to hurt you."

The air left her lungs in a whoosh. For a moment, all Kate could do was stare. "Me?" she squeaked. She'd only met Callum once. Had she done something to offend him?

"Because by doing so, he'd hurt me." Robin caught her hands in his. "If you die, sweet Kate, I'll more than likely be thrust back into the portrait."

"No." Kate wasn't sure if she was denying the threat or the thought of Robin imprisoned again. Her heart hammered in her chest. "He hates you so much that he'd kill me?"

"*Titania* hates me that much." Robin sighed. "Obviously Callum told her he'd seen me and she wants me gone again."

Kate shook her head. "I can't believe this."

"Think, Kate. Ever since we returned . . ."

The ice on the steps. Her fall at work. The river. Kate jerked upright. "Dear God, those weren't accidents."

"I have to face her, Kate. Now, before she tries again."

Icy dread coated her skin. He was right. "You mean *we* have to face her."

Robin hesitated. "I wish you didn't have to be involved."

"But I am." Swallowing the lump in her throat, Kate squeezed his hands. She wasn't about to let him face Titania alone even if she could. "If you go, I go."

Though he nodded, he didn't look pleased. "I don't want you hurt."

"And that's why you won't make love to me?"

He dropped her hands and stood. "I never meant for this to happen, Kate. I never wanted to hurt you. But I have to go. To . . . to continue would only make the parting worse."

His words held a certain logic. If she *could* hurt worse than she did now. But Robin obviously hurt, too. If not making love would help him, she had to give in. "I understand." Rising to her feet, she vowed he wouldn't see her misery. "Then we need to find Nic right away."

"I'll call his gallery." Robin left her bedroom, and Kate quickly changed from her gown and constraining bandage into a comfortable T-shirt and jeans.

Being around Robin without touching him would be agony, but she'd managed to do it once. She could do so again. She had to for his sake.

But nothing said she had to like it.

She found him leaning against the kitchen counter, the receiver held against his ear, his free hand combing through his hair. "Can I leave a message for him?" He sounded frustrated.

"Look, tell him Robin Goodfellow called," he continued. "I'm a friend." The reply made him stand straight, a frown creasing his brow. "He needs to call me right away. It's urgent." He paused. "Then give me his home number. You—"

He pulled the receiver from his ear and glared at it. "He hung up on me."

"I take it he wasn't very helpful." Kate pulled two Cokes from the refrigerator and handed Robin one. "Doesn't your charm work over the phone?"

Slamming the receiver down, he accepted the can. "No, I need to face the person. He said Nic wasn't there, didn't know when he would be there and he couldn't say when Nic would get the message." Robin ripped open the tab and downed half the can in one swallow. "And he wasn't about to give out Nic's home number."

A lump formed in Kate's stomach. "Then I guess we have to go there."

"I guess we do." Robin gave her a wry smile. "I'm sorry. I'll get a better deal on the plane tickets this time."

"No." Kate wanted a little more control. Who knew where they had to go from there? "We'll drive. We should be able to get to Dallas in about a day or so."

"When do we leave?"

"In the morning. I need to get some things done first." Kate bit her lip, making a mental list. The bank, the gas station . . . "Will we be gone long?"

"I don't know." Robin's sober expression didn't give her the reassurance she wanted. Well, she had a week until she had to return to work.

With luck, they'd be done by then.

She shivered. Of course, that meant Robin would stay in the magical realm and Kate would have to go on without him.

Or if Titania succeeded in forcing Robin into the portrait again, Kate might not ever be back at all.

Kate cast a quick glance at Robin in the passenger seat of her car. They were just past the Texas border and he'd barely spoken all day—or looked at her for that matter. He had this distancing himself from her stuff down pat. Unfortunately, it wasn't so easy for her.

So much for the passionate nights spent in his arms, the laughter he'd brought into her life, or the lovemaking that was better than Godiva chocolate. She sighed and he turned, meeting her gaze.

Or maybe not.

If she'd been a candle, the heat of his gaze would've melted her into a waxy puddle. As it was, her insides clenched in response. Maybe he wasn't as detached as she thought.

Her heart skipped a beat. Good. She knew—had always known—that she'd have to lose him someday, but she didn't want it to happen while he was still right beside her.

"Do you need to stop and stretch?" she asked.

He shook his head. "I prefer to get there as soon as possible."

Kate disagreed. The sooner Robin found his friend Nic, the sooner they'd be off to the magical realm . . . and the sooner she'd have to say good-bye forever.

With a grimace, she turned her attention back to the road. At least the traffic hadn't been too bad. They'd covered the miles in good time. If they maintained this speed, they should reach Dallas before too late.

A loud retort echoed in the car and Kate flinched, expecting to be hit with a bullet. Instead, the car jerked sharply to the right as she heard the sound of a tire flopping against the pavement. Great.

She eased the car into the breakdown lane and stepped out to survey the damage. Her right rear tire was completely flat. Just what she needed.

Robin joined her, searching the surrounding area, his gaze concerned. "Did Titania—?"

Shaking her head, Kate gave him a wry smile. Her car and tires were far from new. "Sometimes, Robin, a flat is just a flat." She opened her trunk and pushed their bags aside to get at her jack and tire wrench. Stepping back, she faced him. "How would you like to learn to change a tire?"

The bolts were fastened so tight, it took her and Robin working together to twist them loose. By the time they finished both of them were covered with black grime.

Robin tossed the flat into the trunk and slammed it shut with more force than necessary. "What now?" he asked, his tone indicating he expected the worst.

Kate paused. Her spare was nothing more than one of the temporary donut things. "I should stop in the next town and get a new tire."

"Then stop." He stalked to the front seat. "I'll make sure you get a good price."

He was sure being nasty. Kate slid behind the wheel and gave him an angry glare. What was his problem? Horny and no place to go? Jeez, it wasn't her fault they weren't having sex. If being around her was so difficult, he could always walk to Dallas.

Night had fallen by the time Kate found a tire store and arranged to have her spare replaced. Waiting outside the store, she glanced up at the stars, aware of Robin behind her, leaning against the building.

"We probably should stop for the night," she said.

"I can drive."

"No, thanks." She turned to give him a teasing smile, but he didn't smile in return. Instead, he pushed away from the building and stalked across the parking lot.

This was getting old. Kate watched him, frowning. *She* was the one Titania was trying to kill. He had no right to be so angry.

Thinking of Titania sent a shiver over her skin and Kate scanned the nearby area, but saw nothing out of the ordinary. Thank goodness she hadn't seen Callum once since the incident at the school. If she never saw him again, she'd be happy.

And if Robin would act more like himself and less like a jerk.

They ate a quick meal at a fast food place across the street, then picked up the car with its new tire and headed for a motel near the freeway. The motel wasn't fancy, but it was affordable so long as they only took one room.

Kate hesitated, then agreed. She had nothing against sharing the room with Robin. In fact, she'd prefer to share much more. He should be thankful she insisted on twin beds.

"One room?"

He didn't sound thankful. The glare he sent her upon opening the door only made Kate stand straighter. She stormed
into the room and tossed her bag on one of the beds. "Get
over it, Robin. We've shared a room before. I think we can
handle this."

Without waiting for an answer, she pulled out her toiletries
and entered the bathroom. If she stayed angry, then maybe
she wouldn't cry.

Damn him.

When she emerged, he was standing in front of the window, his back to the room. "It's all yours," she said, pulling
back the blankets. After driving all day, she was tired, but
she doubted she'd sleep. Not with Robin in the same room.

"Thank you." The monotone of his reply only irritated her
further and she tossed the pillow at him.

"What is your problem, Robin? I've agreed to find Titania.
I've agreed to keep my distance. What more do you want?"

"What do I want?" He whirled to face her and she caught
her breath at the anguish in his expression. "I want *you*, Kate.
I want to kiss you, hold you, make love to you."

Her pulse leapt and she stepped toward him. That was
what she wanted, too. "I have no problem with that."

"I do." He didn't sound happy about it. "I don't want to
hurt you any more than I have already. I never should have
touched you in the first place."

"I'm glad you did." Kate moved one step closer, her heart
in her throat, her nipples tightening against her nightgown.
No matter what happened, she'd never regret loving Robin.
Eventually, she would have to give him up, but she wanted
every moment until then. Why couldn't he understand that?

He dropped his gaze to her breasts, then curled his hands
into fists. "Kate, just let me be your friend."

"You are." She stopped in front of him. "You always will
be."

"Kate." Her name emerged as a groan and he extended his

hand toward her face, then dropped it again. "I can't. If I touch you, kiss you, I won't stop."

"I wouldn't ask you to." If their separation made him so angry, why continue with it?

He didn't reply, but she sensed the tension in his body as his gaze searched her face and paused at her mouth. Heat oozed through her body and she moistened her lips, wringing a moan from Robin.

"Kiss me," she murmured. She needed his mouth on hers, his arms around her.

Desire flooded the room, so potent the air almost crackled. Robin continued to stare at her, his eyes dark. All he had to do was bend his head just a little.

"No." He crossed half the room before she could blink. "Go to bed, Kate." He entered the bathroom and shut the door behind him, the latch click permeating the thick silence with a sense of finality.

Kate remained frozen for several long moments. Why was he being so noble? Did he honestly think he was saving her more pain?

With an ache in her chest, she padded to her bed and sank onto it. Maybe he thought he could keep her from falling in love with him. She looked toward the bathroom door. "Too late, Robin. Too late."

Kate only made two wrong turns in Dallas before she located Nic Stone's gallery, and even then she had to park some distance away. Robin stood beside her as she studied the outside. Aside from a wooden sign that declared the gallery's name, the building didn't look any different from the others lining the street. Somehow she'd expected a more elaborate studio.

"Shall we go in?" she asked.

Robin nodded and led the way inside. He'd remained withdrawn all day and Kate let him sulk. What with her own sense of loss and frustration, she wasn't in the best of moods herself.

"Is Nic Stone here?" Robin paused by a man near the

inside entry. Shorter than Robin, the man was also older and balding, though he attempted to hide it with a few thin strands strategically draped across the patch on top. He was dressed impeccably in a tailored suit complete with a handkerchief in the pocket. Kate wasn't surprised to discover his shoes shone brilliantly. No doubt he polished them daily.

The man's face reflected his displeasure as he glanced at Robin's faded jeans and polo shirt. Obviously, a snob of the first order. "Mr. Stone is not available."

"Is he going to be here?"

"I couldn't say." The man's tone indicated he couldn't care less either.

"I called earlier and left a message. I'm Nic's friend, Robin Goodfellow. Did he get my message?" Robin stepped closer, his frustration clear.

"I really don't know."

"Look, I—"

Kate caught Robin's arm and tugged him back before he hit the man. She never thought Robin one for violence, but at this point, she'd rather not take any chances. "We'll look around for awhile. If Nic comes, please let us know."

Pulling Robin after her, she proceeded into the building. "Why didn't you just charm him?" she asked.

Robin ran his hand over his face. "I should have. I'm not thinking clearly." He looked at Kate as if his confusion was her fault. If he suffered from wanting her as much as she wanted him, then maybe it was partially her fault. But he'd brought it on himself. *She* wasn't the one backing off.

"Let's look around while we're here. You can always charm him later." She turned toward the displays. Paintings lined the walls, some beautiful, some dreadful. "Nic certainly has some strange tastes," she said.

"He's supporting new artists, remember?" Robin stood beside her to study a conglomerate of swirled black and purple. "Is that supposed to represent something?"

Kate studied the name plate. "It's called *Agony*."

"I can see that. It agonizes me." Robin continued down the hallway. "Ah, here's Nic's work."

Joining him, Kate smiled. Yes, she recognized the artist's style. All his paintings contained people, but none were like the portraits he'd done in his previous lifetime. These reflected a more modern approach, the settings contemporary.

She hesitated before one of a young couple walking beneath a grove of trees. The man held the woman's hand, but his expression caught Kate's attention. Her chest tightened. Once upon a time Robin had looked at her like that . . . with warmth, desire, fondness. Would he ever do so again?

"Kate?" His voice was low. He stood behind her, but she didn't dare look at him. She didn't want to see the impassive mask he wore.

"Nice painting." She choked out the sentiment and brushed past him.

"Kate." He sounded as if he wanted to say more but didn't follow her. Instead, he remained before the painting as Kate moved farther inside.

Better not to think of how things were. Soon—sooner than she dared to think—Robin would be gone. Forever. A sob rose in her throat but she swallowed it. No tears allowed. No feeling sorry for herself. She'd known what to expect from the beginning.

She paused before an odd-shaped mirror labeled *Self* and viewed her reflection. That she could do so without critical thoughts was a step in the right direction. Robin had given her a sense of self-worth. No one could take that away from her.

Not even Titania.

The afternoon dragged by until Kate knew each piece of art thoroughly and still Nic didn't appear. Where was the man? Didn't he work for a living?

"The gallery is closing." The man who'd greeted them appeared behind Kate. "You'll have to leave."

"Hasn't Nic arrived?" Kate asked.

"He has no set schedule." The man turned back toward the entrance.

Robin went to the man's side. "Could you call him and tell him I'm here?"

"I'm afraid that's impossible. Mr. Stone doesn't like to be disturbed."

"He's going to be disturbed when he finds out you didn't tell him I'm here." Robin's voice held the hint of a threat and the man faced him, lifting his eyebrows.

"As I said, you must leave now."

Robin didn't say anything, but the tautness of his posture hinted at his frustration. Moving beside him, Kate touched his arm. "Robin, your charm."

He exhaled slowly, then nodded. Facing the man again, he radiated a power Kate recognized. "I suggest you call Nic and tell him I'm here."

"I can't."

"Why not?" Robin demanded.

"I don't have his home number." The man sounded ashamed at admitting that fact. "I already left a message with his voice mail."

Kate rolled her eyes. Why couldn't he have said that in the beginning? Pompous ass. She motioned Robin toward the door, then aimed a quelling glance at the gallery's manager. "Thank you *so* much for your help." Not waiting to see his reaction, she hurried for the entry. Heck, the man had his nose so far in the air, he probably wouldn't even recognize sarcasm.

As soon as she and Robin stepped outside, the man locked the door after them with a resounding click.

Kate sighed and looked at Robin. "Friendly fellow."

"Not at all." He paced away from her, then turned to stare at the gallery.

The sun hovered on the horizon as the pedestrian traffic thinned out. Kate grimaced. This was not going as planned.

A loud bang made her jump. Before she could look down the street, Robin wrapped his arms around her.

"Are you all right?" The concern in his voice warmed her.

"Fine." She didn't move, didn't want to make him realize what he'd done. "I think it was just a car backfiring."

He released his hold, but she didn't step back. Reaching

out, she grasped his forearms to keep him near. "What do we do now?"

Easing from her hold, he started down the street, away from where their car was parked. Kate ran after him. "Wait, Robin. What are you doing?"

"The only thing left." He didn't slow his stride. "A spell."

Fourteen

A spell? A shiver ran along Kate's nerves. Why had Robin sounded so ominous?

He pointed to a small park on a corner ahead of them. "I need the power of nature to do it."

"What kind of spell?" He sure wasn't giving her much information.

"A summoning spell."

Okay, that probably meant he planned to summon some-one. Nic? "You're calling Nic?"

"In a manner of speaking."

They reached the park and Kate paused to catch her breath. "Why didn't you do this to start with?"

"Because it will also let Titania know where I am."

Kate frowned. "Doesn't she already know? She seems to find us easily enough."

"But it takes her time to do so." Robin stared into the sky. "By using my magic, she'll know instantly where I am."

"Oh." Kate's racing pulse didn't slow at the knowledge. The last thing she wanted was Callum after her again. "Then maybe you shouldn't."

"I have to." The seriousness of Robin's expression sent

her heart plummeting. He glanced around the park, then moved to a small clump of trees. Evidently, he could gain the power he needed from them.

Placing his hand on the trunk, he stood in silence for several long minutes. Kate shifted her weight from foot to foot, unease creeping along her backbone. What did this spell involve? Eye of newt? A virgin's blood?

She grimaced. Now *she* was the one acting stupid.

Robin stretched his other hand toward the sky. "*Winds that roam the world wide, bring Nic the Fae to my side.*"

A fierce blast of wind followed his words, almost toppling Kate off her feet. She grabbed a nearby light pole and stared at Robin in amazement. His other magical abilities didn't produce this result. Or the trepidation that grew within her.

He stayed in place until the wind died, then dropped his hand and came to face Kate. "Will that bring Nic?" she asked. Could a handful of words really be magical? All his other powers came from his touch, except perhaps his charm. But that was a part of him.

"Yes." He bit off the word. "It will also bring Callum."

Kate swallowed the lump that rose into her throat. "Who will get here first?"

"I don't know." Robin suddenly smiled, revealing a hint of the man she knew so well. "Don't worry. Now that I know what to expect, I can handle Callum."

"I'd rather you didn't have to."

"Me, too." He ran his hand along her cheek. "I won't let him harm you, Kate. I swear it."

She didn't answer. She couldn't. The lump returned to her throat and threatening tears made it even more difficult to speak. Meeting his dark gaze, she gave him a half-hearted smile. She believed him. More than that, she believed *in* him.

"Kate." His voice held a husky note. Kate imagined sparks in the air. She could feel them dance over her skin as their gazes held, the city around them fading into the background.

She could hear her heart beating. Or was it his? Or did they beat together, sharing their life force, their souls? Words rose to Kate's lips. "Robin, I—"

Before she could finish, he dropped his hand and turned away. The moment dissipated in the falling dusk.

She released a shaky breath. Better not to tell him of her love. It wouldn't change anything. He still had to leave. He was still immortal. To speak would only make things more difficult for both of them.

With a sigh, she moved to a bench and sank down upon it. If only . . . No, she was done with if only's. She'd survive this somehow. She'd go on without Robin, without her house, without a family. Because now she knew she could. If nothing else, her time with Robin showed her she was stronger than she ever thought she could be.

Robin fought with himself over his behavior. In trying to save Kate further pain, he was tearing himself apart. As much as he tried to ignore her presence or pretend the passion didn't linger between them, he only wanted her more.

He paused a few steps behind the bench and watched her. She was wonderful and braver than he'd credited her. How many women would have endured all she had and yet continued? None that he'd known. Other women had taken his lovemaking, enjoyed it, then moved on. Not one had given him the trust and caring Kate did.

His presence put her life in jeopardy, but instead of railing at him, she looked at him with such desire that his blood boiled. He'd been nothing but selfish where she was concerned, especially making love to her when he'd vowed he wouldn't.

But he wouldn't regret that . . . at least, not for himself. That memory would sustain him for years to come. Yet, his actions also hurt Kate, which was the one thing he didn't want to do. Some friend he was.

He extended his hand to touch her hair, then drew it back, drawing his fingers into a fist. He'd done her enough harm. If he cared for her at all, he needed to stay away.

Grimacing, he paced to the other side of the park. How long until Nic arrived? And how far away was Callum? Robin had no doubt the water sprite was doing Titania's bidding.

A car roared down the street and Robin whirled to face it, every sense alert. By the time it stopped and a man stepped out, Robin's tension eased. He knew that shape.

"Nic." He crossed the park to greet his friend.

"I'll be damned, it *is* you." Nic gripped Robin's forearm in a familiar clasp. "I thought the call had your signature, but it's been centuries. Where have you been?"

"It's a long story." Nic looked much the same as when Robin saw him last over two hundred years ago. Obviously, he was presenting his normal face at this point in time—an apparent age in his early 30s, lean and more muscular than Robin recalled, a bold nose and chin, and long brown hair cut in a modern style.

"Now that doesn't surprise me." Nic grinned. "And I suppose it involves beautiful women as well."

Robin found himself smiling in reply. "As a matter of fact..." He led Nic toward the bench where Kate stood watching. "Nic, Kate Carmichael. Kate, my friend, Nic."

"I should've known." Nic shook Kate's hand, holding it a moment longer than Robin thought necessary. "Robin has extraordinary taste."

"She's my friend." Robin stepped to Kate's side, glancing pointedly at Nic's hand.

"Friend is it?" Mischief appeared in Nic's gaze before he released Kate's palm.

Kate nodded and smiled. "I'm glad to meet you, Nic. I sure hope you can help us."

"Us?" Nic looked from Kate to Robin, raising his eyebrows.

"Robin says you can tell us how to find the entrance to the magical realm. Can you?"

Nic stepped back. "The magical realm? I don't know what you're talking about."

"It's all right, Nic. She knows about me. She knows about you." Robin caught Kate's eye and shook his head. He hadn't intended to approach his friend so abruptly. "We need to talk." A blast of wind buffeted his hair and he eyed the encroaching darkness. "But not here."

Nic waved toward his car. "Come on out to the house. We can talk there."

"We have to get our car. Can we follow you?"

"Certainly." Kate preceded them and Nic caught Robin's arm as he passed.

"What's going on?" Nic asked. "You've never told a mortal about yourself before."

"Kate's different." Robin smiled wryly. That was an understatement. "And this situation is very different."

"I can't wait to hear about this." They walked together to Nic's car.

"I'll explain at your place." Robin couldn't shake the odd sensation that danger hovered close by. He searched the night again, but saw nothing unusual in the gathering shadows.

"I'll hold you to that."

Nic took them to Kate's car and they changed vehicles.

Kate didn't speak at all while following Nic to his home. That was unlike her.

When Robin glanced at her quizzically, she gave him an encouraging smile. "I like your friend. He thinks I'm strange, doesn't he?"

"No, he thinks you're beautiful." Which didn't please Robin as much as it should. He knew Kate was beautiful, inside as well as out, but wanted to keep her all for himself. He sighed. He would never distance himself with those thoughts.

But then he didn't really want to.

Upon reaching Nic's estate, Kate whistled softly. "I guess he's doing all right."

High walls surrounded the main building, linked by an ornate iron gate that opened to allow them to follow Nic inside. A long drive led to a sprawling stucco home, lights pouring from the windows.

Kate stopped the car in front and they stepped out and waited for Nic to join them.

"I see you're doing well," Robin said. Of course, Nic usually did make his way in the mortal world.

"I'm a recognized talent again." He grinned. "And I'm still alive this time."

"Aren't you always alive?" Kate asked.

"I have to die occasionally." Nic walked toward the front steps and they joined him. "And usually my work doesn't receive any real recognition until I've been gone a few years."

She paused, looking at the house. "I'd say alive is definitely the way to go."

"My sentiments exactly."

"You're back." An attractive young woman appeared in the entry, shorter than Kate, with a straight mane of blonde hair that fell the length of her back. "Where did you go so quickly?"

"Anna, this is my friend, Robin Goodfellow. And his friend, Kate Carmichael." Nic went to wrap his arm around the woman's shoulders. "Robin, my wife."

"Wife?" Robin bit back his surprise. Nic had only married once before in his many lifetimes and vowed never to do so again.

"You never know when you're going to fall in love." Nic gave his wife a look that said more than words and pushed open the door. Obviously Nic had succumbed to that human weakness again. Amazing.

"Welcome to my home." He hugged Anne's shoulders. "Dinner still warm?"

"Just have to nuke the potatoes."

Robin stepped to Kate's side before they followed Nic inside.

"He seems very content with his life," Kate murmured.

"I told you he was odd." But Robin had to agree. He found it hard to remember when Nic last appeared so entrenched in his mortal persona.

And for the first time Robin envied him.

Over dinner, the way Nic sat beside his wife, touching her gently or exchanging smiles that bordered on combustible only added to Robin's internal torment. Though Kate sat close enough to touch, he didn't dare. One touch, however casual, would only lead to more touches and those would be much less casual.

"Have you been married long?" Kate asked, her voice sounding strangled.

"Just over a year." Anna beamed at Nic.

"That's . . . ah . . . great." Kate dropped her gaze to her half-eaten meal and Robin resisted the urge to pull her onto his lap and kiss her with all the passion simmering inside.

"Care to discuss your problem now, Robin?" Nic asked.

Robin hesitated. How much did Anna know? Nic hadn't shared his identity with his previous wife.

"It's all right." Nic took Anna's hand. "I have no secrets from Anna. Unless you prefer . . . ?"

"No." But Robin found it hard to begin. Aside from Kate he'd never shared who he was with a mortal. "You might remember I was headed for the realm when we last met."

"I remember." Nic sat back in his chair. "You had that huge portrait Tommy painted with you."

The portrait. The horror of existing yet unable to move or speak chilled Robin's blood at the memory. "Titania cast me into the portrait for two hundred years." He spoke with more intensity than he intended.

Nic bolted upright. "By the Stones, Robin. Two hundred years?"

A warm hand took his and Robin turned to find Kate offering her bewitching smile as well. "It's over," she whispered. "I won't let her put you back in there."

As if she had a choice. Still, her fierceness dashed away the chill and her concern warmed his blood. "Oberon modified the spell so someone with the sight could see my name and by speaking it aloud overcome the spell. Kate freed me." His beautiful sweet Kate.

"You mean you'd still be there if she hadn't?" Anna asked, her eyes wide.

Robin nodded. "There's no love between Titania and myself. She can't kill me but this was close enough."

"I'd say." Nic pushed back his chair and stood as if unable to sit any longer. "Yet you want to go back to the realm?"

"I have to." Robin withdrew his hand from Kate's, regretting the loss of her touch at once.

"My study's this way." Nic indicated a hallway. "I need a drink. You can finish there." He waited for Robin to join him, then nodded at his wife. "Perhaps you'd like to show Kate the garden?"

Not waiting for an answer, he led Robin to a large room lined with light oak bookshelves and decorated with overstuffed chairs, a large desk and a bar. The room looked more human than any Nic had lived in before. Nic went straight to the bar and poured two glasses from a half-filled flask.

Robin accepted the tumbler from his friend. "You're adapting well to the ways of mortals."

"I prefer mortals." Nic downed the contents of his in one swallow, then turned to the bar for a refill. "After what Titania did to you, I think you would as well."

Robin's first impulse was to deny it, but he paused, reflecting on the past few weeks with Kate. He'd enjoyed his work with the children, cooking meals, sharing laughter and loving Kate, especially that. "It has its good points."

He tossed back the brandy, allowing the spirits to burn their way down. If only the liquor would obliterate his memories like it did for humans. No, not that. He'd never give up his memories of Kate. They would be all he had to sustain him once he faced Titania's wrath.

Nic dropped into a chair. "Tell me why you want to go back. It's insane."

"I'm tempted to agree." Robin paced the room. "But I have to face Titania again."

"And let her imprison you again?"

Robin grimaced. "Kate freed me from the portrait, but didn't break the spell entirely. I can't move more than fifty feet from her without being pulled to her side."

"She's a lovely woman. I don't see that as a bad thing." Nic's eyes gleamed with humor.

"It isn't." The image of Kate in his arms, returning his kisses caught at Robin, bringing an ache to his chest. "But

Titania knows I'm free. She's trying to kill Kate and return me to the portrait."

"By the Stones." Nic emptied his glass again, then set it on an end table. "And you wonder why I prefer mortals."

"I won't let her harm Kate." Robin thumped his fist against the hard wood desk. "I see no alternative."

"Hell of a choice." Nic studied Robin intently. "You care about her, don't you?"

"Kate? Of course." He didn't meet Nic's gaze. "She's my friend."

"You've never had a woman for a friend before."

"I know." Robin walked to the bar and poured another tumbler of brandy, suddenly needing the burning sensation again.

"And you've never cared about a woman before. Not like this."

If Robin hadn't known better, he could've sworn amusement danced in Nic's voice. He looked around to find Nic grinning. "Kate's different."

"So you said." Nic rose and clapped Robin on the back. "Welcome to the real world, Robin. About time you fell in love."

Robin jerked away, rounding on his friend. Love? Love was a mortal suffering, not for the Fae. "I'm not in love."

"Looks that way to me."

Biting back an urge to wipe the smug smirk off Nic's face, Robin frowned. "You're the one in love, not me. After Peggy's death, you swore never to marry again."

"That was five hundred years ago. I didn't think I'd ever feel that way about a woman again, but then I met Anna." Nic's expression grew soft. "I'd be lost without her."

"And when she dies?" His emotions were so tangled, the question emerged before Robin could recall it.

Nic froze, then looked at Robin, his gaze cold. "Then I'll grieve and wish I were mortal so that I could rest alongside her forever."

"You'd give up immortality for her?" Though Robin hated

losing friends, he'd never wanted to give up who . . . what he was. "You'd watch her age?"

"To watch Anna grow old, to hold her every night is a privilege." Nic tilted his head. "You sound afraid of it."

"I've seen women age. They become old crones." Robin shuddered, the past memories still haunting.

"Only if you never cared about them to start with." Nic returned to his seat. "And you've never cared, Robin, not until now. When you love someone, you see things differently."

"I care about Kate." Robin scowled at the sudden lurch in his gut. "That doesn't mean I love her."

"Doesn't it?" Nic's calm stirred the tempest inside Robin.

"I don't know what love is."

"Of course you do. You had a mother."

"She died so long ago, I barely remember her."

"Your fath—no, forget that."

Nic knew how Robin had longed for a true relationship with Oberon and how little he'd received. "You see, I can't love anyone," Robin said.

"Not so." Nic leaned back and swung his legs onto a footstool. "Trust me when I say you'll know if you fall in love."

"Then you admit I'm not in love with Kate." Sweat formed on Robin's brow. Why was this point so important?

Nic gave him an enigmatic smile. "Not yet anyway."

Kate gasped as Anna turned on the back lights revealing a massive garden blooming in a barrage of color. "It's beautiful," she exclaimed.

"It's my weakness." Anna led the way down the steps. "I love to putter in here while Nic paints."

"It shows." Kate was lucky to keep a philodendron alive, let alone the lilies and amaryllis lining the brick path. A mixture of scents hung in the air, giving the night a sensuous feel.

She caught herself before she stumbled into Anna, who'd stopped and was staring at a rear window. "Nic's study?" Kate asked.

Anna nodded and looked back at Kate. "Can I ask—is your friend one of the Fae? Like Nic?"

"He is." If Nic trusted Anna with his secret, surely Kate could as well.

"Is he going to take Nic away?"

"Away?" That explained the haunted look in Anna's eyes. "Of course not. We just need to know how to find the entrance to the magical realm. Robin's been out of touch so long, he doesn't know where it is."

"I see." Relief layered Anna's reply. "I thought . . ." She shook her head. "I don't know what I thought."

Kate laughed. "It's obvious Nic loves you. I doubt Robin could drag him away from here."

"Good. I love him too much to let him go." The determination flowing from the small woman made her appear taller.

Kate's smile faded. And she was just the opposite. She loved Robin enough to let him go. She resumed walking and Anna fell into step with her.

"Robin Goodfellow. Why does that name sound so familiar?" Anna asked.

"Perhaps Nic has mentioned him."

"He's talked about Robin, but never said his full name." Anna frowned even as she ran her hand carefully over a budding hollyhock. "It makes me think of medieval times for some reason. Is he an artist, too?" She stopped abruptly and turned to Kate, her eyes wide. "Good heavens, he's Puck."

Kate shrugged. Robin didn't care for that nomenclature. "Shakespeare called him that. He's Robin to me."

"He's not at all what I would've imagined."

"No one could imagine Robin." To come up with someone that handsome required more creativity than Kate possessed.

"Have you known him long?"

Most of my life. Kate tried to recall when she'd released Robin from the portrait. Two weeks ago? Three? Yet she'd known him for so much longer than that . . . had spoken to the portrait since her arrival at Nana's. "It feels like I have."

"And you're willing to go with him to the realm?" Anna shook her head. "I'd be afraid."

"I have no choice really." Kate quickly explained their circumstances, yet she'd still follow Robin if he'd asked her, whether the spell bound them or not.

"Amazing." Anna faced Kate, her smile warm. "You're welcome to stay here as long as you like. Our security system is top of the line."

"Thank you." Tears sprang to Kate's eyes and she blinked them back. To be able to talk freely with someone, to feel so warmly welcomed touched a loneliness she thought she'd shed. "I'm not sure if a security system can keep out Titania though."

"I still want you to stay, at least for a couple days." Anna met Kate's gaze. "It's so good to have someone to talk with, who understands."

Impulsively, Kate hugged the woman. "I know exactly what you mean." She'd often longed to discuss Robin with someone, but who would believe her?

They exchanged embarrassed smiles as they parted and resumed walking.

"Do you think being magical is what makes them special?" Anna asked.

"I don't know." Kate considered the question. Robin was so much more than that. "I think Robin would be special even if he wasn't magical."

"I see how it is." Anna laughed. "So, how long have you been in love with him?"

Startled, Kate looked around at Anna and walked straight into Robin.

Fifteen

Kate gasped and stepped back. Had he heard Anna's remark?

"You exceeded our limit," he said, a hint of a smile on his lips, yet he looked at Kate as if she'd grown two heads. The intensity of his gaze sent her pulse dancing. What did it mean? That he'd heard and approved? Or something else?

"I'm sorry." Kate swallowed. "I guess we'll head back then."

"Have you enjoyed your talk with Nic?" Anna asked as they fell into step.

"Very much." Humor glimmered in his eyes for the first time in days. "It's been too long."

"Take all the time you need."

"Anna's invited us to stay for a few days." Kate jumped in as the light faded in Robin's face. "They have a security system that should keep us safe for a while."

"We'll be taking a risk." Robin spoke with finality.

Kate shrugged and turned away, hiding her dismay. She wanted to know Nic and Anna better. "It's your decision."

Nic came to greet them before they reached the house. "Now that's a disappearing trick." He clapped Robin on the back as he grinned. "Took me a minute to figure out where you'd gone."

"Just keeps things interesting." Robin's levity returned. "Anna invited us to stay for a while."

"Of course you'll stay." Nic beamed at Anna even as he punched Robin on the shoulder. "It's been over two hundred years. I don't think we'll catch up in one night."

"Well, most of it was spent in a portrait."

"But knowing you, you still have stories to tell."

Kate's cheeks warmed. Robin probably did have tales to tell from his years in the portrait and some of those tales involved her. Darting a worried glance his way, she caught her breath when he winked at her. Somehow that didn't comfort her.

They entered the house and Robin paused by her side. "Don't worry," he murmured. "Your secrets are safe with me."

"Thank goodness." She risked a smile and her heart skipped a beat when he returned it.

"But I imagine you're both exhausted after driving all this way." Anna led the way down a long hallway. "Let me show you your room."

"Do you have two rooms?" Robin asked.

Kate's spirits dropped as quickly as they rose. So much for getting close to him again.

Anna looked around, her expression reflecting her surprise, but she nodded. "Of course."

The rooms were beside each other—a consideration of their distance restrictions—and Kate loved her bedroom. If she couldn't share with Robin, she wouldn't suffer here among the decorations of mauve and pink. Silk flowers sat in a basket near the bed, looking so real she was tempted to smell them.

"Will this be okay?" Anna paused by the doorway.

"This is fine." Kate added a nod for emphasis. "It's beautiful."

"I . . . I'm sorry about the confusion over rooms. I thought you and Robin . . . I mean . . ."

"Don't worry. Not too many days ago you would've been correct in your assumption." Kate sighed. "Robin thinks he's protecting me."

"Protecting you?"

Kate didn't blame Anna for not understanding. She barely understood it herself. "He doesn't want me to be hurt when he leaves me. For some reason, he assumes if we don't make love anymore, the pain will be less."

"That's stupid," Anna said emphatically.

Kate laughed. She had to agree. "It makes sense to him, I guess."

"Of course it does." Anna rolled her eyes. "He's a man." She smiled. "Well, get some rest if you can."

"Thanks, Anna. Good night."

"Night."

But sleep didn't come no matter how many sheep Kate counted. Restless yearning simmered in her veins. Damn Robin. Damn all noble men.

Kate rolled to her side and stared at the curtains covering the sliding glass door to the rear garden. A smaller window by her bed was open, allowing the sensual scent of gardenias to drift in and add to the ache low in her belly.

It wasn't fair for Robin to introduce her to such pleasures, then deny them. Unable to lie still any longer, she rolled out of bed and went to pull open the sliding door. The night was still warm, so different from the spring evenings in Colorado.

Stars dotted the heavens, beckoning her outside. The patio bricks felt cool to her bare feet but Kate welcomed the gentle breeze that brushed over her, caressing her hair, molding her nightgown to her body.

Closing her eyes, she imagined Robin touching her with the same tenderness, his hands hot against her skin. Her nipples hardened and she groaned with need. She had half a mind to go to his room and seduce him into making love to her.

Except that he'd hate her in the morning. Though she thought it ridiculous, he obviously felt honor-bound to protect her from him. She shook her head. Who was going to protect her from her?

She turned to return to her room, then froze as she spotted Robin standing by his patio door, barely visible except for the light provided by the full moon. He didn't speak, but she felt his gaze on her as potent as his touch.

Her breasts swelled. Her blood carried passion to the center of her desire as she returned his stare. Yet she didn't utter a word. Her mouth had turned to cotton, her throat to barren desert. Her heart hammered so hard in her chest she half-feared for her recently healed ribs.

She took one step toward him, but no more. After the previous evening, she wasn't about to beg again. If he wanted her, he'd have to make the first move. *Oh, please make that move.*

But he didn't.

Yet he didn't turn away either. Instead, his gaze devoured her, lingering on her curves—her hips, her breasts, her lips. He wanted her. She knew that with sudden certainty.

Was it enough?

Feeling lightheaded, she reminded herself to breathe, yet the air seemed strangely thin. If she fainted at his feet, would he touch her then? She smiled at the thought.

Robin remained unmoving, as still as a statue. Finally he raised his hand, then curled it into a fist and dropped it again. "Good night, sweet Kate." In two steps, he entered his room and closed the door.

Kate continued to stare at the place where he had been. Her senses still vibrated with desire. With an effort, she forced herself to cross the short distance to her room and step inside. Sliding the door shut added a finality to her longing.

Dropping to the bed, she stared at the ceiling. He might want her, but he didn't love her. Whether or not he'd heard Anna's statement didn't matter. Kate wanted to be with him regardless of the risks. Obviously he didn't feel the same way.

A single tear slid down her cheek. Why should she expect anything different?

Thank goodness, Nic and Anna broke through the tension surrounding Kate and Robin. The men often disappeared into Nic's study to discuss old times, which gave Kate a chance to chat with Anna.

Though Kate would've been hard pressed to explain it, she felt as if Anna had been a good friend for years rather than the hours they'd known each other. They worked together easily preparing a barbecue supper since Nic had insisted they cook shish kabobs on the grill.

The meat and vegetables had been marinating all day. Kate couldn't wait to taste them once they were grilled.

"Where will you go from here?" Anna asked as she sliced cooked potatoes into a bowl.

Kate looked up from cutting vegetables for a salad. "The magical realm, I suppose. We can't avoid it forever."

"Then what will happen?"

That made Kate pause. "I don't know. I wish I did. I'm afraid of what Titania will do to Robin. What if she puts him back in the portrait? Or something worse?"

"I don't know what something worse would be." Anna gave a delicate shudder. "To be alive yet not would be torture."

Kate nodded. She was feeling tortured herself today. Robin had barely spoken to her and not once met her gaze. Perhaps it would be better just to get this all over quickly. His method of helping her was going to kill her.

"All done with that?" Anna nodded toward the salad bowl.

"Yep. What's next?"

"Would you go tell Nic he can start up the grill?"

"Sure." Kate headed for the study, then paused in the dining room to gaze out the sliding doors. The day had dawned bright and beautiful, but now churning clouds filled the sky, their queer gray-green color like nothing she'd seen before.

The wind had picked up, the trees bowing beneath it. A powerful blast came through the screen door with enough strength to topple a vase of fresh-cut flowers onto the floor. Kate jumped at the crash and turned to gather the broken pieces of glass.

Anna came running in. "What happened?"

"The wind blew this off the table. Do you believe—?" Catching sight of the alarm on Anna's face, Kate looked outside again.

A huge, swirling black funnel hung from the sky, then dropped to the ground with a roar.

And it was headed straight for them.

"Oh, my God." She'd seen tornadoes in the movies or TV newscasts, but this was real. It moved fast—quicker than she thought possible—and the noise rose in decibels, drowning out the words Anna shouted at her.

When Anna pointed down the hallway, Kate nodded. They needed to get the men.

Anna hurried away, but as Kate stood upright, the screen door suddenly broke away, spinning into the yard while the wind reached into the room to toss the chairs like straws. First one, then the other crashed into Kate, tumbling her backward so that she smashed against the large wood buffet.

A wave of blackness washed over her and she pushed herself into a sitting position, blinking to clear her vision. Where had the tornado come from so quickly?

Titania.

The name leapt into Kate's mind. No, impossible. Even the Fae couldn't control the weather.

Yet the wind seemed to tug at her as she staggered to her feet. The flowers from the broken vase lifted off the floor and spun around her. Kate swallowed and tried again to follow Anna.

Before she could cross the room, the heavy wood dining table slid toward her. "No." It would smash her against the buffet. Kate searched for an escape route. Only one existed. Outside.

She had no choice. She dashed through the opening.

The table crashed against the buffet where she'd just stood. If she hadn't moved . . .

The roar filled the air, sounding alive. Kate looked for the funnel. My God, it was almost upon her. And huge. It blocked the horizon from view.

Where could she go?

Her hair whipped in front of her face as branches pelted her ceaselessly. Nic had to have a cellar, a basement. She needed to get inside.

Only the table blocked the entrance now. She'd have to crawl over it.

Before she could step forward, the window exploded, showering the yard with glass, and the table rolled toward Kate as if pushed. This couldn't be happening.

She dashed into the garden, rushing past bushes that pummeled her, dodging branches until her foot caught an uneven brick and she toppled to the ground amidst a bed of marigolds. Struggling to her feet, she grabbed a limb on a nearby tree.

The wind attacked with a ferocity that seemed directed at Kate. Was this how she would die?

Rain erupted from the sky, soaking Kate in a matter of moments. Anger rose over her panic. Dammit, she was not going to die out here. This was Texas. Nic had to have a storm shelter or at the very least a basement.

Releasing her grasp on the tree, Kate battled her way through the garden. Where was the house? She couldn't see through the waving bushes and trees. Where was Robin? If he hadn't been pulled to her side, then he couldn't be too far away.

She shouted his name, but the wind sucked it away into the chaos.

Her ears popped as the pressure changed and she heard glass shattering nearby. The house.

Turning in that direction, she stumbled forward, then gasped as something caught her arm. She whirled around, tugging her arm free, then eased a sigh when she spotted Nic.

He bent his head to her ear. "This way. I have a storm

shelter." He took her arm again and led her through the up-rooted yard to a distant corner.

"Is Robin there?" Kate asked.

Nic shook his head, as if indicating he couldn't hear her. Kate nodded and concentrated on remaining upright in the storm. Of course, Robin was there and Anna, too. They'd all been together when the storm hit.

Reaching a set of doors in the ground, Nic tugged one open and waved Kate past him. She half-staggered, half-fell down the steps leading into a dimly lit room.

Anna came to meet her. "Are you all right?" She had to shout until Nic closed the door after him, reducing the roar to a manageable level.

"I'm fine." Kate eyed the cavern. It wasn't very large, though it did contain some chairs and shelves lined with supplies. A generator in the corner provided the power for the single lamp. But something . . . someone was missing. "Where's Robin?"

Nic grimaced. "He went looking for you. I told him to stay here."

Robin was still out there? She ran toward the steps, but Nic caught her around the waist and swung her back.

"You're not going out there. The tornado is on us," he said.

"But I have to find Robin. I can't leave him in that. He doesn't know tornadoes . . ."

"He'll be okay, Kate." Nic didn't loosen his hold. "He's immortal."

She met his gaze despite the tears building in her own. "There are worse things than dying."

Obviously startled, Nic released her and Kate broke for the stairs again. Before she'd gone two steps, hands caught her waist again. "Let me go, Nic. I can't leave him out there."

"I'm here, Kate."

At Robin's voice, she turned to find him behind her, his hair tousled, face scratched and breathing strained. Relief turned her knees to gelatin and she threw her arms around his neck. He enveloped her in a hug equally as tight as her own. "Where were you?" she demanded.

"Where were *you*?" he countered. "I couldn't find you so I ran. I thought I'd be pulled to you, but it took forever." He ran his hand over her hair. "Thank the Stones you're all right."

"You, too." Her voice emerged in a whisper.

The doors above suddenly rattled as if trying to open. Kate's heart rose to her throat. Robin hurried them to the back wall. Anna ran into Nic's arms and he embraced her, nestling close to the wall.

The rattling dimmed and Nic kissed Anna with a growl. They melted against each other with obvious passion that brought a flush to Kate's cheeks. Looking away, she stepped out of Robin's hold before she did something crazy like kiss him senseless.

She'd only taken one stride when he caught her arm. "Kate . . ." Her name sounded strangled.

As she turned, he pulled her close again and claimed her lips in a fierce kiss that spoke of hunger and need. Fire flared to life in Kate's veins and she returned his kiss with equal fervor. God, she'd missed this . . . missed him.

When Robin lifted his head, she met his gaze. Did he regret it? Desire smoldered in his dark eyes and she reached up to touch his cheek, to guide him to her again.

He didn't resist. Instead, he kissed her again with more tenderness, using lips and tongue to communicate his passion. The world receded until the moment became only Robin and the touch of his mouth on hers, the heat within and that radiating from him.

One of the shelter doors suddenly flew open and Kate jumped as Anna cried out in alarm. Together Nic and Robin rushed for it, holding the rail along the wall with one hand while they struggled to close the door with the other.

Anger filled the wind, rushing inside to nudge Kate backwards. She clenched her fists. How did one fight what couldn't be seen?

The wind diminished as the men managed to close the

door and secure the latch once more. Nic hurried down to hold Anna again. Kate watched Robin approach, her pulse erratic. What would he do? Was his kiss nothing more than the heightened tension of the moment?

He hesitated, his gaze searching her face, then stepped forward to embrace her. Kate buried her face against his chest as tears threatened. "Robin." She couldn't say anything more. Did he realize how much she'd missed this?

"I know." He caressed her hair. "I know."

Nic cleared his throat and they looked around sheepishly, but Robin kept his arm around Kate's shoulders. Thank goodness. She needed his strength at this moment.

"Nice weather you're having," Robin said with a twist of his lips.

"Only the best for you." Nic shook his head. "I don't know where this came from. The conditions weren't even right for it."

Kate glanced at Robin. "Titania couldn't do this." Suddenly she wasn't so sure anymore. "Could she?"

"Not alone, she couldn't." Robin's expression was grim. "But I doubt if she had trouble getting assistance."

Nic looked equally grave. "If Titania did cause this, then you're in more trouble than I thought, my friend."

A frisson of apprehension crept along Kate's spine. "Is there any way you can avoid facing her, Robin?"

"No." His response was so adamant that Kate blinked in surprise. He ran his finger along her nose. "She won't rest until she kills you or has me. I prefer she has me."

Considering the alternative was death, Kate wanted to agree, but couldn't. "I don't want her to hurt you."

"Don't worry." He gave her a reassuring grin. "I can handle Titania."

And that's how you ended up in a portrait. Kate grimaced, but didn't pursue the subject. She had no clue how to outwit the faerie queen.

The doors rattled again and everyone swung their glances up the steps. The wind howled in a loud protest, then everything went quiet, leaving a silence as noticeable as the previous roar.

Nic and Robin exchanged looks, then Nic headed up the stairs. Gripping the hand rail, he eased open one of the doors and inched his head up to look outside.

"I'll be damned." He dropped the door open and motioned for the others to join him.

Sunshine blinded Kate as she reached the opening and she narrowed her gaze. Stepping outside, she viewed the sky in amazement. Blue sky, white fluffy clouds, birds soaring in the distance. No sign that a tornado had even existed.

Except for the disaster in Nic's yard. Trees lay uprooted, bushes and flowers were destroyed. Every window in the house was broken.

"I don't believe it." Kate's voice trembled and she bit her lip. The others didn't need to know how unnerved this episode left her. Titania had created a tornado to kill Kate.

Kate swallowed hard. Talk about search and destroy.

Robin squeezed her shoulder, his smile offering encouragement. Kate drew on his strength, fighting the urge to run and hide. As long as Robin stood by her side, she could handle anything.

"If the car isn't damaged, I think we need to keep moving," he said.

"I agree." Nic led the way over the shattered remains of his once beautiful yard to the house. "Our security system isn't much use against natural disasters."

Once inside, he surveyed the damage to his home. Seeing a torn painting on the floor, Anna rushed to it with a soft cry. She picked it up and turned to Nic, her eyes watering. "It's ruined."

He crossed to her and took the painting from her hands. "I'll paint you another one."

Anna nodded, though her smile was watery. "Nic gave that to me soon after we started dating," she explained to Kate. "It's of a park where we liked to walk."

"And not irreplaceable," Nic added. He kissed her. "Unlike you."

Robin kept moving toward the front entrance and Kate followed, her stomach twisting into knots. What would she do if her car was destroyed? She liked that car. It might be old, but it started on cold mornings and she never worried about parking lot dings.

Good thing.

Viewing her car on the front driveway, she wanted to cry. Her side windows were blown out and a tree limb had somehow managed to wedge itself in one backseat window and out the other. "Oh." She sank onto the front steps, staring at the vehicle.

Robin circled it. "I don't think it's that bad."

She raised her eyebrows. Who was he kidding?

"Help me here, Nic."

Nic went to join Robin and together they tugged the limb out of the vehicle, scattering more glass on the pavement as they did so. Robin glanced inside, then stood up and motioned Kate over. "It's only some broken windows."

She joined him slowly, aching at seeing the damage. "How do we know it'll start?"

"One way to find out." He brushed out the glass, then slid into the driver's seat.

"Wait, you don't have the keys." As the engine roared to life, Kate bit back the words. What was she thinking? He didn't need keys.

"Let me see if it drives."

Kate stepped back, then winced as Robin drove the car several feet along the driveway, just missing a toppled tree. When he stopped, she ran down to meet him. "Good. I'll drive."

Mischief danced in his eyes as he rose out of the car. "I can drive for a while. You're exhausted."

"Robin, at this point my nerves could not handle your driving. Trust me."

His slow smile sent warm pulses to her belly. "I do." Touching her elbow, he led the way back to where Nic and Anna stood. "We need to go now."

Anna nodded. "Let me see if I can find your stuff." She

hurried into the house and Kate followed her. Aside from broken windows and scattered branches, the bedrooms weren't heavily damaged. Aching to see the beautiful room in such disarray, Kate jammed her stuff into her bag, snared her purse from a distant corner and met Anna in the hallway.

"I think I have everything," Kate said.

"I grabbed whatever I could find." Anna smiled sadly. "I know we just met, but I'll miss you, Kate."

"I understand." Kate felt as if she'd found a good friend, too. "I'm going to miss you, too."

Linking arms, they returned to the front stoop to find Robin and Nic sweeping up glass from the driveway. "We're ready," Kate said.

Nic nodded, though he didn't look pleased. "Good luck, Robin."

Anna embraced Kate. "Come back after . . ." Her voice trailed away.

"I will," Kate said. If she could. Though she'd only known Nic and Anna for a short time, she liked them both. "I'm sorry about . . ." She waved her hand at the damage surrounding them.

"We'll be all right. No one was hurt and that's what counts."

Nic hugged Kate, too, pulling her close to whisper in her ear. "Keep loving him, Kate. You're what he needs."

"Don't worry." She gave him a wan smile. "I couldn't stop if I wanted to."

"You know where you're going, right?" he asked Robin.

"Kate knows how to find the city. I can find the entrance from there."

"Be careful." Nic said.

"As careful as we can be." Robin grasped Nic's arm. "Anon, my friend."

"We will meet again," Nic said emphatically.

Robin grinned. "Of course."

He joined Kate at the car, the grin leaving his face the moment he settled inside.

"*Will* we see them again?" Kate asked as she steered her car away from the house.

"I hope so." Though Robin kept his tone encouraging, his face was bleak.

And Kate was afraid the bleakness hit closer to the truth. After all, they'd just survived a tornado. What would Titania do next?

Robin frowned at Kate. The way she drove, staring at the road without blinking worried him. "Want me to drive for a while?"

They'd kept driving since they left Nic's house, pausing only for gas and food. Kate even allowed Robin behind the wheel when exhaustion took its toll. From appearances, she was nearing that point now.

"Not yet. I want to make it to Baton Rouge. It's not much further." She shook her head as if to clear it. "But I would love a Coke." She pointed to a highway sign indicating a fast food restaurant at the next exit. "How about I stop there?"

"Good." Robin needed to stretch himself. Confinement to the car only built his tension higher, which in turn tightened all his muscles. He had no difficulty imagining scenarios of when he faced Titania. However, none of them had yet turned out well.

He needed some way to appease the queen, to get her to remove the spell and leave him alone. But with what he'd seen thus far in her attempts to harm Kate, Titania still hated him beyond reason. That didn't bode well.

If nothing else, he had to convince Titania to remove the spell so he could get Kate to safety. As his first female friend, she mattered to him. He wasn't going to allow Titania to hurt her.

Especially when he could do such a good job himself. Robin grimaced. He'd tried to distance himself and failed. Her kisses and touch gave him the strength he needed for the adventure ahead and soothed the fever in his blood that demanded attention.

Stones, he wanted her with an urgency that surpassed any in his past. And he didn't dare give in to that. Each time they made love, he found himself more and more reluctant to let her go. But he would have to. Fate decreed that.

Kate eased off the highway and followed signs along a two lane road toward the town approximately two miles away. When she rolled her neck, Robin reached out to massage the back of it, unable to keep from touching her.

Her moan of pleasure caused a tightening of his loins. "Like that?" he asked.

"Very much. But if you continue, I'll fall asleep right here." She smiled at him. "Let me get to town first."

A bridge crossed a wide river ahead of them and her smile faded. "That almost looks like an antique," she said.

He had to agree. Most bridges he'd seen were no longer made of wood with gaps between the wooden floorboards. "Almost," he said. "But not quite."

"Of course not." Kate started the car across. "It would have to be a few centuries old to be an antique for you."

They'd just gone over halfway when an odd sound caught Robin's attention. Looking around, his heart froze. He immediately scooted over to press his foot atop Kate's on the accelerator.

The car leapt ahead. "What are you doing?"

The noise grew louder and she turned to look, gasping as she noticed what he'd seen and realized why speed was important.

The bridge was collapsing behind them.

Sixteen

Kate no longer needed Robin's foot on top of hers. She floored the gas pedal. This couldn't be happening. But the trembling beneath her car assured her it was. She leaned forward, urging the vehicle to go faster. Solid ground was only fifty feet ahead . . . twenty . . . ten.

Her car had no sooner reached the relative safety of the ground when the bridge collapsed entirely, leaving the vehicle's rear end dangling over the edge as it rocked gently. Kate didn't look around. Fear held her paralyzed. If she moved, the car would fall, taking them with it.

Turning her head slowly, she glanced at Robin. He looked calmer than she felt, but the thin line of his lips signaled his tension. "Kate, we're going to open the door together and jump."

"I don't think I can." The car's rocking motion added to the nausea in her belly.

"You can." Robin reached across the seat to squeeze her hand. "On three."

Kate released a shuddering breath, then nodded.

"One. Two. Three."

She eased her door open only to have the car teeter. Grabbing the door frame, she threw herself out, landing on the pavement beside the vehicle. Staggering to her feet, she backed up as a metal groan filled the air and her car slid over the edge to bounce down to the river below.

Robin ran over to her before she could look for him and together they inched toward the riverbank. The river owned her vehicle now. Only the rear bumper protruded above the water.

Trembling took control of Kate's limbs and she wrapped her arms around herself in an effort to control it. Robin followed suit, holding her close.

She didn't cry. Resting her forehead against his chest, she beat off the tremors with rising anger. Damn it. That had been her car. She'd had enough of Titania's attempts to kill her. Now she was mad. When she met up with this faerie bitch, Kate intended to punch her in the nose.

"I get first dibs on Titania," she said into Robin's shirt. "Then you can talk to her. *If* she can still talk when I'm done with her."

"You intend to fight her?" Disbelief colored his voice.

"Damn straight." Kate looked up. "I'm sick of this. She's not only trying to kill me, now she destroyed my car."

A corner of his lips lifted. "You want to fight her because of your car?"

"Well, yes, I've had that car a long time. It's—"

Robin shook and it took Kate a moment to realize he was laughing. Her first instinct was to glare at him, then slowly her own smile emerged. "God, I'm losing it, aren't I?"

"I don't know what you're losing, but when you consider your car more important than your life, I would have to agree something is missing." He kissed the tip of her nose. "And that you'd expect to fight Titania and survive is amazing."

"Hey, I'm tough." Maybe not magical, but Kate wasn't entirely without resources.

"So you are." Robin's smile filled her with warmth. "I might even worry for her."

"Ha." Kate glanced into the ravine once more, then looked down the road into town. Her car was gone. Which limited their options even more. "I guess we walk from here."

Robin kept her hand in his as they headed down the road.
"How will we reach the realm now?"

"Maybe this place has a train station." She cast him a
mischievous look. "Do you think you can charm some train
tickets for us?"

He grinned in reply. "I'm certain of it."

She hoped so as her purse had sunk with the car. Rocks
grew in her belly. At this rate, by the time they faced Titania
the only thing she *would* have left would be her life.

For once, fortune smiled on them. The town did have a
train station—an ornate building that dated back to the mid-
1800s—and Robin managed to charm two tickets from the
teller without any difficulty.

Guilt nudged Kate at letting Robin use his charm, but at
this point they had little choice. Every minute they wasted
brought danger closer.

Kate waited impatiently for the train's arrival, eyeing the
station's few residents. She was about to the point where she
was afraid to go to the bathroom alone. Hell, the toilet might
attack her.

She grimaced. Invisible dogs, tornadoes, and collapsing
bridges. At least Titania had imagination.

What would she do to top her latest attempt? Release the
Sta-Puff marshmallow man?

As Robin settled into a seat on the train beside Kate, he noted
how bright her eyes appeared in her pale face. Despite her
denials, fear lingered. He didn't blame her. His own nerves
were badly frayed.

He'd feared that Titania's attacks would send Kate into a
mental state where she could no longer function. When she'd
erupted with anger after this last episode, he'd wanted to
dance with joy. His Kate was much stronger than she knew,
filled with courage and the vitality of life.

And he intended to see she remained that way.

Judging from the disasters thus far, it took Titania about
a mortal day to locate them. The train should have them at

their destination within that time. Once in the magical realm, Titania would have to face Kate personally to do her harm and Robin wasn't about to let that happen.

Somehow he would keep Kate as far away from the queen as their restraints allowed them. At the image of Kate fisting Titania in the face, he grinned. Though he'd like to see that, the consequences were too grave to consider letting Kate have her way.

"Will we get there safely?" Kate asked, breaking into his thoughts. "Do you think she'll wash out a bridge or tracks or something?"

Robin raised the seat arm dividing them and wrapped his arm around Kate, pulling her close so that her head nestled against his shoulder. "We'll be fine." Titania needed time to find them. Though the train would take a full day to reach its destination, it would be constantly moving. That would confuse the Fae Queen and give them a chance to reach Orlando safely.

He kissed her forehead, drawing strength from her warmth. "Why don't you rest? It's a long trip yet."

"Good idea." She snuggled into a comfortable position, then closed her eyes.

Robin watched her drift from awareness into slumber. What was it about this woman that had him constantly thinking of her when he should be preparing for the confrontation ahead? Nic's words kept repeating in Robin's mind . . . teasing him, tormenting him.

If he loved Kate surely he'd know. He liked her, cared about her, but love . . . love had no place between an immortal and mortal. Only Nic ever dared to give in to it and Robin remembered all too well how his friend had suffered several hundred years ago when the woman he'd loved had died.

Robin wasn't about to let that happen to him.

"I can't believe it's in here." Kate stared at the back drop to the ticket booths in front of them.

"Nic assured me this is the place," Robin said from beside her.

"I guess it makes sense." Eyeing the familiar characters on the booths, Kate shook her head. She should've known. Disney World.

Where else would the entrance to the magical realm lie?

"Do we go in now?" she asked.

When Robin didn't answer right away, she glanced at him to find his gaze intent on her. She frowned. "What?"

"It's getting late."

True enough. The lights were already appearing on many of the distant rides as dusk settled.

"I prefer to be well rested before I face Titania," Robin added. "Let's come back in the morning."

Kate had no problem agreeing. As much as she wanted this over, she treasured every moment with Robin. Soon—too soon—she'd have no more of them. "Only one problem." She grimaced. "We have no money for a motel room."

"I'll take care of that." He caught her hand and pulled her away. "Let's go."

Being Robin, he managed to convince a young couple leaving the park to drop them by a motel nearby. By the time they arrived there, Kate would've preferred to walk. The young woman spent the entire drive exclaiming over Robin's English accent and giving him come-hither looks. Kate curled her hands into fists, resisting the urge to smack the woman.

"I never used to be violent," she murmured after they exited the car.

"Violent?" Robin raised an eyebrow.

"Ah, nothing." She didn't want to explain about her jealousy. Turning, she viewed the L-shaped motel. It wasn't much, but it was a place to stay. "Can you get us a room?"

"It's as good as done." However, they'd forgotten about the onset of spring break. When Robin emerged from the office, he held a key, but his expression was bleak. "We have their last room for one night only."

"Isn't that what we wanted?" she asked, following him across the parking lot.

His reply was noncommittal. Maybe he was hesitant to face Titania. Kate sure was.

Then he pushed open the room door and stepped aside. Upon entering, Kate froze. "Oh." The room was clean, but small and dominated by a double bed.

One bed.

Though Robin had returned to being her friend, he'd still shown no sign of wanting to make love again. How could they possibly share a bed and not touch each other? Maybe Robin could, but Kate couldn't.

"I see," she added.

"I'll sleep on the floor." Robin's voice held no emotion and Kate glanced at him. He refused to meet her gaze.

"You won't be rested that way." She stepped farther inside. "I'll take the floor."

"No, Kate, I—" Robin came to grip her arms and electricity crackled between them more potent than any static shock she'd ever received. He stared at her, his eyes dark.

Desire churned in Kate's belly. She placed her palm against his chest. "Robin?"

The air sizzled as their gazes locked. The only sound was that of their rapid breathing.

Robin closed his eyes and turned away. "Want to go for a walk?"

Disappointment acted as cold water on her rising passion. Kate bit her lip and waited until he glanced over her shoulder before she replied. "Sure, why not?" What else did she have to do?

The cooling air felt good against her hot skin. Evidently, Robin intended to maintain his stupid nobility. She ought to be thankful he'd at least lost his belligerent attitude.

But that didn't help her longing to be one with him. Each time they made love, she felt a blending of their souls. Maybe that was what frightened Robin. Kate wanted it, needed it. That portion of Robin would be all she had when he was gone.

She turned to walk along the edge of the parking lot toward an empty field and Robin fell into step. For a long time, neither of them said anything.

What was there to say? Good-bye. Take care. Kate shook her head. She wasn't going to do that. No matter what happened Robin would always be a part of her.

"You all right?" he asked.

"Fine." Well, not really, but as close to fine as she expected to be for a long time. Tomorrow they'd enter the magical realm and face Queen Titania. Just thinking about it made her chest constrict.

What would the realm be like? What would Titania do? After her attacks on them, Kate didn't see her blithely giving Robin his freedom. What price would he have to pay? Kate grimaced. Maybe she didn't want the answer to that question.

"Are you frightened about tomorrow, Robin?" Was he feeling this same queasiness?

He didn't respond right away. "Not frightened. More nervous."

"I think I'm frightened."

Catching her hand, Robin lifted it to his lips for a gentle kiss. "I will do all in my power to protect you, milady."

Warmth oozed up her arm as she smiled at his foolishness. "I know. But I can handle myself, y'know. Titania won't hurt me." Silly words, but fitting for the moment. She never wanted him to release her hand.

"Only if you don't punch her." He grinned and started walking again, keeping her hand firmly in his.

"Ah, so that's why you're nervous."

"Actually, I'm nervous about meeting my father."

His father? "Oberon?"

"I've never been sure if I completed the mission he gave me." Robin peered into the distant darkness.

"Mission?" He'd never mentioned a mission before.

"Oberon came to me when I was a young man of sixteen years and said I was to live among the mortals and reward those who deserved kindness and punish those who did wrong."

"Sounds like a lot of work." And a little frightening. Which group did she fall into? Neither?

"I've never felt comfortable with judging mortals, though some cases clearly call for punishment, like with Adam."

Kate blinked. "Adam? Did you do something to him?"

When Robin didn't answer, she squeezed his hand. What *had* he done to Adam? "Robin?"

"He received only what he deserved." His smile held no warmth. "But since I've been with you I haven't pursued this mission. I've enjoyed fitting into your life."

He stopped abruptly as if he hadn't meant to say that, but Kate was glad he did. "I've enjoyed having you in my life," she said quietly. "Even the chaos."

Pausing, Robin turned to her in the darkness. "But what will Oberon think? I haven't done as he asked. To be honest, I haven't wanted to."

"I don't know." Sudden anger rose at Oberon, who was far from being a real father. "If he truly cared about you, he'd want you to be happy, to find a life that suited you."

"Perhaps." Robin drew his hand away and resumed walking, his tone indicating disbelief.

She ran after him. "Do all faerie fathers expect this from their children?"

"Oberon is the only father among the Fae."

"Excuse me?" The only father? That couldn't be right. "Where do they come from then?"

"They're immortal." He didn't slow his stride. "They always have been and always will be. The only way to have children is with mortals. Oberon impregnated my mother to experience fatherhood."

"And did a poor job of it, too."

"Not for a member of the Fae." Robin stopped, his back to her, his face to the forest. "He taught me how to handle my magic, gave me my mission and left me to do it."

Kate frowned. Despite her father's quest for the faerie gold, he'd been better than that. Though she often felt inadequate, she'd always known he loved her. That's why he had to be dead. He wouldn't have deserted her like that.

"I'm sor—" She broke off as Robin whirled around, knocking her to the ground. He stumbled and dropped beside her. *What the hell?* She tried to sit up, but he pushed her back down with one hand.

"Someone's shooting at us."

Shooting? She scanned the dark trees nearby. "I didn't hear anything."

"He must be using a—what is it—a quieter?"

"Silencer?"

"Yes."

"Are you sure?" Wouldn't she have seen something? Felt something?

"Yes."

His clipped replies assured her of his seriousness. Her heart skipped a beat. "Titania?" When she'd imagined the next way the queen would strike, she'd never consider a gun. It was so . . . human.

"Someone doing her work." Robin sat up slowly, but waved at Kate to stay down. "Though this isn't like her. I imagine Callum is doing this on his own." After staring toward the trees for several long moments, he blinked. "It's a human. Callum must've hired him."

"Does that make a difference?" She'd never seen this expression on his face—anger mixed with deadly purpose.

"I can deal with him." He inhaled sharply as he climbed to his feet. "Stay down."

"Are you all right?"

"Just landed hard." He faced the woods and held up one hand while he placed the other against his abdomen. Electricity crackled in the air, raising Kate's hair, and dancing over her skin.

She caught her breath. What was he doing? How powerful was he?

A sudden explosion erupted within the forest, creating a column of fire that rose above the tree tops. "My God." Kate jumped to her feet to stand beside Robin. "What did you do?"

"His gun malfunctioned."

She stared at him. Did she really know this man? "Is he dead?"

After glancing at the trees again, Robin shook his head. "Injured. I doubt he'll be shooting anyone else."

Horror rose in her throat. "Would you have killed him?"

"That's not how I usually work." Her tension eased until he turned his dark gaze on her. "But to protect you, Kate, I would."

She didn't know whether to be flattered or frightened. "Robin, I—"

"Let's get inside." Putting his arm around her shoulders, he led her back toward the motel. "I don't want to take any more chances."

Prickles rose on the back of her neck and she quickened her pace. Now that he'd said that, she couldn't shake the image of a target painted on her back. Thank goodness they were entering the magical realm tomorrow.

Of course, she still had to survive tonight.

While she tried to hurry, Robin kept moving slower. She glanced up at him. "Come on."

He nodded, then stumbled as they neared the motel.

"Are you sure you're all right?"

He nodded again, but his breathing sounded labored. Something was wrong.

When Kate pushed open the door, he staggered past her and she grabbed his torso to catch him. Her palm encountered something wet and she flicked on the lights so she could glance at her hand.

Red.

Her chest tightened as she looked at Robin. A large red stain covered his shirt as if he'd spilled a glass of cherry Kool-Aid. But it wasn't Kool-Aid.

It was blood.

Seventeen

~

"Oh, my God. Oh, my God." Kate stared at Robin, her heart threatening to leap from her chest. "You're shot."

He looked down at his bloody shirt. "So it appears."

"Why didn't you tell me?" Even as she spoke, Kate snared his arm, led him to the bed and made him lie down.

"There wasn't anything you could do but worry." Lying back with a groan, he closed his eyes.

Worry didn't cover it. Sheer panic vibrated along her nerves. Dashing into the bathroom, Kate grabbed a towel and doused it with cold water, then returned to Robin.

He lay still, his face so pale that her breath caught. "Robin?"

"I'm fine." He opened his eyes to look at her.

Inhaling again, she sat beside him and lifted his shirt. Blood covered his chest, making it difficult for her to locate the wound, but she found it finally beneath his ribs. She placed the towel on top of it and pressed. Pressure for a wound—she remembered that much.

"We have to call 911." Her voice trembled almost as much as her hands.

"No."

"Robin, you're shot." Was the loss of blood making him delirious?

"I'm immortal. I'll be fine."

Kate lifted the towel to peek beneath. The bleeding had slowed but not stopped. She reapplied pressure and Robin winced. "You'll be fine," she retorted. "Yeah, right."

"I didn't say I don't feel pain." Thin, white lines around his lips confirmed that fact. "But I'll heal. Quickly."

Seeing his chest covered with blood wasn't likely to convince Kate of his immortality. Fear, even worse than when her life was endangered, gripped her. "Robin, I couldn't bear it if . . ." She choked, unable to finish. She couldn't lose him this way.

He caught one of her hands and brought it to his lips. "I swear to you, Kate. I'll be my charming self by morning."

His confidence gave her hope. "Promise?"

"I swear it on the Stones."

Though not sure what the Stones were, Kate knew he held them in high esteem. And he was magical. She'd seen previous evidence of that. After all, he'd healed her.

But this was worse—much worse—than some broken ribs. Reluctantly, she nodded. She'd hold off calling an ambulance for now, but if he didn't show signs of healing soon, she would take action.

"I'll get another towel." When she returned and removed the soaked towel, she blinked in surprise. The bullet lay on top of his skin and the wound had started to knit together. Maybe he would be all right. The tight band around her chest eased. "It looks better."

"Told you so." Robin gave her a smile that faded as he inhaled sharply.

"What is it?" Was he hurt somewhere else?

"The healing isn't always a painless process." He blew out his breath. "This burns worse than the time I was stabbed."

"Stabbed?" Kate swallowed hard, wanting to wrap him in her arms. "When?"

"Centuries ago. Around seventeen hundred and fifty, I

think." He shivered suddenly and Kate eased the blankets back, then covered him.

"Rest now." She lifted the soaked towel and turned for the bathroom.

"Stay with me, Kate." His voice held a plea she hadn't heard from him before.

"They'd have to drag me away." She smiled with reassurance, meaning every word. She wasn't about to leave his side until convinced he'd survive. "Just let me rinse this out."

When she returned a few minutes later, his eyes were closed again, but his breathing appeared less labored and the skin on his face not as tight. Removing her shoes, she turned off the light, then slipped beneath the covers and placed her arm carefully over his chest. If something started going wrong, she wanted to know about it.

"Thank you, sweet Kate," he whispered.

"Thank *you*." As she said the phrase automatically, the enormity of his actions hit her so hard that she gasped.

"Kate?"

"You took that bullet for me." He'd pushed her out of the way while stepping into danger himself.

"I knew I'd survive it." His voice were husky. "I won't take that chance with you."

Her throat grew tight with emotion, making a response impossible. Instead, she hugged him gently as tears trickled down her cheeks. On the day Robin appeared from the portrait, she'd thought her life was ruined. Now she knew how much more she had to be grateful for.

What was a house when compared with the friendship Robin gave her or the passion he'd awakened?

"I love you," she murmured, unable to stop the words any longer.

Only Robin's steady breathing answered her. Half-disappointed and half-relieved, she snuggled closer and shut her eyes. Perhaps it was just as well. She had no future with a member of the Fae. If Titania's attempts to kill her continued, Kate wasn't sure she had a future at all.

• • •

Robin stirred, awakening slowly. The warm form next to him and Kate's familiar scent soothed him, holding off any reason to open his eyes. Her arm rested across his chest and he smiled at the possessive gesture.

As he enjoyed the feel of her arm on him, he became aware of aches permeating his body as if he'd run for hours. Memories of the previous evening returned in a rush and he flung his eyes open and sat up.

Daylight filtered into the room with the pink shimmer of early morning. The room was quiet. Nothing moved. Kate breathed evenly beside him.

With a sigh, he lay back. No rush to get up yet. This would be the last morning he'd greet the dawn beside Kate. A sense of loss stole over him, so powerful he ached with it.

This woman affected his emotions like none other he'd ever met. He cared about her, liked her, and wanted her with a fervor that hadn't diminished over time.

As he turned to his side to watch her sleeping, he noticed the condition of his shirt. Well past saving. He discarded it with a thought, then glanced at his abdomen where he'd been wounded.

No one would be able to tell he'd been shot the night before. His skin had healed over the wound without a scar or bruise. Though his body ached, his internal organs had repaired themselves as well. *A definite plus to immortality.*

Even more important, he'd saved Kate. Though he would've preferred not to have been shot, the bullet lodged within him enabled him to locate the shooter and explode the remaining bullets in his gun. It stopped the gunman, but at that moment Robin would've enjoyed a more hands-on physical approach. If he hadn't sensed the danger . . .

Kate sighed and he shifted his gaze to her face. Every time he looked at her she appeared more beautiful. As she'd learned to accept who she was, she glowed with vitality. She wouldn't have problems with men finding her attractive ever again.

That thought didn't please him.

He didn't want to leave her. Not now, not ever. To share

mornings with her, to laugh, talk and make love with her, to watch her grow more lovely every day. Even into old age.

His normal terror at that idea didn't surface. Instead, he imagined Kate maturing, her face reflecting her earned wisdom, her hair color giving way to white, and he still found her beautiful. Kate was more than her appearance. She was the most giving, loving, exasperating woman he'd ever met.

Was Nic right about Robin's feelings for her? Robin cared about her. Did he love her as well? He wanted to stay with her, enjoy her, make love to her for the rest of her life. Was that love?

Somehow he'd always imagined the emotion would hit with the impact of a runaway stallion and he would know in an instant. What he experienced now was deeper, warmer, and more terrifying than what he'd expected.

Maybe he did love her. He definitely wanted her. Just watching the gentle rise and fall of her chest as she slept stirred his body to life—a body denied her passion for too long.

When he'd first decided to distance himself he'd thought it a good idea. Now he couldn't remember why. Their parting would be painful for them both no matter what happened. They'd shared too much already. The bond he'd tried to escape already surrounded them.

He drew his finger over her face, tracing the arch of her brow, the line of her cheek, the outline of her lips—lips meant to be kissed, lips designed to kiss back. "Sweet Kate."

As she stirred, he bent to touch his mouth to hers, seeking comfort. He found more than that as passion boiled the blood in his veins.

Opening her eyes, Kate smiled. "Robin." She lifted her hand to touch his chest. "Are you all right?"

"You tell me." Bending to kiss her again, he no longer tried to be gentle. Hunger and need drove him now, as well as the need to be one with the only woman he'd remember for all eternity.

Her enthusiastic response encouraged him, stoked the fire in his loins. She opened her mouth and her tongue met his as she wound her arms around his neck. Her breathing grew ragged. Or was it his?

He grew hard, burning for her. Rational thought threatened to disappear altogether, but he made one desperate attempt to hold onto it. Was this fair to her?

Drawing back, he examined her face. Joy glowed in her eyes. Her full lips were swollen, yet she managed to smile at him, an enigmatic lifting of her lips that stirred him more. "Kate, will you be sorry if—?"

She didn't let him finish by placing her finger over his mouth. "If you *don't* make love to me now, I'll regret it the rest of my life."

Excitement mingled with his desire. Drawing her finger into his mouth, he sucked on it and she groaned. She kicked back the blankets and pressed her body along his, cradling his erection against her pelvis.

Needing no encouragement, he removed her clothes and proceeded to lavish attention to her body—her wonderful full breasts, the slight indention of her belly button, the moist center between her legs. Soon Kate was writhing on the bed, her hands hot against his skin, her head thrown back as she cried his name in a voice heavy with desire.

She reached her peak quickly, but he didn't let her rest. He'd neglected her for too long. Her body responded wildly to his hands and mouth, arching several times before he joined with her in one swift movement.

Her muscles clenched around him in yet another explosion, threatening his already tenuous control. Remaining motionless, he enjoyed the sated expression on Kate's face. As her breathing slowed, he reached out to tease her puckered nipples and her soft moan of pleasure urged him onward.

He moved within her, slowly at first with long, deep thrusts, teasing her, tormenting himself. As her hips rose to meet him, he increased his pace, reveling in her response, in the feel of her around him, in the building ache of his desire. Lovemaking became a total sensory pleasure with Kate.

As she erupted once more, he allowed himself to share it with her, crying out her name. When movement became possible again, he lowered himself to rest atop her. She danced her fingers lightly over his back as he nuzzled the tender spot beneath her ear.

"That was wonderful," she murmured.

"It's always wonderful with you." All the other women he'd known faded into obscurity next to Kate. She was all that he could want.

"I wish we didn't have to leave."

"I know what you mean." He rolled off her onto his side. "I'd prefer to spend the day in bed." He grinned, but in truth she kept him in a fever, his need for her easily aroused.

"Well . . ." Mischief danced in her green eyes. "We don't have to be out of here until noon."

He responded at once to that suggestion with an immediate erection. "Excellent." He extended his hand to draw lazy circles around her breast until the nipple tightened in a hard little nub. "I can think of ways to pass the time."

She reached down to caress him and he stifled the groan that rose in his throat. "So can I," she replied with a wicked grin.

All other thoughts vanished beneath her touch, leaving only one. He bent forward to tease her peak with his tongue, making her gasp.

He intended to enjoy every moment of this morning.

Though Kate ached after several hours of intense lovemaking, she didn't regret one second of it. All Robin had to do was touch her or look at her and she wanted him again. Was it due to the days of abstinence or the simple fact that she would always need him?

Probably the latter.

They took their time preparing to leave the motel, sharing their passion again as they showered together. Upon emerging into the room, Kate held out her arms and faced Robin. "Where are my clothes?"

Though his eyes darkened as he looked at her, he ran his hand over her. Bikini underpants and a lace-rimmed silk bra caressed her curves. Not the kind of underwear she usually wore, but Kate had to admit, they made her feel sexy.

"And?" she asked, lifting her eyebrows. The desire on Robin's face added to her feelings of sexiness.

With a grimace, he produced a pair of soft blue jeans that hugged her hips and a close-fitting green shirt with a low-cut neckline that revealed a hint of her cleavage. He even added socks and her favorite tennis shoes.

Kate went to view her image in the mirror, surprised at the woman in the reflection. Something was different, yet she couldn't put her finger on it. Her figure, her hair, her face—all looked the same, but for once she had to agree with Robin. She looked pretty damned good.

Was it the color in her cheeks? The light in her eyes? Kate smiled. It didn't matter.

Robin came from behind to put his arms around her and met her gaze in the mirror. "You're beautiful," he said huskily.

"And you're the most handsome man to walk the face of the Earth." She turned within his hold to face him.

He smiled, though sadness lingered in his eyes. "I guess we deserve each other then."

Her chest tightened. "Yeah, we do." She leaned forward to accept his gentle kiss, her heart aching. If only such a thing were possible.

When he raised his head, his expression looked bleak. "We have to go."

"I know." They couldn't put off the inevitable any longer.

Upon stepping outside, Kate blinked in the sunlight. Their morning of bliss was over. The magical realm—with Queen Titania and Robin's future—waited.

All too quickly, Robin secured them a ride to Disney World and charmed their way inside. Kate stood on Main Street, unable to take in everything at once—the rides, the stores, the exhibits, the hordes of people, the screams of terror and fun.

She'd always wanted to come here as a child. Now that she'd finally arrived, her only thought was of leaving.

Robin linked his arm through hers. "Come on, Kate."

They walked with the crowd along the decorated street. Despite the tension knotting her stomach, Kate peeked into each building they passed—the tourist shops, restaurants, clothing stores, fudge booths. At any other time in her life, she would've enjoyed this.

As she spotted a photography studio, she stopped, caught by the sample photos of couples together.

"Can we get our picture taken?" she asked, hardly daring to hope. At least she'd have something to remember Robin with . . . not that she needed a physical reminder. Her heart would never forget him.

He hesitated, then nodded.

As they entered the shop, Kate glanced at Robin. "You will show up on film, won't you?"

His smile warmed her. "I think so. I've never done this before."

The photographer seated Kate on Robin's lap, their faces close as they faced the camera. Several flashes later, they stood and the photographer told them to return in an hour.

"What do we do for an hour?" Kate asked once they emerged outside.

"Hungry?"

Her stomach rebelled at the thought. "Not really."

"What about a ride?" The gleam in Robin's eyes made Kate turn to see what impressed him.

"A roller coaster? Oh, no. I don't do well on those." She didn't mind the fast part. It was the upside-down, high-up-in-the-air part that bothered her.

"I'll hold you tight." Taking her elbow, Robin pulled her toward the ride. "Trust me."

Well, he *had* saved her life. But was it worth a roller coaster ride? *Don't be silly.* He couldn't have been on one before. She had no right to deny him this small thing.

However, forty-five minutes later, when she found herself in the seat beside him, Kate wished she'd let him go on his own. She wouldn't have minded waiting below.

Of course, with their distance restraint, he would've probably been yanked from the car before it descended the first hill.

The cars jerked forward and she seized the rail over her legs in a death grip. Robin laughed. "Look, there's the entrance." They climbed slowly to the first pinnacle. "I can see our motel."

Kate snapped her eyes shut, the height making her dizzy. "I don't want to know."

"Come on." He hugged her shoulders. "It's wonderful."

Though reluctant, she peeked out from beneath her lashes. They had to be miles above the park with the entire place spread out below them. Even the trees were dwarfed. In horror, she squeezed her eyes closed again. Her stomach was already upset. Why did she need to make it worse?

Suddenly, the cars dropped over the top and Kate screamed. She couldn't help it. Robin's laughter joined in. Unable to see the track and anticipate the curves, she found herself flung first this way, then that as the roller coaster sped around curves and over hills. And people called this fun.

"Final hill coming up," Robin shouted above the wind. "Are you all right?"

"No," she replied.

He laughed, but squeezed her hand where she maintained her grip on the rail. Reaching the top, the cars dropped again.

Before Kate could scream, Robin pulled her down against the seat and lay over her. "Keep down," he ordered.

She opened her eyes at that, catching a brief glimpse of several geese flying over them, easily within touching distance. At the speed she and Robin were traveling, they would've been badly hurt by that impact if Robin hadn't pulled her down.

The cars slowed to a stop and the attendant ran over. "You two okay?" he asked.

"Fine," Robin said abruptly. He gripped Kate's hand and helped her from the car. Which was a good thing with the way her knees were shaking—as much from the ride itself as the close encounter. She would never, ever ride a roller coaster again.

He didn't say, but she knew the birds were no accident. Titania hadn't given up.

"We have to go now." Urgency colored his voice.

"Just let me get the pictures first."

He nodded, his face grim. Kate squeezed his hand. Even in Disney World they weren't safe. Would she be any better off inside the realm?

After returning to the photography store, Kate found the finished pictures to be even better than she'd hoped. Her love for Robin shone in her face and his expression held such tenderness she wanted to cry. The photographer had enclosed them in an oval outline, blacking out the rest of the picture. She had to have it.

"How much are they?" Though they had no money, these deserved payment.

As he named a sum, she glanced at Robin, but his attention was on the photo. Looking up, he gave Kate a sad smile. "Can we pay you for these later?" he asked the photographer. "If you'll give us your card, I'll make sure you're compensated for this."

His charm worked flawlessly and they left the store with the man's business card and the photos in Kate's pocket.

Without thinking, Kate headed for Sleeping Beauty's castle. Where else would the entrance to the land of the Fae reside? As they reached a crossroads, Robin touched her shoulder. "You're going the wrong way," he said.

"It's not in the castle?" Where else could it be? With her luck, probably in the same lagoon with Peter Pan's crocodile.

"You'll see." He led her to the line for another ride . . . a different kind of ride.

Kate stared at the colorful building. "It's a Small World?" Well, of course.

Once their boat moved away from the loading ramp, Robin unfastened the strap holding them in. "We'll have to jump."

Jump? Why didn't that fill her with encouragement? "Where?"

"You have the sight, Kate. You'll see it."

Though the various exhibits of children in different lands

were cute, Kate was thoroughly sick of the song by the time she spotted a circular blue glow hanging over the water near the tunnel wall. "Is that it?"

Robin nodded and rose to his feet. "Jump into it."

As the boat neared the spot, he leapt toward the glow . . . and vanished.

This was it. Swallowing the lump in her throat, Kate stood on the seat, clenched her hands . . . and jumped.

Eighteen

Kate stumbled as her feet struck solid ground, but Robin was there to catch her shoulders and steadied her. "We're here," he said quietly.

Blinking, she scanned the land surrounding them. It looked normal with vast, green meadowland decorated with flowers and edged by thick forests, yet the colors were more vivid in a manner she couldn't explain. Not fluorescent, yet not exactly normal either.

Glancing behind her, she saw only the faint shimmer of the oval glow to indicate the portal back to the mortal world. Behind it, the meadow stretched on to a range of snow-capped mountains that disappeared into shining clouds.

The sky provided a true indicator that she no longer dwelled in a world she knew. The entire firmament resembled a rainbow—part streaked in blue, another streaked in pink, others in purple, yellow, orange and red. The sun—or whatever provided the light for this realm—glowed behind the heavens, making it resemble a stained-glass window. Truly colorful . . . and amazing.

Birds flew overhead, magnificent creatures easily the size of eagles but they, too, were brightly colored in deep blues and yellows. Songs emerged from the trees ahead, obviously produced by animals, yet resembling the blended tones of the Vienna Boys Choir. Everything here was so much *more* than normal.

You're not in Kansas anymore, Dorothy. "This is the magical realm?" she spoke in a whisper, though not sure why. Perhaps it was due to her awe. No wonder Robin wanted to live here.

"This is it." Pride filled Robin's voice expression as he surveyed the area. "I've only been here once before, but I found it to be everything I expected."

"Except for Titania," Kate added.

He gave her a wry smile. "Except for her. If we could've continued to avoid each other, I might have made my life here."

Kate's stomach clenched. If Robin had stayed here, she never would've met him, never experienced the greatest joy of her life. Though she wouldn't wish him in the portrait for any length of time, she thanked the heavenly powers that had given her the faerie sight.

She stepped farther into the field and almost stumbled over something. Bending, she lifted a tiara from the ground. Only the Celtic design etched into it told her what it was. Her ring. Titania's circlet.

Glancing quickly at her finger, she noticed the ring she'd worn since the day Nana gave it to her was gone. Had it grown larger when she'd entered the realm?

Eyeing the circlet, Kate frowned. What if it hadn't grown larger? "Did we . . . shrink?" The question sounded silly and she wanted to retract it immediately.

"Honey, I shrunk the kids." Robin winked at her. "You're now the true size of the Fae." He held his hands apart to show her the distance of about six inches.

Kate gulped and searched the land again, half expecting a giant to emerge. The Fae had magic. She didn't.

"Don't worry." Robin laughed. "We're the largest things here." He paused. "Well, in this area anyhow."

Oh, that made her feel better.

She glanced at the circlet again. After that one horrible night, Robin had never mentioned it, but she knew he deserved it more than she. If Oberon hadn't given it as a gift to Robin's mother, he might never have suffered Titania's wrath. As much as she loved that ring, she still had her memories of Nana. If this plain crown could save Robin from further misery, she had no right to it. She should've done this long ago.

She placed it in Robin's hands. "I want you to have this."

His gaze searched hers as if trying to discern her true feelings. "Are you sure?"

"Very sure." She smiled. "You've given me many more important things." Like a sense of worth, of feeling valued, of realizing she could survive more than she thought.

"Kate, I—" He broke off, then kissed her softly with such restrained passion it brought tears to her eyes. "Thank you."

She nodded, not trusting herself to speak.

"Come on." Holding the circlet in one hand, he took her hand with his other and walked across the meadow toward the trees.

Upon entering the forest, he moved with purpose. Kate had to walk fast to keep up with him, often lagging behind as she stared at the wide variety of vegetation. "Do you know where you're going?"

"There's a grove close to here where the Fae gather. I hope to find Oberon there."

"Will . . . Titania be there?"

He grimaced. "Possibly."

Squeezing his hand, Kate released a tremulous breath. She wasn't at all sure she was ready for this. "I won't let her hurt you again," she declared. Surely a human had some power over the Fae.

Robin gave her a smile tinged with amusement. "I appreciate that."

"Well, I won't." Maybe she wasn't magical, but she loved him. That had to be worth something.

He brought her fingers to his lips. "And I'll protect you as well."

A shiver of delight ran up her arm. "Maybe . . . maybe she'll release the spell and let us both go."

"I'd like that." His gaze held such heat that Kate tingled with anticipation.

"Me, too." Her heart skipped a beat. Was it possible that they could be together?

The moment hung suspended in time as they stared at each other, the only sounds that of their erratic breathing. With a groan, Robin placed the circlet over his arm and stepped forward to cup her face in his palms. "Kate, it's not going to be pleasant. I would do anything to spare you this"

"I don't know that I'd let you do that." His mission had become hers as well.

"Dear, sweet Kate." He kissed her with an equal mixture of fury and passion, frustration and sweetness, angst and hope. Melting against him, wrapping her arms around him, she never wanted him to stop.

Love for this unusual man who believed in TV commercials and 555 phone numbers and became drunk on Coke welled up within her. If only this moment could last forever. If only Titania didn't hate him. If only . . .

Kate choked back a sob. She was doing it again. "If only's" solved nothing. Though she didn't like it, she had the strength to face whatever came her way—be it faerie magic or losing the only man she'd ever love. She could survive alone now.

Resting his forehead against hers, Robin sighed. "We have to go on."

"I know, but I don't have to like it."

He stole a quick kiss, then resumed walking. He didn't glance back at her, as if doing so might weaken his resolve—something Kate understood all too well.

Falling into step with him, she matched him stride for stride, but didn't speak. All the words had been said.

They paused at the edge of a large grove filled with bright flowers and soft green grass. Music drifted from somewhere, but Kate couldn't pinpoint the location. Light and airy, the notes of the flute suited this place.

In the distance, she spotted two large thrones cut into rocks covered with ivy. In fact, she only saw one problem. "Where is everyone?"

Robin grimaced and glanced at the sky. "It's early yet. I guess no one has arrived."

"Early?" By her reckoning, it was late afternoon.

"Time is different here." He gave her an indulgent smile. "It moves slower than in your world."

"I see." She didn't really and didn't want to examine it too closely. Some things were better off not understood.

"The Fae meet near dusk and dance into the night," he added.

Walking farther into the grove, she imagined the dancing Fae as she inhaled the flowers' fragrant perfumes, the mixture tickling her nose and making her sneeze. Maybe too fragrant. This entire place appeared surreal. Any moment now a white rabbit was going to hop by and check his watch.

"It's beautiful here," she admitted.

"But?" When she glanced at Robin, he smiled. "I can hear it in your voice."

She smiled wryly. "But it's not home."

"No, it's not." An expression of nostalgia appeared on his face. Was he remembering her tiny apartment with the same fondness? Or the time he expected the pizza delivery man to sing and dance when he arrived? Or when he followed the stove top instructions for preparing oatmeal yet had cooked it in the microwave and exploded the entire bowl? Or better yet, the laughter they'd shared and the nights in her bed?

She never expected to miss that apartment, but if she could be there now with Robin by her side, she'd never complain again.

A sudden alertness in Robin's posture drew her attention and she turned to see a man approaching from across the grove. Oberon?

Something in the man's walk seemed familiar. Had she seen the Fae king before? *Not likely.*

He came close enough for her to make out his features

and she staggered backward with a gasp as if someone had punched her in the chest. It couldn't be.

But she'd never forget that copper-colored hair, cleft chin or brilliant green eyes.

"Kate, what is it?" Robin came to her side at once.

Shaking her head, she struggled to speak. The man was almost to them now. She swallowed and gripped Robin's arm, still unable to believe the evidence before her eyes.

"It's my . . . my father."

Robin looked at the man in surprise. "Your father? I thought he was dead."

"So did I."

And he hadn't aged a day since she'd last seen him. By rights, his hair should be gray, his face lined, yet he still looked like the thirty-nine-year-old man who'd left in search of gold.

Had he found it? Was that why he'd remained here instead of returning to his only child?

He reached them and extended his hand to Robin, giving Kate only a cursory glance. "Titania sent me to meet you. I'm Philip Carmichael."

"You're mortal." Anger colored Robin's words, but Kate knew it was on her behalf.

"Afraid so. I'm visiting." Philip smiled, reminding Kate of their last days together when they'd played and talked about finding the fortune.

Tear stung her eyes, but she stepped forward to face him. "And I'm *Kate* Carmichael." She lifted her chin, daring him to dispute her claim, her voice heavy with sarcasm. "Good to see you, *Dad*."

"Kate?" His eyes widened and he stared at her. "Little Katie? No. It's impossible."

"It's me. Want to see my appendectomy scar?" She didn't try to keep the bitterness from her voice. "Everyone told me you'd deserted me but I wouldn't believe them. I said you had to be dead, but here you are. I guess I was wrong after all."

"No." He shook his head. "It can't be. You were thirteen when I left."

"True, but that was twelve years ago."

"Twelve years?" The color faded from his face and he stumbled backward to land on his backside on the ground. "That can't be."

"What? That I grew up?" Though her heart ached at seeing him so distraught, she had only to remember the years of pain she'd endured to revive her anger. "It happens to little girls, even ones deserted by their fathers."

He stared up at her. "I . . . I've only been here four or five months . . . six at the most."

"It's been twelve years," she said firmly. "Did you forget me? Was that it?"

"No, no, I couldn't do that." He went to rise and Robin took his elbow to help him.

The traitor. Kate glared at him.

Robin came to touch her shoulder. "Kate, remember what I told you about time here?"

She frowned. "Something about it being different."

"Slower. Time moves slower here. It's probably only been four or five months for your father while in the mortal world twelve years have passed."

Her head ached. She didn't do well with abstract things, let alone something like this. "But he left me. What if Nana had refused to take care of me?" To her horror, her voice trembled. "I would've gone into foster care."

"Katie, honey, I'm sorry." Her father extended his hands to her. "I didn't know."

She stepped back, shaking her head. "Do you know how hard I cried night after night, year after year until I had no more tears left?" Her voice trembled with anger and agony. Those horrible years returned in a rush of memory . . . memories she didn't want to recall. "I thought you loved me, that you'd come back for me."

"I do love you." Moisture filled Philip's eyes. "With God as my witness, Kate, I would've returned if I'd known . . ."

Tears hovered beneath the surface, threatening to erupt.

She wanted to believe him—needed to believe him. "And all for some stupid gold. Did you find it?"

"No." He sounded subdued. "I know it's here, but I haven't found it yet. For some reason the queen here likes me and keeps dropping hints of the gold's location. I expect to discover it any day."

Kate didn't speak. What was there to say? His search for gold meant more than she did.

"I wanted the gold for you, honey, to give you all the things I promised."

"I didn't want the damned gold." Her tears burst free as years of pain erupted. Didn't he understand? She'd never wanted him to go in the first place. "I only wanted you."

"Ah, Katie, honey." Her father wrapped her in his arms and the sobs of a young child took over, rising from where Kate had buried them years ago. "I'm sorry, honey," he murmured, rocking her as if she were a little girl once again. "I'm so, so sorry. I've been a fool."

She sobbed until the tears were gone, giving way to hiccups. He hadn't deserted her. He did love her. And he was alive. *Alive!*

Pushing away from his damp shoulder, she gave him a watery smile. "I love you, Daddy."

His cheeks showed signs of tear tracks as well and the grin he returned was equally tremulous. "I'll never leave you again. I promise."

She laughed at that. "Dad, I'm twenty-five years old."

He grimaced. "I guess I'll have to get used to that. I missed so much." His voice dropped as sorrow filled his expression. "So much."

Spotting Robin a few feet away, a grin on his face, Kate went to take his hand. "Dad, this is Robin Goodfellow."

"I know." Philip crossed over to join them. "Titania isn't too pleased with you right now, Robin. For the past few days, she's done nothing but mutter about how you evaded her spell."

Robin shrugged. "She never has liked me much. I take it she's expecting me?"

"I'm supposed to take you to her."

Kate's stomach clenched. "Dad, we can't let her hurt him again. He was in that portrait for two hundred years."

"The portrait at Zelma's?" When Kate nodded, Philip glanced at Robin again. "No wonder you look familiar. And Katie set you free?"

"She was able to see my name written in magic and said it aloud, thus releasing me from my prison." Robin reached out to caress her cheek. "But that didn't break the spell completely. I've not been able to get far from her." His gaze met hers. "Not that I've minded."

"Ah, the Carmichael blood. The sight has been a blessing and a curse to us," Philip said.

Robin frowned. "Has your family always had it?"

"As far as I can remember. It's said we were given the ability for a good deed done for a member of the Fae." Philip shook his head. "I'm not sure it was such a wonderful reward. If I didn't have it, I wouldn't be here now, I wouldn't have left my child for so long."

"I'm not sure I agree with that," Kate said. She glanced at Robin. "Without it, I never would've found Robin." And she wouldn't change that for all the gold in the world.

"I see." Philip sounded thoughtful as he studied the two of them. "Is he important to you then?"

"Very important." Would her father understand her love for Robin? To Philip she was still his little girl and not a grown woman. She gave him a slight smile. They both had adjustments to make.

Philip fixed his gaze on Robin. "Then I hope he's worthy."

"He is." Kate linked her arm through Robin's. Surely her father would help them. If Titania liked him, that could only be to their benefit. "We've come to get Titania to break the spell."

Robin squeezed her arm. "More important, she needs to leave you alone." He turned to Philip. "This queen you've befriended has been trying to kill Kate for the past few weeks."

Her father paled. "Kill her? Why?"

"So I'd be returned to the portrait."

Philip's eyes took on a fierce glow, his lips pressed firmly together. He turned to Kate. "Have you been hurt?"

"I'm fine," she assured him. "We've had some . . . uh . . . adventures, but thanks to Robin the worst I've experienced has been some first rate terror, a sprained ankle, and a drowned car." The car made her angriest.

Nodding, Philip touched Robin's shoulder. "I owe you."

"There is no obligation." Robin sounded strangely stiff. "I would never let any harm come to Kate."

He moved closer to her, yet over her head he exchanged gazes with her father. For several long moments, no one spoke, until Philip smiled. "Then I thank you."

Men. Kate sighed. She loved them both, but certainly didn't understand either of them. "What's next? Can we avoid Titania for a while? Robin wants to see Oberon first."

"I haven't seen Oberon in days," Philip said.

"Does he know I'm free?" Robin asked.

"I doubt it." Philip grimaced. "He was gone when Titania learned about it."

Robin nodded, but Kate sensed his disappointment. Having her father back made her want him to share in that joy. "Where can we find him?" she asked.

"I don't know." Her father shook his head. "He comes and goes as he wishes."

"I'm here."

At the sound of a deep voice, they all turned to see a magnificent specimen of a man standing nearby. Definitely Robin's father. Though he appeared only slightly older, the features were the same, with dark intense eyes and a winning smile. Only this man radiated power in the same way Robin exuded charm and sensuality.

"Wow," Kate murmured. Dealing with one Robin was a heady experience. Dealing with two might overload her senses.

Robin approached the man. "Oberon." He stopped before him. "Father?" he asked with hesitation.

Oberon immediately enveloped him in a bear hug that

lifted Robin's feet off the ground. "My son. It is good to see you again."

"And you." Robin broke into a wide grin.

Kate couldn't stop smiling. She inched closer to her father's side and squeezed his arm. Maybe things would turn out all right after all. She had her father and Robin had his.

As they stepped apart, Oberon and Robin clasped each other's forearm. "Thank the Stones you're free," Oberon said.

"In a manner of speaking." Robin turned to indicate Kate. "Kate freed me, but I'm tied to her now."

He led Oberon over to stand before her. Though not much taller than her, Oberon had an aura that made him appear much larger. He studied her intently. Did he find her lacking?

Kate straightened and met the faerie king's gaze defiantly.

"Your daughter, Philip?" Oberon asked.

"Yes, Your Majesty."

"She's a beautiful woman." Oberon winked at Robin. "But I'm sure you've noticed that, son."

Robin met Kate's gaze, the warmth in his own kindling heat throughout her veins. "Aye, she's beautiful and so much more."

Oberon gave him a strange look that Robin didn't appear to notice, but Kate did. Did the king disapprove of his son's fondness for her? Too bad.

He didn't have to like her to save Robin. "Can you help us with Titania?"

"You don't know what you ask, lass." Oberon patted her cheek as if she were a child and she turned her face away. Maybe she believed things could work out, but that didn't make her stupid.

"Titania has a mind of her own," he continued.

"Well put, husband."

As one they whirled toward the icy tones. Kate's heart rose into her throat as she spotted a beautiful woman clad in a knee-length gown of shimmering material. The gown appeared to be translucent, yet it covered her well, hinting at her secrets. Sexy, very sexy.

She was small, but, like Oberon, appeared taller. A golden, ornate tiara rested on her head. Her brilliant gold hair flowed to her waist in gleaming tresses and her bright sea-blue eyes glowed with power. Definitely someone Kate didn't want to face.

As if she had a choice.

"No one tells me what to do," the woman added, fixing her angry glare on Robin.

Kate gulped. This woman was all she'd feared and more.

Titania.

Damn.

Nineteen

Robin exhaled a slow breath. So much for delaying their meeting. He viewed Titania with distaste, but followed the dictates of protocol. Dropping to one knee before her, he brought her fingers to his lips and bestowed a brief kiss.

Her gaze revealed her hate and anger and his heart sank. He wasn't likely to emerge from this clash any better than their last encounter. Grasping the circlet, he raised it in both hands and presented it to her.

"Your lost circlet, Your Majesty."

"My circlet." Her voice softened slightly as she took it. "Not lost, but given away as a trinket to some mortal whore." She fixed her hard gaze on Oberon, then returned it to Robin. "I suppose you think I will listen to you now. Only if I so desire."

He remained kneeling, unable to rise until she bid him to do so. No doubt this pleased her. She would like nothing better than to have him at her beck and call, but she'd learned at their first meeting that he would have none of that. He might be a bastard, but he was *Oberon's* son.

"Your Majesty, if I might make a request."

That he dared to speak obviously offended her, for she

didn't reply. Instead, she turned away. "I wish to sit." She headed for her throne, then paused and waved her hand at Robin. "Come."

Biting his tongue, Robin stood and glanced back at Kate. Her father had his arm around her shoulders. Good. From the expression on her face, Robin knew she wanted to be beside him. His courageous Kate. She would intervene if she could and that would only invite Titania's wrath. She needed to stay as far away from Titania as possible.

He nodded at Philip. They had achieved an understanding during their brief meeting. They both cared about Kate and would protect her with their lives, if necessary. When Philip gave a curt jerk of his head in reply, Robin eased a sigh of relief and followed Titania to her throne.

His spirits rose when Oberon came to his side. "Be strong, my son."

"I will." Aye, he had to be strong. He had too much to lose.

Titania placed herself on her rock-hewn throne—all the easier to look down on him. Robin had been surprised upon first meeting the queen to discover she was extremely petite. But she radiated power in waves. He knew now just how much power.

His courage strengthened when Oberon placed a quick kiss on her cheek, then lounged on his throne at her side. He would help if he could, but the burden rested on Robin. His future—his life—would be decided today.

This time he waited to speak, but held himself tall, refusing to flinch beneath her imperious stare. She wouldn't intimidate him or push him into foolish words. He had to obtain his freedom . . . for himself, for Kate.

"You didn't bring your portrait this time," she said finally.

"No, Your Majesty." He'd learned from his mistakes.

She waited, as if baiting him to say more, but he remained silent. His anger had brought about his punishment before. He intended to think more clearly this time.

"You said you have a request?" She looked down her slender nose at him.

"Yes, Your Majesty." He took one step closer. "If I may?"

When she nodded, he drew a deep breath. "I respectfully ask Your Majesty if you would be so kind as to remove the spell you placed upon me."

"It appears to me you removed it yourself." Anger vibrated beneath her words and Robin hesitated. He had to choose his reply carefully.

"Not in its entirety, Your Majesty. Your magic is much too powerful for that. I am now tied to the mortal who released me. If you would graciously remove the spell, we could lead our separate lives."

"Why would I want to do that?" Her smile held no warmth. "It could prove amusing to have you forced to live as a mortal and suffer through their tiresome existence."

"I've done that most of my life, Your Majesty. It is not the inconvenience you would want it to be."

"But what about when your mortal dies? What happens then?"

Robin heard an exclamation behind him, quickly cut off. He didn't dare look around. Philip had to keep Kate quiet. The less Titania noticed her, the better.

"I presume I would return to the portrait," Robin said.

"Did you enjoy your stay in there, Robin Goodfellow? Was it fun to watch others and not be able to participate?" Mockery coated her words.

"It was unbearable." He struggled to keep his voice even, despite the overwhelming memories of that time. If not for the small pleasure of watching Kate mature from a young girl into a lovely woman, he would've surely gone insane. "As I'm certain you well know."

She descended from the throne and circled him. Pausing in front of him, she reached up to stroke his cheek. "You are very charming, young Robin. I've heard tales of your prowess through the years. I'm certain you'd like to charm me into doing your bidding."

Robin kept his gaze straight ahead, fighting the urge to shake off her touch. "I wouldn't dare try, Your Majesty." Her magic was much more powerful than his.

"You remind me of your father long ago." She patted his cheek until he met her gaze. "Will you share my bed and pleasure me as he can? Will you try to charm me into giving you your freedom there?"

She made her point clear. What better way to degrade him and insult his father? If Robin bedded her, lowered himself to pleasuring her, she'd remove the spell. But he couldn't . . . wouldn't. To do so would betray everything he'd shared with Kate.

He almost laughed. At one time, making love to a woman had been as natural as breathing, but that was before Kate. "No, Your Majesty."

Her pat changed to a slap that knocked his head to the side. She whirled around and stalked to her throne. "Very well, I'll remove the spell."

Robin stared at her, stunned. Had he heard correctly?

"I need to come up with something more creative," she continued. "That last spell was too easily undone." She darted a glance at Oberon.

Terror wrapped its tendrils around Robin. Being in the portrait had been torture beyond anything he could imagine. What did she intend to do to him now?

He drew in a deep breath. *So be it.* "Will you return the mortal to her home?" As long as Kate was unharmed, he would endure whatever he had to.

"Of course. I have no use for her."

Thank the Stones.

"Just who the hell do you think you are?"

Robin flinched at hearing Kate's angry voice and turned to see her running toward them, her father in pursuit. Robin hurried to catch her shoulders, forcing her to face him. "Kate, no."

She wrenched away and stalked to the front of the throne to face Titania. "Robin has done nothing to you. He can't help it if his father gave away your circlet. You've no right to blame him."

Her eyes blazed with fury. Robin allowed himself a brief moment of admiration. Not only beautiful but brave.

And, unfortunately, foolish.

Titania had agreed to set her free. If Kate continued to antagonize the queen . . . "Kate—"

"Continue." Titania's voice was deceptively calm. Robin noticed the glimmer of anger in her eyes and his chest tightened. If he threw Kate over his shoulder now as he wanted, the queen wouldn't let them go.

Kate needed no encouragement. "You were wrong to cage Robin in a portrait. You were wrong to try to kill me and put him back there."

"I am never wrong." Titania rose to her feet. "I am Queen of the Fae."

"That doesn't make you God."

"Doesn't it?" The queen descended a step so her gaze was even with Kate's.

"You have no right to manipulate people's lives like that. What did Robin do to you? All he wants is to see his father. You must be pretty insecure if you have to forbid even that most basic instinct."

Sparks danced in the air around Titania. Robin groaned. Time to grab Kate and run. Not that he'd get far. He inched closer to her.

"*Insecure?*" Titania's voice rose with every syllable. "I trust you do not wish to return to your home, mortal."

"I do, but I refuse to stand by and let you put another spell on Robin." Kate raised her chin defiantly. "He doesn't deserve it."

"He deserves to *die*," Titania shouted. "He's an atrocity among the Fae and should be destroyed. But since I can't kill him, you'll have to do."

Robin anticipated her actions and threw himself at Kate, knocking her to the ground seconds before bolts of lightning shot from Titania's fingertips to where Kate had stood. "You should've kept quiet," he murmured, holding Kate tight.

"I can't let her do that to you." Despite her trembling, Kate met his gaze as they sat up. "I can't."

Her eyes held such warmth, such caring that his chest ached. "Sweet Kate."

"Titania."

They looked up at hearing Kate's father speak. He stood before the queen, his hands outstretched, palms up. "I beg of you not to harm my daughter."

"Your daughter?" She looked at him in surprise. "Your *daughter* needs to learn to control her temper."

A good lesson for Titania as well. Robin kept his arms around Kate as they stood, but the queen's attention stayed on Philip.

"She grew up while I was away," he replied. "You never told me of the difference in time between your world and mine."

"Didn't I?" Her pretense at innocence didn't fool Robin. He doubted it fooled Philip either. "An oversight, of course."

"Of course," Philip said quietly. "She speaks from the heart, Your Majesty. After all, you've been trying to kill her." He curled his hands into fists, the only outward sign of his obvious internal rage. "Surely she has reason to be upset."

"And would you die in her place, Philip?" The coldness on her face indicated this was no casual question.

He didn't hesitate. "Yes."

She stretched her arms toward him and Kate nearly leapt from Robin's hold. "Daddy, no."

To Robin's surprise, Titania lowered her arms. "I don't want to kill you, Philip. I want to kill *her*. *She* is the one who has insulted me."

She swung toward Kate and Robin quickly stood between them. "That is not an option," he said firmly. "Not now, not ever." He glanced at Oberon. Why wasn't his father doing something? Though the king watched them closely through narrowed eyes, he remained reclining on his throne.

An evil smile appeared on Titania's lips. "Ah, now the real Robin emerges. I knew you couldn't stay servile for long."

"Not around you, Titania." He dropped all pretense of respect. "It's not in my nature."

"Ah, yes, that tainted mortal blood."

"No doubt." If being Fae meant he had to spend eternity kowtowing to her, he'd rather be mortal.

Kate stepped around him to face the throne and he thrust his arm in front of her. What was she doing? Hadn't she learned how volatile the queen could be?

"Titania." Kate bit her lip. "Your Majesty. All we're asking is for you to remove the spell on Robin, then we'll go back to my world and you'll never have to see us again."

"A tempting proposition." Titania appeared to consider the idea, but Robin already knew she'd dismiss it. "But I'd still know he was out there somewhere."

"Please." Kate's voice quivered, making Robin want to pull her into his embrace.

The queen lounged back on her throne. "You sound like you care for this misfit."

"I . . ." Kate glanced at Robin with an emotion in her eyes that tugged at his heart and stole his breath. "He's my friend."

"Friend?" Though Titania appeared at ease, Robin waited for her to pounce. She was obviously playing with Kate. "A good friend?"

"Yes."

"Good enough that you plead his case, risk my wrath for his freedom?" That had already been answered by Kate's actions, but the queen waited for Kate to nod. "Good enough that you would die to ensure his freedom?"

Kate hesitated only a moment. "If that's what it takes."

"No!" Robin whirled on her and grabbed her shoulders. The thought of Kate sacrificing herself filled him with agony. He'd rather spend eternity as a rock than have her lose one moment of her life. He inhaled sharply, compounding the ache in his chest. By the Stones, he *did* love her.

"No," he repeated more quietly but with the same forcefulness. "I won't allow you to do that."

Familiar defiance blazed in her eyes. "I don't see where it's your choice."

"If you sacrificed yourself for me, I'd spend the rest of

my life in a living hell." His voice grew deeper with each word. "Is that what you want?"

"Sounds perfect to me," Titania said

Robin didn't look at her. He cupped Kate's cheek with his hand. "Kate?"

Her eyes watered, but the tears didn't fall. She met his gaze. "And I can't bear to think of you in a portrait for eternity."

Pulling her into his arms, Robin swallowed the thick lump in his throat. Now that he'd found the one woman he never believed could exist for him, Titania would ensure they were separated . . . one way or another.

"Titania, enough of this foolishness." Oberon spoke up, the power in his voice filling the grove, and Robin glanced at his father. Could he help? Or would his interference now only make his wife angrier? "You've had your fun with Robin and his friend, now remove the spell and be done with it."

"Foolishness?" She rounded on the king. "Robin deserved his punishment for his disrespectful treatment of me. I am Queen of the Fae, his sovereign, whether he chooses to acknowledge it or not."

"I agree Robin spoke hastily when last he was here, but you have to remember he's spent his entire life among mortals. He has learned since then." Oberon's tone became soothing. "And the mortal woman knows nothing of our ways. Tolerance is called for."

Titania jerked her head away to focus on Robin and Kate again. "Tolerance? Of a mortal and a half-breed? You ask much, husband."

"And I will make it worth your while, wife." Sensuality oozed thick in his words.

Tapping her finger against her lips, Titania said nothing for several long minutes. As he waited, Robin's heart beat in rhythm with Kate's and he tried to memorize her every detail . . . the feel of her in his arms, the scent that was uniquely Kate, the days and nights spent together.

"I am due a penance," the queen said finally. "They have both treated me abominably."

"One penance," Oberon added.

Someone would suffer this day. Robin closed his eyes briefly. And he would not let it be Kate.

"Perhaps I could keep the mortal woman as a servant." Titania tilted her head, studying Kate. "She looks strong. I would have to remove her ability to speak, though. She's much too outspoken."

"No, Your Majesty." Philip stepped forward and went to one knee before the throne. "If you need a servant, then use me. We have formed a friendship. Would that not be more pleasant?"

"Hmmm."

"No, Daddy." Kate jerked free of Robin's hold and ran to her father.

Robin followed her and faced Titania. "This is all for naught, isn't it? We both know what you want." A chill spread through his veins. "I will be your servant, my queen, at your beck and call for the rest of eternity."

As Titania's eyes lit up, Robin forced himself to bow. "However," he added as he straightened, "Kate and her father must be returned home without any fear of retribution."

Titania stood, her smile sealing his doom. "So be it." She laughed. "To have you as my servant will be very amusing. Perhaps you will finally lose your proud ways."

"Robin, don't." Kate caught his hand and he turned, then flinched at the anguish in her face.

"I have to." He squeezed her palm. "This is the only thing that will satisfy her."

"But—"

Touching his finger to her lips, he silenced her protest. "At least I'll be free." He grimaced. "More or less."

"Stand before me, Robin Goodfellow," Titania ordered.

With a sad smile at Kate, he complied. His future would belong to the queen, but he didn't mind as long as Kate went home, free from Titania's attempts on her life.

The queen extended her arms and murmured several words

quickly. At once a confining heat enveloped Robin. He couldn't breathe . . . couldn't move. The world blurred around him. He didn't remember it being like this before. Had she tricked him? Was he doomed to something worse than a portrait?

As suddenly as the heat arrived, it disappeared. Robin glanced around him, amazed to find nothing had changed. Kate stood nearby, her expression concerned, her father beside her. The throne with Titania and Oberon sat before him.

"The spell is gone." Titania descended the steps and offered her hand to him. "Now I must have your pledge."

He didn't dare look at Kate. Dropping to one knee, Robin again brought Titania's fingers to his lips. "I pledge my life to Your Majesty to serve you to the best of my ability for as long as you desire it."

"Very good." Her smile promised he would soon regret his words. "Now to return the mortals to their miserable, short existence."

Robin bolted to his feet. "Titania, Your Majesty, may I have a few minutes with Kate first?" Things were happening too fast. He had much he needed to say. He couldn't let Kate leave without telling her how much she meant to him. "Please?"

The queen glanced from him to Kate, her expression revealing nothing. Finally she nodded. "I am feeling gracious. A few minutes only."

"Thank you, Your Majesty." Robin didn't waste time. He executed a precise bow, then snared Kate's hand and led her away from the thrones.

When he stopped, she seized his forearm. "Robin, don't do this."

"It's already done." He'd sealed his life sentence with his own words.

"But I'm the one who mouthed off at her."

He had to smile. "This time. During my first visit, I was very arrogant and said some things I shouldn't have, worse things than you dared to speak. She wants me to be punished for that, Kate. It's me she hates."

"I'm sorry." She looked down. "I ruined everything."

"No." Reaching out, he lifted her chin. "This is better than I had expected. I can live with this." Though living without Kate might prove more difficult.

"I'm not sure I can." Her voice wavered, tearing at his already aching heart.

"We knew from the beginning this would happen." Though knowing it and facing the reality were two different things. "But I don't regret one moment of our time together. You taught me more about mortals than anyone else during the centuries I lived among them." And more about himself.

Her eyes watered. "And you taught me, too. I know who I am now. I don't need anyone else's approval to feel worthy."

"Kate." He groaned her name. "Sweet Kate." Unable to resist, he pulled her close and kissed her, trying to convey his love with his lips. She tasted sweet, her response as frantic as his own. Her body fit his perfectly. He never wanted to let her go.

"Your time is over." Titania interrupted his bliss and Robin looked around. Not yet. He still had more to say. "Tell your mortal good-bye," she added.

Even as Titania spoke, Kate started to disappear, her eyes wide. "I love you," she said quickly. She clung to him as long as possible.

"I lo—" Before he could finish, she was gone. Agony pierced him. Would she know what he'd waited too long to say? What he'd failed to realize until it was too late?

Clenching his fists, he went to face Titania, struggling to keep his tone calm despite the trembling in his limbs and the resentment simmering deep inside. "Couldn't you have waited a few more minutes?"

"Why? So you could vow your undying love?" Titania laughed and reclined on her throne again. "Your words would've been soon forgotten."

Kate wouldn't forget. Robin narrowed his eyes. Unless . . . "What do you mean?"

Wicked humor danced in Titania's eyes as she leaned forward. "You wouldn't want your mortal to suffer, would you? Not when you care so much about her. I merely altered the memories of both the woman and Philip." Her smile indicated how much she enjoyed telling him this.

"She won't remember her time here," she said. "In fact, she won't remember that you even existed."

Twenty

Robin staggered back. Not remember him? Would Kate forget all she'd learned about appreciating herself and her beauty? Would she forget the nights they spent together?

"No," he whispered.

"Yes." Titania obviously enjoyed his pain. Her malicious smile broadened. "Don't you agree it's better for her this way?"

He couldn't agree . . . not now, not with a fist squeezing his heart.

"Now she can find some mortal man and settle down with him, give him whining mortal babies."

That image didn't help. Robin wanted to be the one to touch Kate, to make love to her, to silence her cries of passion with his lips. He wanted to share the miracle of birth with her. He turned away, desperate to be alone.

"I desire some fresh raspberries, Robin. Fetch me some."

Glancing over his shoulder, he bit back his first reply. So his sentence began. "Very well, Your Majesty."

He hurried away. Reaching into the prickly bushes for berries couldn't compare to his current agony. The berries grew by the stream that meandered through this part of the realm and he walked slowly in that direction.

"I'm sorry, son." Oberon appeared by his side and matched Robin's strides.

Robin whirled on him. "Why didn't you speak up sooner? Things might be different."

"I knew what Titania wanted, what it would take to pacify her. So did you." Oberon touched Robin's shoulder. "I would not have allowed her to harm your friend."

"She erased Kate's memory." Maybe that didn't constitute physical harm to Kate, but it pained Robin. A lot.

"She has to get in her little twists."

"Maybe she's right." Robin hated to consider that possibility. "Maybe Kate is better off not remembering." He sighed. "But I wanted her to remember me, to remember what we shared."

Perhaps he was being selfish. Yet to think all that he and Kate had been through could be erased so easily burned in his gut.

"You love her very much."

It was a statement more than a question, but Robin nodded.

"I didn't know I could love." He sighed. "Then I met Kate."

Oberon remained silent as they wound their way through the forest. "I know I am limited in the battle between you and Titania, but can I help somehow?"

Send me to be with her. But Oberon couldn't. Titania's magic equaled his and couldn't be so easily undone. Besides, Robin had given his pledge. "No," he finally replied.

Robin froze in mid-step as an idea emerged. "Yes, there is one thing you could do." One thing that would help Kate even if she didn't remember him.

"Name it."

Robin met his father's gaze. "Find Nana's will for Kate." He could, at least, do this for her.

Clasping Robin's forearm in the standard greeting, Oberon grinned. "Consider it done."

• • •

Kate awakened in her bed, strangely disoriented. Blinking, she glanced at the clock. Oh, no, she was late for work!

Sliding from the bed, she paused halfway to the bathroom. Wait, it was spring break. Or was it? For some reason, she couldn't recall which day it was. Time seemed jumbled somehow.

She clicked on the radio and crawled back under the covers to sit as she listened. Friday? It was Friday already? Where had the week gone? The last day she remembered was . . . was at school. The field day. An accident with Timmy Robinson. She'd been hurt. Was that why her mind felt so foggy?

Apparently, her injuries had been minor as nothing hurt. She rested her chin on her bent knees. No, something hurt, but she couldn't say exactly what. Her chest ached as if she had lost something important.

Of course, Nana's house. That was it.

Or was it?

Kate glanced around her bedroom. Everything looked familiar, yet different as if something was missing. How odd.

With a shrug, she rose and dressed for the day in jeans and a sweater that fit her like a glove and accented her hair color. Facing her reflection, she nodded. Not bad.

She emerged from her bedroom as a man stepped out of the adjoining room. For a moment her vision blurred as if she expected to see someone different, but the face escaped her. Still she knew this man, but had never expected to see him again. "Daddy." Her heart leapt.

He was alive? When had he returned? When she was hurt?

"Katie, honey." He came to hug her fiercely. "I'm sorry for taking so long to return."

Her eyes watered. For some reason the anger she expected didn't rise. Her father was home, alive. That was all that mattered. She tightened the hug. "As long as you're here now. I've missed you so much."

"Not half as much as I've missed you." He stepped back

and glanced around the room. "And now you're all grown up. Is this your place?"

"Such as it is." She motioned for him to follow her into the kitchen. Coffee. She definitely needed coffee. "When did you arrive?" Why couldn't she remember something as important as that?

Philip hesitated. "Last night, I think."

"Are you having trouble remembering things, too?" Kate glanced at him as she prepared the coffee maker.

"Things are hazy. I can't picture places and times."

"Don't you remember returning home?" Why would they both be so confused?

He shook his head. "I have a vague memory of seeing you, of realizing how much I've missed." He sighed and sat at the small kitchen table. "I feel as if I have a wall in my mind. I don't even remember where I've been."

"You've been gone for twelve years, Dad." How could he not remember any of it?

"Twelve years?" He stared at her, then dropped his head onto his hands. "Dear God, Twelve years."

She squeezed his shoulder. "I'm sure you'll remember something soon." But would she? Why was her brain so foggy?

"At least, I'm home now." He covered her hand with his own.

"Good." For years she'd longed for her father to return. Now that he had, why didn't she feel more ecstatic? Happiness danced through her veins, yet something tempered it with a heavy dose of depression.

Listening to the steady drip of the pot, she studied him. He certainly didn't look twelve years older though. "Wherever you were you didn't age much." She grinned. Maybe he'd stumbled onto Shangri-La. "You hardly look older than me."

"Maybe I should have my temples grayed." Philip smiled at her and Kate laughed, then caught herself as if laughing were a betrayal. A betrayal of what?

"Are you okay?"

"I don't know." She shook her head. "I feel scatterbrained as if I'm forgetting something very important."

"Maybe you're not getting enough sleep."

"Maybe." Hell, she couldn't even recall going to bed last night. This was bad. Maybe she should see a doctor. Had she hurt her head in the accident? She vaguely recalled being in the hospital, the pain in her head, then hands touching her and making the pain go away. Whose hands?

The coffee finished and she poured two cups, gave one to her father, then drank as fast as the temperature would allow. She felt more awake, but not any more clear-headed.

Philip peered at her over the rim of his mug. "What are your plans for today?"

"I'm not sure I should go anywhere. I'd probably get lost." Recalling the pile of clothes in her room, she grimaced. "Laundry, I think. There's a facility in the building."

"Now that's exciting."

"And you? Want to help?"

"Actually, I thought I'd go job hunting." He stared into his coffee.

"Really?" Hope bloomed. "No more faerie gold?"

"No more. I think it's more important I stick around my little girl for a while."

Her smile wavered slightly. "Thank you, Dad." To have her father back made up for losing Nana's home, yet still didn't fill the aching hole in her heart. Why?

What was wrong with her?

Philip departed to find a newspaper and start his job search and Kate gathered the dirty clothes into a basket. Some items were missing. How could she have lost them?

Pausing at her dresser, she touched a small pink shell lying on a doily. Why couldn't she remember where it came from? More important, why did seeing it make her feel so melancholy?

With a sigh, she trudged to the laundry room, thankful to find it empty. For all she knew, she might be losing her grip on sanity. Was she dangerous?

Loading the clothing into a washing machine, she automatically turned everything right side out and checked pockets before tossing each article in. She jammed her hand into the pocket on a pair of jeans, then hesitated as she encountered slippery plastic.

A bag.

She pulled it out and stared at the insignia on the plastic. Disney World? When had she ever been to Disney World?

Her hand trembled as she reached inside the bag, almost as if she expected the contents to bite her. She withdrew two photographs and gaped at them. It was her with . . . with . . . Robin.

Memories erupted in her mind with the force of an explosion, knocking her to the floor. She gripped her head, her breathing rapid as she fought to withstand the pain—both mental and physical. Images flashed through her brain— Robin appearing behind her, dancing, kissing, making love.

She remembered. She remembered everything.

"Oh, my God." Closing her eyes, she rested her head against the cool wall. Titania had sent Kate back and kept Robin as her slave. He was gone.

Forever.

Now the gaping wound in her heart made sense. Tears trickled down her face and Kate wrapped her arms around herself, allowing the sorrow over the loss of the only man she would ever love.

When the sobs ceased, she swiped at her damp cheeks and rose to her feet. She wasn't going to spend her life in tears. Robin wouldn't want that. He'd expect her to get on with her life even if he wasn't in it.

And maybe she would.

But not anytime soon.

After filling the washer, she climbed back to her apartment and walked through the rooms, each filled with precious memories. No wonder it seemed so empty. Robin's vitality was missing.

She dropped onto the couch where he'd once cuddled her on his lap and kissed her senseless. "Damn." Her bottom lip quivered and she fought back the urge to cry again. No more.

She was a stronger person now. The least she could do for
Robin was use the confidence and sense of worth he'd given
her.

A short rap on the door brought her to her feet in an
instant. Had Titania relented and let Robin return? Kate
threw open the door, then grimaced upon spotting Adam.
"What do *you* want?" His attempt to have her arrested destroyed any lingering warmth she'd had for him.

"Can I come in?"

In response, she stepped back and held the door open. He
limped inside and she noticed he wore a black, knee-height
foam boot on his right leg. "What happened?"

He looked chagrined. "I tripped getting out of my car and
broke my ankle."

Kate bit back a smile. Robin's punishment, no doubt. "I'm
sorry," she lied.

Stepping aside, Adam motioned two men to come in after
him. They carried a large rectangular object covered in
brown paper that they rested against the wall. Kate's heart
skipped a beat and she glanced at Adam in surprise.

He waited for the men to leave before he spoke. "I owe
you an apology."

Taken aback, Kate raised her eyebrows. "Do you?"

"We found Nana's revised will. She'd put it in an envelope
to mail to her attorney and it slipped behind the bureau in
the entryway. I found the letter when I sold the bureau."

Kate's breath caught in her throat. "And?"

"She didn't leave you the house."

"What?" That didn't make sense. Why would Nana make
a new will if not to leave her the house?

"For some reason she wanted you to have the portrait over
the fireplace. Said you'd appreciate it most."

The portrait. Kate crossed over to it and tore open the
brown wrapping, her hands shaking. Robin's face peered
back at her and she gasped. Yes, she would appreciate this
more than anyone else.

"However, I've since had everything appraised for sale
and we learned more about this portrait. I can't believe it's

sat over the fireplace for all these years." Adam sank into a nearby chair and stuck his leg out in front of him. "It's an original by Thomas Gainsborough."

She'd heard the name but couldn't place it. "Who?"

"He's the artist of *The Blue Boy*."

Oh, she did know that painting. Glancing at the portrait, she grinned. Robin's friend Tommy. Of course.

"That portrait is worth thousands of dollars, Kate. I'd like to suggest a swap. I'll sign over the house to you in exchange for that painting."

"No." Kate didn't need to consider that offer. Robin meant more to her than any house.

Adam's eyes widened. "Do you understand what I'm saying? I'll give you the house."

"I understand." She touched Robin's face. "But Nana was right. This painting is very, very important to me."

"And what do you intend to do with it? Display it in this elegant apartment?" Adam waved his hand at her tiny quarters in disdain.

"Exactly that." She'd never sell it. She couldn't. Turning to face Adam, she extended her hand. "Thank you for bringing it, Adam."

He stood unsteadily. "You're crazy, Kate."

"Maybe so, but I won't give up this painting." She didn't expect him to understand.

Limping to the door, he paused with his hand on the frame. "Last chance, Kate."

"Thank you, Adam, but no."

Muttering to himself, he stalked out of the apartment, slamming the door after him.

Kate didn't hesitate to remove the rest of the paper until Robin's image faced her, the twinkle in his eyes so familiar she half expected him to step out of it. "Robin Goodfellow," she said at once. She had to try it. When nothing happened, she spoke louder. "Robin Goodfellow."

Still nothing.

Of course not. Robin wasn't imprisoned there this time.

Now he worked as a servant for the Queen of the Fae. For eternity.

And Kate was stuck here in her world.

Without him.

"My feet ache. Massage them." Titania ordered.

"Yes, Your Majesty." Robin bent to the task, which was no better or worse than those he'd completed since turning his life over to the queen.

"You've been too cooperative, half-breed." Titania nudged him with her foot. "I expected more rebellion."

"It's not worth it," Robin muttered. Since Kate's departure a few days ago, he'd found it difficult to summon any resistance to the queen's outrageous orders. What did they matter? What did anything matter? Without Kate in his life, he no longer eagerly approached each day as a new adventure.

Nearly three months would've passed in the mortal world. Time was slipping away. What was Kate doing?

"Have I broken you already?" Titania laughed. "I had no idea it would be so easy."

Robin didn't answer. What could he say? Losing Kate had ripped his life apart. Nothing Titania could do would equal that.

Titania kicked him suddenly, knocking him back to the ground. Looking at her, he kept his expression bland. "Does that mean I'm finished?"

"Oooo." She glared at him. "Go. Get out of my sight."

Climbing to his feet, Robin bowed. "Yes, Your Majesty." He hurried into the forest, seeking the quiet spot beside the stream where he liked to sit when the queen didn't claim his time.

But even that didn't help him find peace of mind.

If he were truly magical, couldn't he have found a way to appease Titania and be with Kate? What good was magical charm when the one person he wanted to charm was a dimension away? With the Fae immune to his magic, he was every bit as helpless as a mortal in this world.

He'd come originally to find his father and Oberon's presence was the only thing that made living here bearable. Robin couldn't recall why he'd once wanted to stay here. One day among the humans held more excitement, more feelings than an eternity here.

Standing, he grabbed a rock and hurled it into the stream. "By the Stones, I've been a fool."

"Nice to hear you admit it." Oberon emerged from the trees. "You're learning."

"Learning?" Robin didn't keep the derision from his voice. "What? What I am and am not?"

"Exactly." Oberon reclined on the rock. "That's all I ever wanted you to learn. It's what you *had* to learn."

Robin sank down beside his father in disbelief. "But what about the mission you gave me?"

Oberon shrugged. "Something to keep you busy. I've always been proud of you, Robin."

"To keep me busy?" Robin had spent most of his life worrying whether he'd done as Oberon would've wanted. And it was only to keep him busy? "I thought it was a mission, that I had to please you."

"You've more than met my expectations in regard to that. I only wanted you to be aware of the good and evil in humans. For a reason, Robin. You've never been comfortable in your own skin. You lived a mortal life, but considered yourself a member of the Fae." He met Robin's gaze. "Which are you?"

"I wish I knew." Robin spoke before he thought, then hesitated. He did know. His heart had made that decision for him. "I'm much too charming for my own good." He winced at saying that. Titania had told him much the same thing.

"I can do some special things, but in my heart I'm a man," he continued. "I don't belong here. I once thought I did, but now I know my life is among the mortals."

Oberon sighed. "I suspected as much. Your affinity with them is more than anyone here has experienced. Except maybe Nic."

"You're not disappointed?" Robin searched his father's face for a sign of his feelings.

"No. Our paths are not the same. I am Oberon, King of the Fae. These are my people. This is my land. I go among mortals for amusement, nothing more." He smiled. "It is not the same for you."

"True." Robin's life belonged among the humans . . . and with Kate. Grasping for hope, he caught Oberon's shoulder. "Is there a way I can return?"

When Oberon didn't answer, Robin tightened his grip. "Is there?"

"Titania will never agree to let you return." His father began slowly. "Not without a penalty."

"What does that mean?"

"There is only one way this idea may achieve success."

Robin waited, unable to look away. "And?"

"You would have to give up your immortality." Oberon placed his hand over Robin's. "You'd be truly a mortal."

Dropping his hand, Robin blinked in surprise. He hadn't thought it possible. "Mortal? Can I? Would I . . . ?"

Oberon grimaced. "Being half mortal, it is a possibility, but you would live a limited life, my son, age, and die as all mortals do."

That idea didn't frighten Robin as much as he expected. He'd seen too much during the past centuries. All he wanted—really wanted—was to share Kate's life with her. If that meant becoming mortal, then he'd do it.

"I'm willing," he said with certainty.

"Think carefully. Your friend will have no memory of you."

"She loved me once. I'll convince her to do so again." He had to believe that. Somehow, some way.

"You'll no longer have your magic. You can't charm her."

Robin smiled sadly. "I didn't charm her before." Kate had cared for him all on her own.

"Then you are certain?" Oberon rose to his feet and Robin followed.

"Yes." On impulse, Robin hugged his father. "I'll miss you, but I have to do this."

"I know." Oberon returned the embrace, then rested his

hand on Robin's shoulder. "Wait until this evening when Titania and I are at the grove. Make your petition then and play along with what I say."

"Thank you." Robin swallowed, then forced a smile. He wouldn't wait until too late again to speak. "I love you, Father."

Oberon blinked several times, then squeezed Robin's shoulder. "And I you, son." With a slight smile, he turned toward the forest. "I will see you anon, Robin Goodfellow."

"Anon," he replied. Clenching his fists, Robin paced the shoreline, gathering the words he would need to address Titania. This had to work.

By the time he approached the twin thrones at dusk, his nerves were drawn tight. One wrong word would keep him here forever.

Dropping to one knee before Titania, he bowed his head. "Your Majesty, I beg an audience."

"Rise." Interest filled Titania's face. Perhaps she enjoyed their sparring. "What do you have to ask of me?"

"If it pleases Your Majesty, I request you free me from my pledge and return me to the mortal world." He'd worked on these words all day.

To his surprise, his father answered. "No, impossible. I won't allow it."

Robin faced Oberon. "May I ask why?" He hadn't expected this.

"The only way to release you from your pledge and return you is to make you mortal. It's unthinkable."

"Mortal? A good-for-nothing, limited mortal?" Titania seized the idea. "But what if he wants to go, Oberon?"

"He's my son. I won't ask him to suffer in that manner."

Robin watched the interchange with interest. Now he understood his father's actions. If Oberon was against it, then Titania would want it even more.

"It's my decision, Sire," Robin said firmly. "I am willing to give up my immortality and magic in order to return."

Gasps from the other Fae standing nearby amused him. Obviously, they couldn't imagine why he'd be so foolish.

But he doubted any of them had ever experienced real love either. Aside from the bond of royalty keeping Oberon and Titania together, most Fae rarely shared anything more than brief liaisons.

"As a mortal you'll die," Titania said, revealing a certain amount of pleasure. "You'll never bother me again."

Robin inclined his head. "True, Your Majesty." That was, undoubtedly, a good selling point. One he had thought about at length. He would grow old—something he'd once dreaded. But if he could age with Kate, he wouldn't mind.

Her eyes lit up. "If he is willing to accept the consequences, then we must honor his request, husband."

"I am against it." Oberon winked at Robin. "But I will not refuse him."

"Then it is done." Titania stood. "I hereby release you from your pledge, Robin Goodfellow." She gave an evil laugh that sent chills over Robin's skin. "And I condemn you to the pitifully short existence of a mortal."

He shivered. Now to return to Kate. To convince her to love him again.

"Robin."

He turned to see Oberon holding a bag in his outstretched hand. "Take this to start you on your new life."

Robin bowed his head. "Thank you, Father."

Oberon smiled. "We'll meet again. Perhaps I need to visit the mortal world more often."

Knowing that helped. "I will look forward to it." Robin faced Titania again. "I'm ready."

Tensing, he centered his thoughts on Kate. Would the transformation hurt? The world spun around him and he closed his eyes. Would he be different? Suppose Kate had loved him only for his magic and immortality. What if she didn't like him as a mere mortal? What if . . . ?

The spinning gripped him despite his closed eyes. He was falling, tumbling. Then he knew nothing but blackness.

Returning to her childhood habit, Kate spoke to Robin's portrait as she set the dining room table. The painting dominated the wall more easily than it did at Nana's, but she didn't mind. His presence reassured her.

"And I'm going to night school now that Dad found a job," she continued. "I'm going to get my teaching degree one way or another." She paused to gaze into Robin's eyes. "I hope you're proud of me."

Her father entered the apartment and set down his briefcase. "*I'm* proud of you. Does that count?"

She went to kiss his cheek. "Of course it does."

"But you still ask that painting."

"I've explained it to you, Dad." Time and time again.

"But I don't remember him. Not at all. Why should you regain your memory and not me?"

Kate returned to viewing the portrait. "I don't know. Perhaps because I knew him longer, because he means more to me. I love him, Dad."

"You can't moon over him forever, Katie. It's been three months since we returned. That fella down the hall has asked you out twice, but you keep refusing him."

"I'm not interested in dating right now." Now that men found her attractive, she didn't care.

"When then?" Without waiting for an answer, Philip moved into the kitchen.

"Possibly never," she murmured. She could never love anyone like Robin.

The doorbell rang, but before she could turn, her father called out, "I'll get it."

She continued to face the painting. "What are you doing right now? Slaving for Titania?"

"Actually, I'm looking at the most beautiful woman in the world."

Kate's stomach dropped. She knew that voice, recognized the laughter in it. She turned slowly, hoping, yet fearing what she'd see.

Robin stood just inside the doorway, watching her intently. Kate blinked. It couldn't be. She stepped forward. "Robin?"

His familiar smile appeared. "You remember me?"

"No one, not even Titania, could stop me." She flung her

arms around his neck as he came to hold her tight. "I've missed you so much."

"Not as much as I've missed you." Robin ran his hand over her hair, staring at her as if he couldn't believe it. She knew that feeling. "I love you, sweet Kate."

Her heart leapt in her chest as she accepted his kiss, melding as close to him as their clothing would allow. Their lips met, promised, teased.

In the distance, she dimly heard her father's voice. "I . . . ah . . . I think I'll catch a movie."

The click of the front door penetrated her senses and Kate grinned at Robin. "You came back."

"I had to." Reaching into his pocket, Robin withdrew a ring similar to Titania's circlet and Kate glanced at him wide-eyed. "Don't worry. I had this one made here."

He took her hand and posed with the ring over her finger. "Will you marry me, Kate? Be my wife for the rest of our lives?"

Joy exploded within her and she opened her mouth to reply at once, but he held up his hand. "There's something you should know first." He inhaled deeply. "I'm mortal now. I have no magic. My life span has become finite."

Her joy dissipated. "Mortal? Why? How?" Sudden realization dawned and she stepped back in horror. "Did you do this for me?"

"No." His smile warmed her. "For me. What was the point of eternity when I'd spend it being miserable? Especially compared to however many years I could share with the woman I love?"

Tears sprang to her eyes. This was why no other man could ever replace him. "I love you so much."

"Is that a yes?"

"A definite yes."

"Good." He slipped the ring on her finger, then drew her close. His kiss claimed possession—hot and passionate—and Kate responded equally.

She'd almost lost this . . . lost her life. Thank the Stones— Robin's precious Stones—for giving her a second chance.

Mating with his tongue, she ran her hands over his back, through his curly hair as he slid his hands down to cup her bottom and pull her tight against his erection. Hungry desire filled her veins and tugged at the knot low in her belly.

"Do you remember where the bedroom is?" she asked, her voice low.

"Vividly." Scooping her up in his arms, he carried her to that room, then slowly slid her along his body to the floor. "I want to make love to you for days."

She grinned, already working the clasp on his jeans. "It's summer break. That might be possible."

His jeans dropped with a noticeable jangle. Startled, she looked to Robin.

An impish light danced in his eyes. "Oberon gave us a wedding gift." He pulled a small bag out of his pocket and poured a pile of gold coins onto the bed.

Kate gasped. "The faerie gold?"

"Aye, enough for a long time." Robin dropped the bag and returned to nuzzling her neck, his hands caressing her breasts. "In fact, I've already used some to purchase a certain house we both know."

"Nana's house?" Already Kate found it difficult to speak as desire rose within her and her breathing increased.

"Does that please you?"

"You please me." As long as she had Robin, life was wonderful.

He tried to take off her shirt, but caught it on her chin. Kate laughed. "Can't do it without your magic, eh?"

In several swift movements, he removed her shirt and bra and fell with her onto the bed. "I'll learn," he murmured against her lips. "I'll learn."

Author's Note

~

Dear Reader,

Thank you for sharing this story with me. I discovered Robin Goodfellow in a book entitled *Things That Never Were*. While I've always thought of him more in the Puck mind-set, the drawing of Robin Goodfellow beside the entry in this book changed my mind. Not only was he good-looking, but the text stated that he was a favorite among women.

It wasn't long after discovering that entry that this story began to take shape. I adored Robin, my sexy, fun Fae prince, and my Rubenesque Kate and hated to write "the end." But I'm not leaving the Fae completely.

My next book for Jove Magical Love will be out in the fall of 2001. *Queen of Hearts* is the story of Ariel, the dethroned queen of the pillywiggins, the flower faeries. Visiting the mortal world to see Kate and Robin's baby, she decides she wants a child of her own. But the Fae can only be impregnated by mortals, so Ariel picks one.

And the fun begins.

I love to hear from my readers. You can E-mail me at *karen@karenafox.com* or write to me at P.O. Box 31541, Colorado Springs, CO 80931-1541.